BUTCHER BAKER BANKER

LINDA COLES

Blue Banana

CHAPTER 1

Victoria Road
Thursday afternoon

The last time Margaret had seen Nelly Raven, she'd been sitting outside in her tiny back garden in nothing more than her flimsy nightdress, rambling away about the washing getting damp on the line. There hadn't been any washing to see, only spongy moss clinging to the brick walls of her boundary and dull grey paving slabs on the ground. Yet Nelly had been adamant the clothes needed taking inside. Margaret had 'helped' her with the chore before assisting the old woman herself. It couldn't have been any more than 8 °C outside, and so she'd gently guided Nelly back indoors, wrapped her in a dressing gown, and added a blanket across her shoulders to warm her through.

"She's losing her marbles," she'd said that night at dinner.

"She's old, what do you expect?" her husband had replied, barely prising himself away from the word game he continually played on his phone. And so she'd conceded it was nature taking its course. It was something old folk did, and maybe she'd ramble on the same when her time came. That's why people called them old-timers, wasn't it?

Nelly never received visitors – no grandchildren, no grown-up children, no one else to keep a protective eye on her. It saddened Margaret that nobody took any notice of the woman, particularly in her later years of life, and she hoped someone would be around to care for her when she needed it most. Nelly was someone's daughter, though they'd be long gone, and a mother, a friend even, but not a soul ever came.

Relatives could be punishing at times but having none would be purgatory. Soon after that night, Margaret and her husband left for a two-week holiday in the Lake District, and while they were away, she decided to make it her duty to keep a watchful lookout for Nelly, just to be neighbourly.

The day they returned, she made a hot steak and potato stew that she knew Nelly would appreciate and carried it the three doors down in a casserole dish with a tea towel over the top. Just out of a hot oven, it could be eaten right away for her evening meal, no need to worry about warming it again. She hoped the Worcester sauce she'd added was to Nelly's taste, didn't produce too much of a kick, that she liked it that way.

Margaret rapped on the old wooden back door and waited, listening for the usual shuffle approaching from the other side. Damn, it had been cold up in the Lake District, but then autumn in Croydon wasn't much warmer. She knocked again and called out to tell Nelly who it was. Still nothing. She turned the handle and opened the door enough to put her head around. She called again, but there was no reply. Concerned now, Margaret entered the tiny kitchen, placed the casserole dish on the table, then headed towards the front of the house, to the lounge, the room she knew Nelly spent most of her time in. Perhaps she'd fallen asleep in front of the TV.

The house felt cold and damp, like it was unlived in, and she wondered why the heating wasn't on. She could see her breath on the chilly air as she made her way further inside, calling out again so as not to frighten the woman. Involuntarily, Margaret shivered.

"Nelly, it's only me, Margaret," she said as she opened the lounge door. A huge moth-bitten, bottle-green sofa and an ancient oak dining table, pushed up against the far wall, almost filled the room.

Nelly didn't appear to be there. Margaret rubbed her arms to warm herself, glancing around at the decrepit contents of the room. She picked up a small card table that had toppled over at some point. Then a stool. It was only then that Margaret noted other items had been dislodged or had fallen over. She looked at the room as a whole: a chair turned over, medication scattered, books fallen from a shelf. It was as if someone had been rifling through Nelly's possessions looking for something. Had Nelly been burgled? Her hand flew to her mouth at the thought. Was the culprit still in the house, perhaps? And where was Nelly herself? Panic took over. She fumbled in her pocket for her phone and quickly dialled 999. While she waited to be connected, she carefully picked her way through the lounge and across the hall to where she knew Nelly slept. The door was open, and she slipped inside. The room was in just as much disarray as the lounge was, photo frames scattered and smashed on the floor. The drawers from the tallboy all open, items of clothing strewn about, some dangling, threatening to fall. The operator asked which emergency service she required.

"Police, there's been a burglary. An old lady on her own, and I can't find her."

Once she was patched through, Margaret gave her location and repeated what had happened, that the elderly homeowner, Nelly Raven, was missing.

"An officer has been dispatched and will be there shortly," an operator informed her. "Are you sure any intruder has left the property?"

"Pretty sure I'm on my own," she said. "I'll wait in the kitchen, at the back of the house."

"An officer won't be long."

Hanging up, Margaret took another good look at the mess around her and headed back to wait. But something was bothering her, something didn't feel quite right. Why wasn't the heating on? And where was the woman that rarely ventured away from her back door? Wondering if perhaps she'd had a fall, she doubled back and checked the bathroom, but that too was empty. Still the uneasy feeling gnawed away at her, and she returned to the lounge to take another look. With daylight fading fast, the early amber glow from the street lamp did its best to light the room. She flicked the light switch on, but nothing happened.

"It's not the weather to have no power," she said to herself glumly.

Walking around the other side of the sofa, the only thing of note was what looked to be discarded clothes: women's trousers, half inside out; a knitted jumper haphazardly strewn; underwear tossed. Confused, Margaret glanced across at the old oak table. Two chairs lay on their backs, with two more imprisoned between the table itself and wall. No doubt it had seen happy family gatherings in the past, though none in recent years. It was as Margaret bent down to look underneath that she first noticed the pale grey-blue of a wrinkled and pitifully thin elderly foot sticking out, and the rest of Nelly's body coiled up in the foetal position under the table.

"Oh heavens, no!" she cried, getting down on to all fours and making her way under to check for a pulse, one she knew she would never find.

Placing two fingers on the paper-thin skin that covered Nelly Raven's neck, she found the frail and naked body was as cold as the room in which she lay.

CHAPTER 2

The police station
Thursday evening

"Just when you thought it was safe and nearly home time," moaned DC Jack Rutherford. "And Mrs Stewart has a cheese and onion pie ready for dinner tonight. Now the crust will go soft; it's not the same heated up later."

DS Amanda Lacey rolled her eyes at him. Even though she was his direct boss, Jack was a good twenty years older than her. Not that it even mattered, but most assumed it would be the other way around. Amanda looked youthful for her age, while Jack had more wrinkles and laughter lines than a retired barmaid. Male moisturiser hadn't been a thing when he'd been younger, not like what men used nowadays – though Jack was still to discover it. The police staff locker rooms now resembled those of a premier league football team with the amount of fancy balms and fragrances that were used in there. The world was going soft, literally.

"We can't control when the dead are discovered," she said, mild irritation evident in her voice as she slipped in behind the steering wheel. Jack tucked into the passenger seat beside her. She'd known Jack, been his work partner, for a little over five years now, and the two of them were close. With his wider work and life experiences, they were an even match in ability. While she held rank, theirs was usually a relationship of level pegging, unless a higher-ranking officer was present.

"It sounds like a burglary gone wrong from what we know," she added. "It appals me that someone has obviously targeted a vulnerable and elderly person. What scum walk amongst us, don't you think?"

Jack grunted his agreement. It wasn't like Amanda to be so vocal, so negative, particularly at the outset of a case. They hadn't even got to the scene for heaven's sake, and she was already making assumptions. It was out of character for her. But Amanda had been taking things hard ever since she and her wife, Ruth, had had a major falling out and started living apart. That had been a little over two months ago, and there was no sign of her current mood abating, nor normal service resuming. The two women were now living in separate houses, Amanda returning to her old property when the tenants had conveniently moved on, while Ruth remained in the matrimonial home. Although she hadn't needed it for long, Amanda had at first accepted the offer of Jack's back bedroom, which was certainly better than a hotel room. When the heart is in the process of breaking, it's best not to be alone. Her recent time away, a brief spell on the Cornish coast to lick her break-up wounds, had been closely followed by a leadership and resilience course. The holiday might have done her good, but the course seemed to have been a waste of time, her current demeanour not showing any evidence of improved leadership. Jack was also yet to see results from the resilience aspect, which he thought sounded way too much like tree-hugging to be anything serious. He kept his head down and braved her stormy moods. When he figured it was safe to talk, he asked, "Who found the body?" It was more for conversation than anything else. He already knew the answer.

"A neighbour. She went around with a casserole, and it's a good job she did otherwise no one would be any the wiser." Amanda indicated right out of the T-junction and headed towards the elderly woman's address, the GPS directing her. It was only a ten-minute drive from the station. "Faye is on her way."

Pathologist Dr Faye Mitchell was a woman the two detectives saw far too often in the sense that she attended the deaths of victims on their patch. Croydon, on the outskirts of London, had its share, and with the increase in fatal stabbings over the last year or two, she was kept busy enough.

"At least someone was keeping an eye out for the old lady," Jack said. "Any family, do you know?"

"I know about as much as you do at this stage, Jack. So no, I've no idea," she snapped. Jack pursed his lips, refraining from adding or asking anything else. While Amanda was still wounded from Ruth's betrayal, her words had the ability to smart like a paper cut. It was sometimes best to stay silent, and he was thankful the address wasn't far away.

Blue flashing lights marked the actual house towards the end of Victoria Road. There were rows of semi-detached houses on both sides of the street, their brick walls scuffed or pebble-dashed and each with white UPVC bay windows. All followed the same uniform pattern leaving it to the owners to add any character. A standard wheelie bin stood in every front garden, if you could call them that. Jack had eaten larger slices of toast than they had greenery. Shears needed rather than a lawnmower. Cars parked on both sides of the road added to the mayhem of the police arrival, and Amanda's car was one more. Pulling his jacket collar up, Jack headed to the front door where a uniformed officer stood on guard and logged them both in. He pulled on a paper suit and boots and waited for Amanda to put her own protective suit on before entering the property. Stood inside the hallway, they each took a moment to take in their immediate surroundings before Jack voiced what they were likely both thinking.

"I'd bet it's warmer outside than it is in here." They stepped carefully through to the lounge where the crime scene investigators were already hard at work. Lamps had been set up and the room was filled with white light, a stark contrast to the charcoal of the gathering night outside. Another uniformed officer approached them and introduced himself.

"PC John Shepherd. I was first on the scene along with PC Gill."

Jack nodded. Shepherd must be new to the station; he'd have remembered seeing a moustache such as his. "Do you wax that?" Jack enquired, pointing towards the man's upper lip where a few bristles seemed almost glued together in an upward curve. Obviously not expecting such a response from the detective, the uniformed officer fought and lost the battle as pale pink starting to glow on his cheeks. Noticing it, Jack let him off the hook and made his way towards the back of the room where Amanda was bending down trying to look at the victim. In the bright light, the elderly woman's skin looked almost translucent, greaseproof-paper thin. Amanda used her phone torch to illuminate the space under the table a little better. The woman lying there was pitifully thin, her bones threatening to pierce her skin, and Amanda wondered how she'd gone unnoticed for so long as to be in such a way. An absence of care, from her neighbours, her family, her community even, had led to what Amanda herself could tell was a malnourished individual. At least one woman had thought about helping, the lady delivering the casserole, and Amanda was thankful for small mercies. She made a mental note to work on making more new friends so that someone might look out for her, if only occasionally, when the time came.

"What's gone on here, eh? And where's your family?" she asked gently as Jack bent down beside her.

"There's photos scattered on the floor. They could be family members," he offered. "I'll go and chat to the woman that found her, she might know of someone." He stood to leave. "Damn, it's cold in here," he grumbled as he left, leaving Amanda wishing she could give comfort and take the old woman's hand in her own.

CHAPTER 3

The elderly woman's house
Thursday evening

The kitchen was as cold as the front room, and Jack rubbed his hands together in an effort to warm them.

"DC Jack Rutherford," he said, introducing himself. "You must be Margaret Mumford. I understand you found your neighbour and called the police, is that correct?"

"Yes, I'm Margaret, and yes, I found her. So sad." The woman's eyes were pink and damp from crying, she held a scrunched-up tissue in one hand, and even though Jack would estimate her age at around forty, the wrinkles around her eyes void of make-up made him question his own calculation. Perhaps she was more his own age.

"Why don't you tell me what happened?" he said, gently pulling a chair out and joining her at the kitchen table.

"She's not been so good," she started. "I think she's losing her memory. You know, old-timers. I found her in the garden in her nightie only a few weeks back. She was as cold as ice, and I brought her back in here, put the fire on for her. I looked out for her when I could, but we've been away, in the Lakes for a break." Her voice trailed off a little, no doubt wishing she'd done more, been more vigilant, not gone away perhaps.

"Did she have family? There are photos on the floor."

"Yes, a son apparently. All grown up of course, though I've never met him or spoken to him. I've got his number in my phone, but I don't know his name," she said, bending for her bag.

Jack noticed the casserole sitting on the work surface that would now go uneaten. The elderly lady could have perhaps enjoyed it had it been a while sooner. Still, at least she'd been discovered now. If they'd waited for an absent offspring to visit, who knows how long she'd have lain there decomposing. Margaret showed Jack the number, and he jotted it in his notebook. "Thanks, I'll give him a call. You say she's not been well... You mean with her memory?"

"Yes. It's been harder to get a coherent conversation from her of late. Perhaps I should have done something, called a doctor or something. But it's too late now." Fresh tears started to flow as she looked straight at Jack, guilt heavy in her heart and evident on her face.

"She was lucky to have you watching out for her, I'd say. Don't fret you should have done more; you did what a good neighbour could."

She nodded her head to accept the compliment. While he waited for her to compose herself, Jack scanned the kitchen. A tin of baked beans, half a loaf of stale bread, a carving knife, marmalade, and a tin opener sat near the casserole that Margaret had delivered. From his chair he noticed the top edge of the beans tin – the label looked like it was starting to fray or shred somehow. Standing, he moved closer and bent down to take a better look without picking it up. Tiny fragments of label dangled delicately, and there appeared to be scuff marks, as if someone had used a pair of scissors to scratch the label off. Then he noticed the carving knife slightly further along. That was the obvious culprit. It looked to him as though she'd tried to cut the tin of beans lid off with the knife rather than the tin opener. The old lady certainly was confused. Dementia could be to blame. And if that was the case, had she let the intruder in herself, perhaps thinking it was her son visiting? She'd have likely been delighted to see him, greeting him with a hug. Could her dementia have got her killed?

"Why don't I walk you back home," Jack offered. There was little else she could tell him, and he'd got the next of kin's contact details to pass on anyway. The woman was not responsible and didn't know anything about a possible burglary.

"Thank you." When she'd gathered herself together and was ready to leave, Jack picked the casserole dish up. "You may as well take this back, there's no point it going to waste," he said, smiling and offering to carry it. "Lead the way," he encouraged, and the two of them walked slowly back to her house.

As she opened her own back door, a welcoming warmth greeted them both. He stepped into the kitchen and placed the dish on the stove hob. A TV chatted, presumably to someone in another room, the contrast of the two homes startling.

"I may be back in touch. I'll see myself out," he said, waving lightly.

Wandering back to Nelly's house, he dialled the number Margaret had handed him and waited for it to connect. It rang out. Nobody was going to answer, it seemed. He wondered if the son knew of his mother's ill health and how she was managing. Maybe he was in hospital, perhaps, or even abroad? Or maybe any family the old lady did have were aware of the situation and didn't care.

Could family members be so callous?

Of course they could. And worse. Jack knew from professional experience just how callous people could be.

CHAPTER 4

The crime scene
Thursday evening

Nelly Raven had been zipped into a body bag and taken to the mortuary. Dr Faye Mitchell had arrived shortly after Amanda and Jack and done the necessary. But, as was her way, Faye never gave anything away other than a rough time of death, and only then if she was really pushed for it. Since the house had been cold anyway, a mere 8 °C, it made things a little more difficult to calculate, but she'd relented and estimated the time of death was between 4 am and 10 am earlier that day. That Nelly had presumably been wearing the clothes that had been found close by, and not her nightdress, added to the evidence she'd risen and dressed herself. Thankfully, there was no initial indication of it being a sexual attack.

"I'll know more later and tomorrow," Faye said before getting into her car. "Over to you, Jack."

"Gee, thanks," he said. Faye raised her hand in goodbye, and he wandered back inside. It seemed every surface was covered with grey powder as the forensic team searched for prints. Even with the disturbance, the items strewn all over the place, it didn't appear anything obvious had been taken. But then Nelly's possessions weren't particularly modern.

"Do you think she had money hidden?" Amanda asked, joining him in the lounge again. "Only, I can't think what else the perpetrator was after. Certainly not the old telly. I doubt Noah would have wanted that for his arc."

"Even if she did, it doesn't seem like they went looking for it because burglars rarely close drawers after searching them, and none of the drawers in the dresser have been opened. And forensics aren't even getting glove prints, unless the person wore nitrile or latex. Give me a rubber glove anytime, at least it shows they wore the damn things." Amanda stood silently thoughtful, chewing the inside of her bottom lip while he rambled on. Jack watched it turn from pink to white to red as blood was moved about under the pressure of her teeth.

"Stop staring, Jack, I'm thinking."

He cleared his throat. "At least the neighbour found her, though she's not hopeful of family members caring. Apparently the son never visited, whoever he is. She gave me a telephone number but doesn't know his name. Sad, don't you think? I hope the old dear left a will someplace, and he's not in it."

Amanda grunted. "There's nothing else we can do here now, but perhaps we'll know more in the morning. Everyone is winding down so we may as well get off too." She checked her watch – it was a little after 7 pm. Back to an empty house of her own, and a microwave meal for one. As if Jack could read her thoughts, he said, "You're welcome to share my cheese and onion pie. Mrs Stewart always makes a family-sized one so there's leftovers."

His part-time housekeeper had been a present from Amanda and Ruth after a stint in hospital. Since his wife, Janine, had died a few years back, he'd been struggling to cope with the upkeep of his own home and to feed himself properly. He'd originally kept Mrs Stewart on as a trial but often wondered now how he'd ever managed without the woman. He was also conscious that she was now in her seventies and wouldn't be fussing around him forever.

"You know she makes a decent pie..." He wiggled his eyebrows at her comically, and he knew instantly she'd relent. "Come on, you know you want to," he said, smiling, and guided her back to the front door. Had they been on their own, he would have slipped an arm across her shoulders, boss or not. Friendship didn't care about rank. The crime scene investigators, however, didn't need to see the depth of their affection. While his friend and colleague was still hurting inside, he'd be the support she needed. After what they'd both witnessed with Nelly Raven, neither fancied an empty house on their own tonight.

"At least the heating will have warmed the place up a bit," he said, shivering as they climbed into Amanda's car.

"May as well leave yours parked at the station," Amanda suggested. "I'll drop by in the morning and pick you up, shall I?" The engine caught, and she turned the heater dial up high. A fine mist clung to the inside of the windscreen, which the heater did its best to clear it.

"Sounds good to me."

He slammed his door shut, and they set off towards Jack's place, the rush hour traffic now all but gone. "You know," he said, "if it was a burglary, that's yet another this month, taking it up to nine by my reckoning. And do you remember that poor bugger that was hit twice in the same week?"

"And you think this one could be connected? Even though there doesn't appear to be anything missing?"

"Who knows. But I do know this: this old lady's situation feels different somehow," Jack said, wagging his finger in a schoolmaster kind of way. "I don't know what it is yet, but I'll bet you it's not a straightforward burglary. You mark my words."

"Well, she wasn't obviously harmed. All old folks bruise easily, and since she was lying on the floor, she likely sustained those nasty-looking purple-blue patches during a fall. I doubt she was attacked, not in this instance, but I wonder if she was frightened and tried to hide?" She indicated, turned into Jack's street, and pulled into his driveway. His house was one of the handful in the row that actually had a garage, most folks had knocked theirs down in order to get an extra vehicle off the road. Parking space on local residential streets was as scarce as a traffic warden's smile. "And that's why she was under the table? But I don't get why she was naked."

"I've no clue about her being nude," he said. "That part doesn't fit; it was perishing in her house." He unlocked the back door. A warm and welcoming smell of home baking greeted them both, and Jack took a deep breath, savouring it in his nostrils. "Now, aren't you glad you took me up on the offer of dinner?" Amanda let the door close behind them and had to admit it had been the perfect decision. Having watched Jack take his coat off and hang it up behind the door, she followed suit.

"See if there's a bottle of wine while I heat the vegetables up," he instructed, suddenly appearing rather domesticated. Things had changed for Jack, for the better, and Amanda busied herself opening a bottle of rosé and pouring two glasses. She couldn't help smiling behind his back as the microwave turntable circled, a pot of mixed veg almost ready to be served. He lifted the pie from the oven, removed the tinfoil lid Mrs Stewart had added so it didn't dry out, and set the pan of white sauce to warm on the stove top. To anyone observing from the outside, they looked like father and daughter about to sit down to a meal.

Their table conversation would be anything but normal.

CHAPTER 5

Baker

Friday morning

Kit Morris sneaked out of his house like he did every morning. At the early bird hour of 4 am, the last thing he wanted to do was wake his family up. It was a life he'd known since he'd started working as a young man in his uncle's bakery, but that was more than twenty years ago. Those were the days, when he'd been allowed to make dough knots and plats before school as a way of making pocket money and then take one home for his breakfast to have with strawberry jam ladled over it while it was still warm. He'd loved the smell of freshly baked bread, found the dough therapeutic to work with and so, when he'd finished his school years, it had been a no brainer to carry on and open a bread shop of his own. And the name fit: Dough Knots. Everyone needed bread, didn't they? No matter what the economy was doing. If it was up, people spent their money. And if the economy was down a little, people turned to comfort food as a pick-me-up, and he'd been ready with traditional ring doughnuts and eclairs to satisfy every sweet tooth. Now with plans for a second shop, he was well on his way to turning dough into money.

It was a fifteen-minute walk from home, and whatever the weather, Kit walked the short distance and allowed himself the quiet time to cogitate. No plastic buds in his ears, no distraction of any kind, just his thoughts. A time to review the day ahead, the week ahead, the future in general, and at the end of his working day, he'd make the same journey in reverse, doing the exact same thinking in reverse. What had gone well today? What was he thankful for? What opportunity might he have missed? But once he was back at his own front door, his small family were his only focus, work stayed outside. Walking now, he allowed himself a moment to think of the three girls in his life, lying snuggled up in their duvets back at home. The thought of Jess and Angie, his two young daughters, safely tucked up in their beds, not far from their mother, oblivious as usual to his early working hour, made him smile. They'd call in later for a kiss on their way to school. It was their routine, and he looked forward to the few moments away from a hot oven to say good morning properly.

As soon as he hit the switch, the bakery was illuminated with a glow far too fierce for such an early hour, but his eyes readily adjusted as he got to work making coffee before the rest of his small team arrived. He flicked the ovens on to heat up and take the edge off the cold. Soon enough, it would be snug, and that was always a welcoming feeling to a cold individual passer-by.

Kit saw no reason why they shouldn't be neighbourly so they unlocked the front door when the clock struck five. If an early customer on their way to work wanted a coffee and a quick chat, that was fine by him since he and the team were on the premises by that time anyway. Since many of his early customers worked nights, either driving a taxi or doing local shift work, he was happy to take their change when nobody else was open, it made business sense. Many of the early folks were regulars, and Kit made a point of knowing their names. If he was going to be seeing them daily, he liked to know a little about them, and at times it made for a boisterous ambience. Still, that was an hour away, and he sipped his strong coffee, waiting for the caffeine to kick in.

He heard the back door open and close, sending a draught around his ankles. It would be Elizabeth, always the next to arrive. Jakub was always in at the last minute, his alarm clock forever in need of replacement apparently. Kit knew the lad had trouble getting up, but if he was intent on working in the baking industry, he'd have to get used to the early starts. Elizabeth's bright, pink-tinged face beamed at him as she headed straight for the coffee machine.

"It's cold out there!" she said, peeling her gloves off so she could handle the apparatus.

"Morning and yes, another cold one," he replied easily.

"I can't believe it's this cold, and it's not even Halloween yet," she added, unwrapping her scarf as water forced its way through ground coffee. She poured milk into a jug and let the steam jet work its magic. Another clunk of the back door. Kit and Elizabeth looked at one another – Jakub, on time. Sure enough, his long pale face entered the room, and he greeted the others in his usual low-key manner. Dressed in black hoody and black jeans, the contrast of his skin tone and his clothing was as stark as the keys on a piano. Kit had wondered why the lad was permanently so pale but had never bothered to ask. While Jakub was sullen at times, he was a decent worker, getting on with his role with vigour and accuracy, and since Kit had no work issues with him, there was little point in prying. Still, it wasn't Kit's style to not keep a watchful eye out.

"Morning," Jakub said, and that was it. The two greeted him back and watched as he grabbed a mug for himself to make his own coffee.

"Right," announced Kit, "it's Friday, and that means a busy weekend ahead, I hope. So, when you've had your coffee, let's get on with it. Jakub, those iced spice buns went down a treat last weekend so let's do half on top again rather than double."

Jakub nodded and put his apron on.

"We should do orange icing for Halloween," said Elizabeth.

"What do you think? Get into the spirit of things. Literally. Plus, they would match your hair," she added cheekily.

"Ha ha. But great idea actually. Jakub, do half orange and half plain."

Again, a nod. The lad had precious little to say at the best of times, and when he was following orders, input wasn't needed. That was his rationale at least.

As the small team busied themselves in their work and Arielle Free played workout anthems on the radio, Kit's mind wandered from his usual positive outlook to what had been troubling him of late. Inside, he was in turmoil. The facade he'd been so diligently projecting was making him weary at times, but he'd kept his thoughts and worries from those close to him. Now, with his hands busy, worry filled every dark corner of his mind, and he let it lie there, heavy while he worked. He allowed himself the time in the hope that an answer would break through.

It hadn't happened yesterday. It likely wouldn't happen today either.

CHAPTER 6

Butcher

Friday morning

Pemdevon Road held some of Ron Butcher's best clients. The definition of best was those that paid their weekly repayments on time and without any hassle. He despised it when an individual thought they could take his money and pay it back when it suited them, delaying because they'd fancied a meal out with the missus. None of that was any of his concern, and he was happy to show them just how the system worked if they fell behind.

Bargain. He couldn't call his interest rates 'a bargain', he knew, and Ron sniggered to himself as he headed back to his van. The first visit was always on Ron, and that was about as dirty as his hands got from then on in. His team was small but talented, and when a client took the mickey or overstepped the agreed boundary, they stepped in. What was the point in agreeing to terms only to flake out and ignore them at the first opportunity? So, Ron had paid his latest customer an early morning visit, one just long enough to put the fear of God into him and leave a gob of spit on the man's left cheek.

Gnarly long fingers reached for the van door, and he slipped inside, checked his hair in the rear-view mirror. He hated getting upset, and the effort of frightening the man had blown his thinning mousy hair in an awkward direction. He smoothed it back into place with the help of a little more spittle and started the engine. Usually he drove a classy black Lexus, something a little more upmarket, but when he was on a working errand such as this, the generic white transit van was ideal. He never knew when it might come in useful. Radio 4 filled the space as he pulled away from the kerb and made his way back to the south side of the town. With the *Today* programme playing, he settled into the drive towards home.

His place overlooked Purley Downs' golf course, a far cry from the miniscule semis and terraced houses his clients lived in. Green space was something he appreciated; it gave him a place to think. He rummaged in his pocket for his vape pen, switched it on, and a sweet vanilla fragrance filled the confines of the van.

The radio presenters were lining up for Thought for the Day as he pulled up in his own driveway fifteen minutes later. It was a stunning red brick detached property on two levels, complete with a tall chimney stack at either end of the long tiled roof. Being on the thinner side, Ron felt the cold during the winter months and so had a fireplace installed in both the lounge and his own bedroom. Mainly because he could. Central heating warmed the rest of the huge dwelling, but Ron liked the feel of naked flames near his skin while undressing and the fragrance of wood as it burned in the hearth. Women, he'd discovered, found it attractive too. While his bedroom was a far cry from a secluded cottage deep in the woods, he'd often used the lure of the open fire to entice his infrequent visitors. While he knew he wasn't blessed with good looks, he'd found ways to make himself more desirable to the opposite sex. Add in a chilled bottle of bubbly and he was away.

He slithered from his seat to the tarmac, slammed the van door behind him, and made his way to the front door. It amused him why so many people never used their own, preferring the back door for reasons he could not explain. He liked being reminded of the grandeur of owning such a place, and the front entrance did just that. He fumbled for the right key then lingered a moment to listen before turning it in the lock. The impressive water fountain in the front garden made it sound like he was by a river, splashing and gurgling as several thin streams of water cascaded down from wedding-cake-style shallow stone bowls. A miniature statue of a naked boy stood atop it all, the water streams giving the impression he was urinating, and birds often drank from the lower bowl. Smiling at the sound, Ron entered his house and called out to see if anyone was home. He shared the place with his son, Felix, who at twenty-five was still happy to live with his old dad and saw no reason to get a place of his own. Since no one replied back, Ron assumed he was out. His phone buzzed in his jacket pocket, and he glanced at the screen.

"Felix, talk of the devil, where are you?" he said, approaching the coffee pot and filling a nearby mug. Ron could hear Felix's heavy breathing down the line.

"Attending to an errand. There's been a problem with a set of papers, and the guy was getting lippy over it. All sorted now. But I tell you, we need to look for another supplier. It's not the first stuff-up that thick sod has done, and it probably won't be the last."

"You been running or something?"

"A bit of a scuffle, that's all. Anyway, I'll leave it with you. Before it's too late, eh?"

"Is that all you wanted me for?"

"Isn't that enough?"

Ron grunted. "How many we got in the system?"

"A couple more for this month. But I'm not tolerating any more stuff-ups. Sort it, Dad. I mean it, all right?"

Felix had hung up. Ron looked at his screen; a picture of his late wife, Lyn, stared back at him.

"I thought I was the boss, but there's no mistaking his mother's genes in him all right," he said, smiling at her. "And as feisty too. Miss you." He kissed the image gently then tossed the phone on to the kitchen counter as if she hadn't been an important part of his life at all.

CHAPTER 7

Banker

Friday morning

To the south-west of Croydon lay a tiny village that was home to some of the most expensive properties in the region. Was Upper Woodcote even a village? A selection of high-end homes, each placed a fair distance from the next, sat dotted around the village green. More commonly known to locals as the Webb Estate, it was a conservation area with trees as old as Adam himself. A prospective buyer would need funds north of a couple million pounds, and even then you'd likely want to modernise what that bought you. Families had owned the properties for generations, and while some might still sport a salmon-pink bathroom complete with bidet, the younger homeowner, and there were a couple, much preferred the more minimalist look. Salmon pink had been replaced with gleaming white and steely grey decor. Glass played its modern part when permission could be gained for a trendy but stylish extension on the back. It was in such a stylish home that you'd find Lee Meady, CEO of a large high-street bank. At forty-eight years old, he was undoubtedly one of the youngest with the title that the banking industry had ever seen. He'd earned his stripes though. Having started as a management trainee twenty-seven years ago and worked his way up, he now held the top spot with a salary one hundred and twenty times that of most of his employees. He could afford to live in such a sought-after location, and indeed this house wasn't his only one. With several properties around the world, available for various sports depending on the season, Lee Meady had done all right for himself.

Having finished tying a thick Windsor knot, he double-checked himself in the full-length dressing-room mirror, grabbed his jacket, and headed downstairs. His wife, Bethany, was sitting elegantly on a bar stool on one side of the kitchen island. The weak early morning sunshine mixed delicately with the pale blue silk of her robe, and for a moment Lee stood mesmerised. He knew if she lifted her head and her eyes met his, they'd sparkle, and he'd be rooted to the spot for the morning. But her thoughts were buried in the newspaper she was reading so Lee reached for a cereal bowl before approaching her.

"Morning, darling," he said, planting a light kiss on the back of her neck, nuzzling in a little. Bethany immediately raised a shoulder as if to squeeze him out of the ticklish space he liked to frequent.

"You know that tickles," she said, laughing a little, "and I wish you wouldn't sneak up on me like that."

"I wasn't sneaking. I greeted you good morning first, but your head's buried in your reading. I can't be responsible for you not paying me any attention," he said, smiling. Taking his bowl, he poured granola before adding yogurt and defrosted blueberries to it. His motto was 'you are what you eat' and a healthy breakfast was the norm on a busy workday. Weekends were more relaxed, and he allowed himself to indulge a little.

"Don't forget, we're out for dinner tonight at Eric and Tanya's. Can you get home relatively early?" she asked.

"I'll make sure of it," he said between mouthfuls. "Is it just the four of us?"

"No, there's six apparently, though I don't know who they are. But I'm guessing they'll be along the lines of either bankers or lawyers, their dinners usually are." There was an air of disappointment in her words.

"You don't sound too thrilled at the prospect."

Bethany raised her eyes to his and Lee stopped short. He'd been right, the blue was fascinatingly clear. "That's because I'm not really. Us four is fine, but two more can be hard work when I'm in a different field all together. Retail management is a far cry from law and banking, so scintillating conversation on those topics doesn't come that easy."

"I shouldn't worry about it," he said, scraping his bowl with the spoon. "You're a gorgeous and intelligent woman, and you don't need to keep up with such dreary subjects." He moved towards her and slipped his arm around her shoulder, pulling her into his chest. She felt glorious. "You've got enough interesting topics to talk about without thinking you need to do our boring 'shop talk'. And Tanya always has plenty to say about her own career." Bethany pulled herself away and couldn't help but roll her eyes. Tanya was a vet at a local surgery.

"Great, so we get to dissect a case or a cat corpse. I don't know which one disinterests me the most," she said, rubbing at her temples as if she had a migraine coming.

"Oh come on, Bethany, this is unlike you. Shall we cancel then? I'm sure we can do it some other time."

"No, it's fine," she relented, "I'm just being whiney. I've a migraine coming, I think. My vision is blurring."

"I thought as much, I can see it in your shoulders. Why don't you go back to bed for an hour, eh? You can't drive like that so call in sick and take a tablet. You'll feel better then," he said, smiling. "In fact, let me get you one of mine, it'll be sure to shift it in quick time. Hang on a second." Lee vanished from sight, leaving Bethany to grab a glass of water. He was back soon enough, a tiny white pill in the palm of his hand. "There you go, swallow it back, call in sick, and go back to bed." Reluctantly,

Bethany took the pill from him and Lee watched as she washed it down.

Satisfied she'd take his advice, he said, "Right, I'd better get off so I can get back in time. If you're no better, we'll have to cancel. Now, rest," he encouraged, wagging a finger affectionately in her direction. As she turned, he watched her body move beneath the silk fabric and marvelled, not for the first time, at what a lucky man he was.

In so many ways.

CHAPTER 8

Jack's house
Friday morning

Amanda had stayed over at Jack's place more times in the last two months than she'd like to admit. It wasn't that she felt uncomfortable around her work partner and friend, it was more the fact she didn't want to admit she hated being alone in her own place.

Without Ruth. The love of her life.

Amanda had found the only way to cope with Ruth's betrayal was to move out for a time, to give herself some breathing space. And while she had that now, there seemed to be too much of it. The space Ruth had filled was empty, and Amanda missed her company every moment of every day. But she wasn't going to rush headlong into forgiving her, not yet, not for what she'd done. It had almost torn her heart out, and her colleagues had only added to the pain and torment by making snide comments behind her back and speculating about her involvement in covering up a murder case. The tittle-tattle had finally been dealt with by the station's superintendent, but Amanda knew it would take time for the gossip and hurt to diffuse through the system as well as her own being.

She headed downstairs before Jack, taking the opportunity to have the bathroom to herself before he made it into a Turkish steam room. At least he'd stopped using Brut, his preference now a splash of citrus courtesy of Calvin Klein according to a bottle on the windowsill. Likely a gift from his now girlfriend, Vivian, it was a tad more palatable. Afterwards, she headed for the kitchen, not at all expecting to find Jack there in his pyjamas and dressing gown at six in the morning. She stopped abruptly and a hand flew to her chest. The top of his head was all that was visible of his upper torso, the rest covered by the morning newspaper. He rustled it noisily as he turned to greet her, having sensed her presence rather than heard her.

"Damn, you made me jump," she said, wafting herself.

"Sorry, I wasn't expecting you down just yet. I heard the shower running and thought I'd make myself a cuppa. Want one?" He stood to make a move, folding his paper and dropping it on the floor by his chair. Overnight shadow covered his cheeks and chin giving him a sandy look, like he'd slept on the beach with damp skin.

"Thanks, yes. Do you always get up so early? Ruth used to go for a..." Her voice trailed off before she finished 'run', and a silence filled the gap between them. Jack placed a comforting hand on Amanda's shoulder and looked her straight in the eyes.

"You know, maybe it's time you two sorted yourselves out."

"Don't go there, Jack," she said warningly.

He raised both hands in surrender. "It's a shame, that's all. You two clearly love each other, so why not start making things right again between you?"

"What did I just ask you not to do?"

"Well, I did. Because I care. About the both of you, and I hate to see you so down in the doldrums. Still," he said, moving towards the kettle, "what do I know? Janine and I only had thirty years together... before she died." It was enough to leave it there, let the comment dangle. If he could have another week with her, another day even, he would do whatever he needed to make it happen. Now was the ideal moment to distract himself and make two mugs of tea while she ruminated on what he'd just said, there was no need to fill the silence as he busied himself with teabags and milk. He could feel the ice daggers shooting into the flesh of his back and then, thankfully, melting away again. When two mugs were ready, he turned to face her and was shocked and surprised to see tears falling down her cheeks. Her lower lip trembled slightly.

"Hey," he said, putting the tea back down and wrapping his arms around her, pulling her into him. "I didn't mean to upset you. I'm sorry if I have." He was tempted to kiss the top of her head, like she was the daughter he'd never had, but didn't. Though perhaps it was a line he had already crossed. Amanda was technically his boss, yes, but not in his kitchen, with him in his bathrobe and her crying. He waited for her to pull away and was surprised when she didn't, so let her stay for a moment or two longer. Finally, she took a deep breath and made her move, wiping her eyes and averting her gaze as she did so. Amanda liked to think she was a tough one, but her skin was as soft as everyone else's on the inside.

"Sorry, Jack," she said quickly, recovering herself. "I should go."

"No, you don't, not yet. Sit and drink your tea first. Plus, if you go now, I've no way of getting to work. My car's still at the station, remember?" he said, smiling. "And I don't much fancy bugging the boss woman by being late. I've heard she's a right dragon's arse at the moment." That made her smile back, even if her face was bubble-gum pink from crying.

"Dragon's arse?"

"Just gossip."

He passed her a mug of tea, and she took several mouthfuls before speaking again.

"It's not been easy."

"I can see that, but it will get better. And I wouldn't mention it but, as I've just said, I care about you both. I know Ruth's hurting too. So, why don't you consider at least talking to her? Meet on neutral ground, have a glass of wine or something and make a start.

Because it won't happen without your effort, now will it? Ruth is waiting for you. Everyone is waiting for you." Amanda stood silently, had she the strength and courage to do so? Jack added another thought, "Plus, you've just been on that resilience course. Didn't they teach you about bouncing back and whatnot?"

Amanda frowned slightly. Had she been a dragon's arse? "I know. But I'm hurting."

"Then help yourself, and take some of that pain away. Little steps," he added gently. Nothing else needed to be said on the matter. Changing the energy in the room, he announced, "Pep talk over, I'm off for a shower. Like I said, the boss can be a right dragon's arse sometimes, and I don't want to be late. Plus, I'm fancying a bacon bap on the way," he said, smiling over his shoulder. Amanda was relieved at the change of subject and forced a smile back, even though it was a weak one.

When she was sure Jack was out of earshot she said, "Dragon's arse? I've not really been a dragon's arse, have I?"

On the other side of the door, Jack stood smiling. He reached over and patted his own back as he quietly climbed the stairs. Maybe, just maybe, there'd be a breakthrough on the horizon sometime soon.

CHAPTER 9

Banker

Friday morning

It wasn't going to be Lee Meady's morning. He'd left the house at his usual 7 am and headed for the station. While he could have easily got a train from Purley, the closest station, trains ran more frequently from East Croydon, so he'd kept up the habit of going there instead. It would make his return journey easier too, so it had seemed the sensible thing to do for the handful of extra miles it took him. He'd been travelling along Barclay Road, close to the station, when he was alerted to a flat rear tyre. On top of that, a light drizzle had begun to fall. He slammed a fist into the steering wheel as he searched for a spot to pull over.

"Damn it!" he shouted.

Nobody wanted a flat tyre, and Lee certainly didn't want one on his way to work, dressed in a well-cut business suit. Scrabbling around on the tarmac in damp conditions was not conducive to performing at his best through a day packed with meetings and conference calls. He checked his watch and wondered if the AA might be able to fix it quickly for him. It was worth a try. Since the tyre had to be swapped over at some point, it might as well be done this side of lunchtime rather than the other. Getting back from work and still having a flat would be even more annoying. Since his first appointment was a conference call at ten, perhaps he'd be able to do it on the move if need be. It wouldn't be ideal, but at least he could hear what the rest of the team had to contribute, even if he couldn't do much himself. It made the most sense. Grumbling about the unfairness of it all, he checked his wallet for his membership card and called the number. Once he was through, he explained what he needed and was advised that the wait was currently sixty minutes. It would have to do. Lee made sure they had his mobile number and asked them to call when they were ten minutes out, as he was going for a coffee. With help on the way, Lee grabbed his umbrella off the back seat and headed off.

There were several coffee places that he knew of nearby but, as he walked, he spotted a familiar logo on a paper bag: Dough Knots. Lee had been in the bakery in the past and knew it wasn't far away. He quickened his step as the drizzle picked up pace. By the time he arrived, miniscule droplets of water were clinging to his suit trouser legs, but at least the umbrella had kept his top half dry. Shaking it out as he closed it, he opened the front door and slipped the umbrella into a nearby holder where the remaining moisture could drip on to a small tray. He brushed at the sleeves of his jacket and the front of his thighs.

"Not a day for a picnic, is it."

It wasn't actually a question but a statement from the man with bright ginger hair that was standing behind the counter. He was smiling at Lee, who approached and agreed it wasn't. He ordered a cappuccino and browsed the display, deciding what to add to it. Glancing around, he tried to observe what the handful of other customers were eating, but everyone appeared to have finished and were making a coffee last until it was time to head off. Maybe they were all going into London, he wondered, getting breakfast before the train in.

"I'll take a doughnut, thanks, and I'll eat it here, with my coffee."

"Coming right up," Kit called over his shoulder as he forced steam into milk. "Off into the city, are you?" Another customer entered, and Elizabeth moved to serve the woman.

"I was. I mean, I still am. But I've managed to get a flat tyre on the way in, so I'm waiting for the AA to swap it out."

"Bad luck," Kit said. "Still, at least they'll do it, and you don't have to get dirty in your suit," he said, gesturing with his nose. "It looks a nice one too." He poured milk over coffee and said, "I'll bring this over, take a seat." Lee headed to a spot in the window and pulled himself on to a bar stool, leaving his briefcase on the floor beside it. A man entered the shop, and Lee couldn't help but notice him. He was likely the thinnest man Lee had ever seen, and he had thin strands of mousy brown hair. A moment later, his own coffee and doughnut arrived by his elbow.

"Thanks."

"You're welcome."

As soon as he sunk his teeth into the soft, warm dough, he let out an involuntary groan, loud enough for Kit to hear, though he didn't say anything. Lee surprised himself as he licked sugar from his lips and took another bite, the sensation lifting his foul mood somewhat. He turned to the man behind the counter again and nodded, and in between chewing, he said, "This is likely the best doughnut I've ever had. Superb. Do you bake them here?"

"Every morning. Glad you like them."

"Can you pack me a box to go, say a dozen?"

"On their way," Kit said, reaching for a box and filling it with twelve more. He walked over with and placed it next to the man's coffee.

"It's a good job you don't have a bakery near my office, I'd be the size of a house," quipped Lee.

"We are opening another shop soon actually. Where are you based?"

"Up in Bank, not far from the Tube station."

"Then we're still your local. For now," he said.

"So, you're expanding then?"

"One so far, another in a few months, but yes, if I can get the funding, I want to open two more next year. Know anyone with money to lend?"

"I should do, I'm in banking. Here," Lee said, taking a card from his wallet. "No promises but tell whoever you deal with at your nearest branch to call me before they make their final decision. From what I can see, you've a damn good product, and as long as your business plan stacks up, it's worth a deeper look than we normally do on paper. If that makes sense." A queue had begun to form back at the counter, and Elizabeth was struggling to keep up as the door opened again and more customers filed in. Kit looked at the card; he was chatting to the CEO of a high-street bank. He kept his awe and surprise in check, not wishing to appear like an impressed fanboy.

"I can see you're busy, don't let me keep you," Lee added, turning back to his coffee. "Let me know how you get on though. I mean it." Kit raised his hand in thanks and headed back to help Elizabeth.

But Lee was intrigued at the steady flow of business, and the damn good doughnuts. The box of twelve would be coming home with him, not going to the office.

CHAPTER 10

Butcher
Friday morning

Another stuff-up meant more aggro, and Ron Butcher hated aggro. While his business wasn't exactly run by the book and aggro came with the territory, it wasn't something he personally enjoyed. That's why he usually passed the task of handling it on to someone else, someone a bit younger. Unfortunately, he'd had to deal with the latest mishap himself, though he'd taken someone along for the grunt work. Back home again, he rested against the kitchen cupboards and took a long drink from his coffee, which could have been a couple of degrees hotter. Cream always reduced the temperature, but it was one of life's luxuries, along with a single spoon of dark cane sugar, and for Ron, there was no other way to consume coffee. He topped his mug up from the pot and settled back to think.

Supplying complete sets of identity documents was a growing part of his business – and extremely lucrative. It was also far easier than dealing with the loans. Someone wanting a new ID paid a chunk up front, while someone who'd taken a loan had to be chased constantly for a dribble of repayments. And these were individuals that had no money in the first place. Why else would they agree to forty per cent interest? They were desperate people, but then so were those in need of documents. And with so many immigrants filtering in via Europe, the demand would only grow, Brexit or not. He reached for his phone and scrolled the list of contacts until he found whom he was looking for. It had been a while, but he doubted the old man would have forgotten him. No one forgot an interaction with Ron Butcher, no matter how fleeting it was.

"Yeah?" The man answered gruffly.

"How's it going, Bernard? Ron Butcher in your ear."

"Ron Butcher. Well, I'll be damned. It's been a while. How did you get this number?"

Ron ignored the question, "How you been keeping?"

"Fine, though I doubt you're calling about my wellbeing. What's troubling you?"

Ron liked a man that didn't dawdle, that made straight for the point. It saved time.

"Thought we might have a chat. I'm looking for a new supplier and thought you might be able to help, perhaps clip the ticket even. You still in the people business?"

The man sniggered before he replied. "You could say that, yes. Though I've diversified a little over the years. But people, yeah, that's me." He chuckled. "When do you want to meet up?"

"What you doing this morning? No point in waiting."

"Free as a bee."

"Eh?"

"No grandkids then?"

"Not yet. If ever. Look, whatever. Remember the Baskerville pub in town? Think it's a Whelan's now. Irish-themed place but they serve London Pride. Say 11.30?"

"That'll do for me."

"See you there."

Ron finished the call and checked his watch. He still had plenty of time. The acid from his coffee was making his empty stomach ache slightly, and he needed something to soak it up. Since he'd been out paying a non-paying client a reminder visit before work, his routine had been upset, and so he'd missed his usual breakfast. Grabbing his keys, he left the house and slipped behind the wheel of his shiny black Lexus, a vehicle that was rather more pleasant to drive than the generic van he'd been out in earlier. Heads turned when he drove his swanky machine, and he liked the notoriety that followed him around. Whether you were crime-living or clean-living, everyone knew Ron Butcher. Graphite Black gleamed as he backed out of his third garage and headed out past the edge of the golf course and into town for breakfast. Radio 4 chatted away in the background with yet another Brexit discussion. It seemed Britain had little else to talk about, and Ron wondered whatever else had gone on in the previous twenty-four hours that had been ignored because it was not as 'of the moment' as the blasted B-word. Now would be the ideal time to commit crime or get a contentious bill through Parliament. He was sick of hearing about Brexit, whether it was Theresa, Boris, or the opposition whining on about it, it made no odds. Democracy was dying, and whether you liked it or not, a referendum should stand. Though it appeared many thought the opposite.

Traffic was slow heading into town, but he wasn't in a rush, and he eventually pulled up outside the bakery. He tightened his jacket closer at the neck and stepped out into a fine drizzle. Hopes of a clear day were gone, the temperature seeming to have dropped a few degrees from earlier. At least a weak sun warmed your bones a little; cold and rain only dampened them. The warmth of the shop hit him square in the face, and he sniffed loudly, grinning at the red-haired man behind the counter as he entered. It was always a pleasant place to be.

"Morning, Ron," Kit said. "I thought you must be ill or something, not being in earlier."

"Spot of business first off, but I'm here now."

"I'll bring it over, take a seat."

As Ron made his way to his usual perch in the corner, he glanced across at a formally dressed man sitting nearby and gave him the once over. It was certainly not an off-the-peg suit he was wearing, Ron knew. He noticed and appreciated the finer things in life. He made himself comfortable.

Ron liked to watch people as they hurried past the window on the way to work, or running errands, or whatnot. It was surprising what he noticed as he perused the outside world, which was now getting bathed in a stronger drizzle, blobs of moisture clinging to everything it touched. A woman dragging a toddler close behind her caught his attention, as did the carrier bag in her hand. How the hell could she afford to be shopping in such upmarket stores when she was a single mum? He must ask her next time he saw her. Maybe she'd got herself a decent-paying job somewhere nice, safe, and secure. Or maybe she was turning tricks again. Kit appeared at his shoulder, breaking into his thoughts.

"Two fresh jam doughnuts and an Americano with cream," he said, setting them down. He added a small pot of dark brown sugar next to them on the bench. "And your cane sugar."

"Damn it, they look good," Ron said, and he tucked into one, a little red jam seeping from the hole he'd just made. Being later in the morning, they were now only just aired, usually they were almost too hot to handle.

"Good?" asked Kit, wiping his hands on his apron.

"I think they're possibly better a little cooler, they have more taste somehow." Ron took another bite. Dismissed, Kit headed back to the counter and stood watching him eat for a moment. Such a skinny man with a sweet tooth, perhaps he was diabetic and didn't know it. Kit had a friend that was just the same; the doctor had called it 'skinny fat' when he'd been diagnosed. Fried doughnuts were not going to do Ron any favours if that was the case. Still, Kit Morris wasn't going to be the one to ask him. He stood watching the back of the man's head of thinning hair. What went on in there, he wondered. Were the local rumours true? He suspected they were, though the man clearly stayed out of trouble with the police.

It made him think of Al Capone – everyone knew that piece of history and what he eventually went away for. At forty-eight, Capone was a little younger than Ron Butcher when he died. He was riddled with syphilis apparently, though he actually died of cardiac arrest following a stroke. Ron looked to have survived to be a few years older, but he was not a healthy-looking specimen either.

Jakub joined him and casually nodded in Ron's direction. "Big businessman. Seen him about."

Everything Jakub said sounded like it had come from a bear's mouth, deep and rough, clipped and somewhat monotone. His voice and demeanour never seemed to match, and since he said precious few words anyway, it frequently came as a surprise when he did speak. Kit thought back to Bubble from *Absolutely Fabulous*, the high-pitched, squeaky voice so far off base from the pretty blonde it was comical, though that was the idea. He found himself smiling a little, and that confused Jakub.

"Funny? How?"

"Sorry, Jakub, I wasn't making fun of you, thinking of someone else for a moment," he said, turning to the young man. "You know him then?"

Did Kit imagine it or did his pale face blush a little? Kit was quick to pick up on the vibe. Maybe Jakub knew more about the man than he was letting on, or perhaps he even had dealings with him.

"Not me. Friend of mine," he said hurriedly. Jakub averted his gaze as he spoke and picked his mug up. "Quick smoke," he added and headed to the back door.

Kit watched his black-clad silhouette leave the room and glanced back to Ron, who was on his second doughnut. He knew what line of business the man was in, that was no secret, everyone in Croydon knew. Maybe that was the answer for him? But was he really that desperate?

"No, you're not, Kit Morris," he scolded himself.

"What was that?" asked Elizabeth as she passed him by. Her question startled him. Inquisitive eyes caught his own.

"Sorry, just thinking out loud." Kit swigged the last of his coffee down and headed out to the back room. As he passed the open back door, he caught a glimpse of Jakub finishing his cigarette, sheltering from the rain under the roof overhang. He couldn't help notice the lad was shivering. Having only ever seen him in his hoody, Kit wondered if he even owned a coat. He grabbed his own from a hook by the door and headed to where Jakub was standing, offering it out. Jakub glanced at it but didn't touch it.

"Take it, else you'll freeze to death. At least until you finish your smoke." Jakub bit into his top lip, obviously thinking about it, so Kit pushed his jacket at him again. "You may as well borrow it, it's doing no good keeping the coat hook warm, may as well be keeping you warm." A thin, pale hand finally took it, and Jakub slipped his skinny arms inside and pulled it closed. Kit saw him visibly relax as the tension from being cold and shivering started to leave his body. The lad nodded his thanks. As Kit headed back inside, he wondered about his situation.

The lad was also short of money, though on a different scale to Kit.

Perhaps they could team up. And solve each of their problems.

CHAPTER 11

The police station
Friday morning

After an emotional start to the day, Amanda Lacey and Jack Rutherford resumed normal ranks and positions in her car, and she drove them the short distance to the police station. Pulling into the car park, Amanda found a space right next to Jack's vehicle, which had been there all night. Wet from the drizzle, which had now upped its pace, the car had a silvery grey sheen that covered up the old, faded black paint job.

"There she is, and still in one piece," Jack said, unbuckling himself. "Rain covers a multitude of sins. She looks almost clean too."

"You ever going to upgrade her, Jack? She's nearly as old as you are."

"No, she's not, just looks it. While she still gets me from A to B without any issues, I'll keep her on. There's no sense in trading up just yet. Which reminds me, talking of old things, Faye will be doing the post-mortem today on the elderly lady from last night. Poor thing, did you see how thin she was?"

"It was hard not to."

"It turns my stomach to think that someone, likely some scumbag youth, frightened the hell out of her and then violated and demeaned her, if only by removing her clothes. Can you imagine what she'd have been feeling right then? She probably died of heart failure."

"What makes you think it's a youth?" enquired Amanda. They were almost at the squad room and their desks. And the coffee cupboard.

"Only because they must have been looking for money or small valuables. TVs are way too big these days and video recorders are non-existent. It's all smartphones and tablets. Tuck it inside their hoody and sell it down the pub stuff. Older thieves tend to have a van, be a bit more organised, maybe a little less opportunistic nowadays."

"An element of truth in that."

"If they've been inside before, they'll want to avoid going back to prison so they try harder at not getting caught. That crime scene had all the hallmarks of a fly-by-night chancer. In my humble opinion, you understand. Add to that she was likely suffering from dementia and the lack of a struggle in the hallway, and maybe she did think she knew him."

"Or maybe she actually did recognise him." Amanda slung her bag over her chair back, and they headed to the coffee cupboard together for their first of the day. Raj, another DC on the team, was leaning against the fridge, mug in hand.

"Morning, all," he said brightly. His customary pale blue shirt looked as crisp as usual; the man was impeccably dressed at all times. His dark brown skin contrasted with the cool colour of his clothes and together with his slim physique gave him a GQ-model look that was the envy of many of his male colleagues. Passing the annual fitness test was never a problem for Raj. Jack had work to do in that area, as did Amanda.

"Morning," they said in unison.

"I heard about yesterday's burglary victim, the elderly lady," Raj said, shaking his head. "Poor thing."

"You know, you've both mentioned burglary, but we don't know for sure that's what it is yet. We've no idea if anything was actually taken, or whether she was hurt by the intruder. And since we don't know anything was definitely stolen, it's possible this is something entirely different."

"Do you really think so, boss?" asked Raj. "How do you explain her being undressed?"

"That may be nothing to do with the crime. She could have been in the throes of getting ready for a shower when the intruder entered. That aspect may not be connected at all."

"And her lying on the floor under the table?" Raj went on. "How do you explain that?"

"Simply frightened, trying to get away, panicked. Then the intruder fled. He or she might not even know the lady is now dead. She could have died an hour after they left."

Jack grunted. He wasn't convinced, but it was a theory. It was easy to jump to conclusions, but then with a crime scene that looked as this one had, it was natural to assume the obvious. Amanda was playing devil's advocate, or the defence to their prosecution. Either way, every angle deserved to be analysed properly, and the truth would eventually float to the surface like cream in coffee, the crime scene investigators would see to that.

"We'll catch them, no matter," Jack said confidently. "*Every contact leaves a trace*, Locard's Exchange Principle. There'll be tiny traces of evidence left at every contact. We might not see them, but they'll be there, and we just have to find them."

"I wish it was as easy as the textbook," said Amanda.

She stood back and left Jack at the capsule machine to make them a mug each. Nine times out of ten, it worked for him perfectly, but that tenth time? Anything could happen, usually just hot water came back. The machine had become his Achilles heel. For a smart man, he amazed her with how often he proved incompetent in the face of such a simple task. But it was to be their lucky day, the fresh aroma of coffee filled the tiny room, and he passed her a perfect mug. She took a sip and expressed her satisfaction with a loud sigh.

"Damn that's a good one, Jack," she said and took a deeper mouthful. "I might have to have another straight after I've finished this one, though no two mugs can ever be the same," she said, more to lift her own spirits than anything else. Jack gave her a sideways smile that he understood and left it at that. It hadn't been that long ago he'd been stood in dressing gown and slippers while his boss cried into his shoulder in his kitchen. It hadn't been the usual start to the day, but still, that's what friends were for. With his own mug full, he followed Amanda over to their desks, and they settled in for the day ahead.

"You seen the email from Faye?" Jack called across to Amanda.

"Yes. Odd she wants to go back to the scene but not unusual. I wonder what she's thinking."

"No clue."

CHAPTER 12

Baker

Friday morning

Kit had hardly had time to breathe but that was the way he liked it. Busy brought cash to the till; quiet brought worry to the mind. However, his money worry was never far away, always niggling away in the back of his mind, sitting in a filing cabinet of his brain. The contents tab of that file reflected on the back of his eyeballs, taunting him like a cape to a bull. In a lull before the sandwich rush, he found himself sneaking a cigarette break outside in the rain like Jakub had, though he had nothing between his fingers other than the handle of a mug. Nicotine wasn't what he needed, but a breather certainly was. The rain had upped its tempo and was now falling hard like fireworks that disintegrate as they hit the ground. Thousands of steady streams of water were falling from the sky, going their own way, and joining up with the shallow river moving around his feet.

Kit thought about the man he had met earlier in the morning, the one from the bank. Could he help with his expansion funding?

That would be one way to grow the business quickly, though he hadn't been entirely truthful on that score. He'd said he was opening two more next year, but that wasn't true. He was struggling to get even the second one open with funds being so tight. Why had he lied? To impress a stranger? It had been unnecessary, but the words had left his mouth before he knew what he was saying. Still, it was done now, and the chances of ever seeing the guy again would be remote. In reality, it should have been store number five next year, not two. It would have been if his business partnership not gone south.

But he did have pressing financial matters to attend to, and a cash injection would help him immensely. The size of it was relative. To a homeless person living on the street, a £10 note would be considered wealth. To a billionaire, a £20,000 bottle of champagne would be considered loose change. Kit fitted somewhere in between. He needed £20,000, that bottle of bubbly in fact, but he was up to his limit at the bank and had already been told there was no more. They were getting tighter when it came to lending to businesses, not trusting the economy to keep sales buoyed, and with so much emphasis on Brexit and little else, Kit had been instructed to make it work with what he had. It was painful for him. His product was excellent, his sales were increasing, but unfortunately they weren't interested. Now there was the machinery outlay he'd paid for. He'd got an excellent deal for three pieces of second-hand equipment, but it had meant paying cash for them instead of taking out finance and paying them back over time. He'd figured it would have been better in the long run; his accountant had disagreed. Now, Kit needed a break in his luck. He'd not done the sums properly, not thought through the implications of financing it as he had. Add to that a failed business partnership, and it was no wonder cash worries were on his mind.

Three years ago, Kit had met Darrel, and the man had bought a twenty per cent stake in the business. Everything had been going to plan until Kit had found him fiddling the books, and he'd kicked him out. A week or two prior to their falling out, they'd agreed a price on Kit's car, to be payable over three instalments. Darrel had paid the first instalment, and Kit had agreed to sign the car over since they were mates and business partners. After he'd caught Darrel fiddling the books, Kit hadn't seen another payment. Darrel still owed him £20,000, and the likelihood of him ever seeing that money was slim to none. He'd no legal leg to stand on since he was officially no longer the owner. As a shareholder, Kit had financed a buyout to sever all ties but the failed relationship with Darrel was a double whammy.

The file in his head, its contents tab flashing at him, screamed 'do something'. He watched the outside door open and close as Jakub sauntered out for a cigarette break of his own. The lad didn't join him, perhaps hadn't even noticed him from under the hood of his sweatshirt. Kit kept his distance and finished his coffee in silence before tipping the dregs into the river and moving back towards the rear door. But standing mulling his problems over had given Kit the germ of an idea. Jakub needed extra cash – all youngsters did, didn't they? Could he get what was rightfully owed to him with Jakub's help? Or was he dreaming? Since Darrel officially owned the vehicle according to the documentation, Kit had no legal right to 'his own' property.

All he needed was a driver, someone who would be willing to drive the car back to him once he got the keys. That was the first obstacle to overcome, but it was not an insurmountable one. Knowing where Darrel lived and worked, he was sure that part would be a doddle, just slip in and slip back out again. He likely wouldn't know his keys were even missing for a while, though when he came to reach for the spare pair and found that they were also gone, he would likely work it out. Would Jakub want to get involved, for a cut? If he sold it right, it would be an easy job. It had been obvious to Kit earlier that Jakub knew more about Ron Butcher than he was letting on.

Now all he had to do was scope Jakub out and hope he was up for getting two sets of keys back.

It would be easy money.

CHAPTER 13

Butcher

Friday lunchtime

Bernard Evans was as insalubrious as Ron was. While Ron was gaunt and twig thin, Bernard was the polar opposite size-wise, with a pink chubby face to match his bulging stomach. It had been some years since the two had last met up as Bernard had been on the run in Europe for his part in a child-trafficking ring. That had been back at the turn of the century, Christmas 1999 in fact, and he'd been living and working across Europe ever since then. He doubted anyone was even looking for him now, not for that crime at any rate. All the evidence had burned to the ground when the house they'd operated from went up in flames. Their then ringleader had died in the fire, but the rest of them had managed to escape, and with open borders across much of Europe, it had been a doddle for Bernard to disappear. Nobody had caught up with him.

He'd learned a new skill while in Poland, where he'd worked trafficking girls in all manner of ways until the industry had become too hot for him to handle. Rather than risk getting caught, he'd found forging identity documents to be something he was actually rather good at and had stuck to that. It was less hassle, meant you got your money up front, and as long as he had the right tools, he could easily transport himself and his business anywhere he needed to. It made commercial sense, and since he wasn't getting any younger, it suited his more sedentary lifestyle. He still had contacts *in traffic*, as he liked to refer to them, should he wish to go back to it, and he occasionally visited one of their establishments for his own greedy pleasure. He couldn't help himself.

Ron disliked the man, but in business, sometimes needs must. He approached the ample figure of Bernard and sat down next to him.

"It's been a while," he opened with. Never one to lie unless he had to, Ron wasn't going to say 'good to see you' if it wasn't true.

Nicotine-stained teeth grinned at him, and Ron tried not to balk at the stale breath that escaped the man's mouth. Dental hygiene was not his skill.

"Ron," he exclaimed. "Sit down while I get you a pint. London Pride, right?"

"In one," he said, turning away from the vapour as the big man headed for the bar.

Service was brisk, and it seemed only a moment later that Bernard was back with two pints of deep-golden amber. Ron took a long drink to cleanse his palate, the somewhat sweet, malty flavour replacing the lingering taste of coffee. At 11.30 in the morning, it was almost too early to enjoy a pint, but a pub was the best place to meet someone like Bernard. The man hadn't changed a dot since he'd last seen him, still as overweight and just as sloth-like. Bernard drained a quarter of his glass and rested his head back with an audible gasp of delight. "So, what's this about?"

"I've run into a spot of bother with a supplier, and I thought you might be able to help fill some orders." Any eavesdroppers would have thought it a normal business discussion – unless they knew what the man was peddling.

"I'm listening, go on."

"Not much else to tell you. Though I should ask your price and inspect a sample."

"Naturally. I'll get a set to you. Is your boy Felix still involved?" It didn't go unnoticed he hadn't quoted a price, but Ron let it go, for now. Bernard obviously knew his stuff or he wouldn't have even enquired about Felix. He'd done his homework.

"He is. Have you met him since you've been back?"

"Not as yet, no, but I hear he has a taste for the job." Bernard gave an exaggerated wink, showing more caramel teeth, and Ron fought to control his clenching stomach. He didn't approve of some of his son's methods, but he did approve of the results. How he got them was up to him, it would be him facing the law if he ever got collared.

"I should introduce the two of you then, since it's his side of the business really. I'll set it up."

"Grateful," Bernard said, draining half his glass. Ron waited for a belch that thankfully never came. "Fancy another?"

Ron wasn't halfway down his own glass yet. "It's my round, I'll get you one," he said, standing to do the necessary and leaving Bernard to focus on the last of his pint. It gave Ron a chance to pull away for a moment and make a call. He instructed the barmaid to pull Bernard's pint slowly and slipped her a fiver for her trouble. Felix answered promptly and Ron said, "I've got someone you need to meet. Get over to the Baskerville as quick as you can."

"It's not called that any more, Dad."

"I know, force of habit, just get over here now." He hung up and waited for the pint. When he turned back towards Bernard, he gave a tight smile and wandered over.

"Is Felix on his way?" Bernard asked. He caught the look on Ron's face and added, "That's what you'd have done twenty years ago. I took a punt you haven't changed."

Ron relaxed a little. It seemed Bernard was no fool, he only looked it.

"Then you know the answer to your own question," Ron said. "How soon can we see a sample?"

"As soon as he gets here."

"You carry them around with you?" Ron asked incredulously.

"You could say that." he leaned in a little and added, "I'm no longer Bernard."

"You did your own?"

"Why not?"

"Risky?"

"Not in the slightest."

"So, what's your name now then?"

"Barry Cribbins." Ron couldn't help himself and threw his head back laughing. The barmaid looked across at the sudden outburst then went back to wiping glasses.

"Let me guess, you always liked Bernard Cribbins, and since you're now Barry, and not Bernard, you added Cribbins to be close, like."

"Works for me. I loved the *Wombles* as a youngster."

Ron couldn't help but smile at that logic. "Let's see then, Barry," he added as an afterthought. Or was it a dig?

As Bernard struggled to retrieve his wallet from his trouser pocket, the door opened and Felix walked in. Spotting his dad, he headed over, all swagger like young men often were. He was a younger version of Ron and just as wiry. Without being invited, he pulled a chair out from a nearby table, dragged it across, and sat down.

"Hello Barry," he said, smiling.

How the hell Felix knew the man and his assumed name, Ron had no idea, but something told him he was about to find out.

CHAPTER 14

Baker

Friday lunchtime

The more he thought about it, the more Kit liked the idea. And surely Jakub would appreciate the money on offer – it was a fair exchange, keys for cash. A simple job, he expected, and if he framed it correctly, one Jakub should feel comfortable about doing. Certainly, there was no harm in asking, it wasn't like he was planning a bank robbery or a raid on a corner shop. The lad would only be helping to return an item to its rightful owner.

While there was a lull in trade, Kit worked his wording out in his head and approached Jakub. Elizabeth was busy out front with a handful of remaining customers when Kit found Jakub eating his own lunch on the back step. The rain had finally stopped falling, but it had left everything gleaming wet in the weak daylight. At just gone 1.30 pm, the day felt like it was already closing to darkness. It was a depressing thought. Kit squeezed past Jakub and sat down next to him, making him shuffle up a little. A lad of few words, he never complained or had an opinion on anything. Kit started off with small talk, the weather.

"At least it's stopped for a while. I hate the rain, don't you?"

Jakub merely grunted, a slight nod of his head in agreement perhaps. Kit moved on, sensing small talk would be non-existent.

"I have a little job for you, a chance to earn yourself some extra cash, if you want it?" he said, facing forward, not wanting to look at him.

That caught Jakub's attention, and he turned sideways to Kit, finishing the last mouthful of his sandwich.

"Job? What job?"

"I need someone to get my car keys back for me."

"Why not you do it?" Such a deep mono voice didn't suit the lad's frame and demeanour.

"Well, here's the thing. The car is at someone else's home, someone who hasn't paid for it. And they have the keys." Kit stayed facing forward.

"You want me to steal them for you."

It wasn't a question, and Kit let the statement hang for a moment while he considered whether to answer it, and if he was going to, what to say. When the silence had gone on for too long, he had no option.

"I suppose so, yes." He cringed to himself. It wasn't going quite how he'd planned it in his head. Perhaps he'd blown it already.

"How much pay?"

He was interested!

"Two hundred. The keys are local."

"Three hundred and I do it."

"Deal. I'll get you the address. I guess you'll want to do it during the night, when the vehicle is home."

"Leave it to me. I sort it. Cash up front."

Kit hoped there was enough in the safe, so many customers paid by card these days.

"Okay. Do you need anything else?"

"No." He stood to leave – for another cigarette, perhaps? Kit watched him amble outside to where he'd been stood earlier that morning and noted the orange flicker as the match caught light. Was that it then? Was it that simple? He'd just organised for an employee to steal car keys for him with no questions asked, aside from how much he'd get paid. Still, Jakub hadn't actually stolen anything yet. The car itself was a different matter. It needed a bit more planning. He'd have to figure out where to hide the vehicle for one thing. But how could he get the paperwork transferred back into his name, preferably beforehand? When Darrel realised both sets of keys had gone missing, he'd likely come looking for him, the obvious suspect. And Darrel would be able to replace the keys fairly quickly as well. With so many cars driving around by remote keyless system, a replacement set would come from a dealership rather than a locksmith, but even so, he didn't envisage it taking long. It was a shame he couldn't just hand over the vehicle's identification number himself, he probably still had it on an old insurance document, and then get a duplicate set made, but too many questions would be asked, and he'd be leaving a trail too. The more he tossed ideas around, the more he came back to the same conclusion: there was no other way around it, he had to involve someone else.

Judging from his quick reaction, Kit suspected it wouldn't be Jakub's first theft. He hoped the lad hadn't been stealing anything more than a sticky bun during his employment at the bakery. He wrote Darrel's address on a Post-it note and took it out to Jakub who had almost finished his cigarette.

"I'll leave the details up to you. It's a black Audi A5. Lives on the drive, though I've no idea about the keys themselves."

"Want me to drive it away?"

"No!" he said, almost shouting. "Just the keys. I've nowhere to put the damn thing yet."

Jakub thought for a moment before adding, "I do."

"That might be the case, but I'm not ready yet. There are documents to sort out first, to prove it's mine. I don't want 'stolen' goods hanging around, so I need to fix that part sooner than later."

It wasn't lost on Kit that Jakub had a solution ready. Just who had he hired? Not the quiet lad he thought he had, that was for sure.

"I help with documents too, if you like."

Heavens, who was he? But Kit was intrigued now. Perhaps it would be easier all round if the lad sorted the documentation as well. After all, he had a bakery to run and could ill afford the time it would take to do the necessary. He assumed Jakub was talking forgeries there too.

"Out of interest, how could you do the change of ownership?"

"I know a man. Gets documents for people. He can do car."

"How much?" Now he sounded like Jakub, though his voice was nowhere near as deep.

"You afford. I ask him. I get keys anyway. You decide." Kit watched as he stubbed the butt out under his foot and ambled back inside, break over. As Kit followed, he wondered when the deed might be done and just how he'd sort the documentation himself, without Jakub's help. Perhaps he hadn't thought this through quite as well as he should have, and maybe Jakub was the solution to the paperwork too. It would cost him though. Cost him funds he didn't have.

He needed the money from that car, a car that was rightfully his, and he doubted Darrel was struggling with cash flow quite like he was. Getting it back and selling it on quickly was the only way to solve his money problems.

He'd better get his thinking cap on if he was going to do it himself.

CHAPTER 15

Banker

Friday afternoon

Lee Meady was hard at work behind his desk as if the slower start
to his day had never happened. The AA had eventually arrived and
changed the tyre for him, so he'd be good to go when he arrived
back at Croydon station later. After a quick shower and change, he
and Bethany would be due for dinner at Eric and Tanya's place not
far from their own. Sitting back in his chair, pen tapping his lower
lip rhythmically, Lee remembered breakfast with Bethany and her
headache. A clever and strong woman with her own career as an
area manager for a retail chain, she sometimes felt out of place at
their get-togethers, feeling her contribution to the conversation
was never quite adequate enough. All three, including Lee, had
gone to university, but she never had. Instead, she'd plunged
straight into retail with gusto, starting out as a seasonal worker as
soon as she'd left school. By the time she was twenty, she'd earned
herself her first store management role and had excelled all the way.

Lee could never understand why she felt left out of the conversation and as though she hadn't much of interest to offer, but he was conscious of her feelings and looked for her input as much as possible. He reached for his phone and pushed his chair away from his desk with one leg. He worried when she had bad headaches, and he hoped she had rested and called in sick as he'd suggested. He knew from experience that when his own vision started to blur and resemble the inside of a kaleidoscope, though without the colours, there was nothing for it but to stop. Driving was impossible. A dark room, a tablet and quiet time for it to pass was all anyone could do. He looked at the time, it was almost 2 pm. Was he calling too early? He didn't want to wake her unnecessarily, and the tablet he'd given her was a strong one. Still, he called anyway, he was concerned. But after six rings it went through to voicemail, and so he left a brief message.

"I wanted to check you were okay, but I'm guessing you're sleeping. Text me when you wake and get this, tell me you're feeling better." He blew a kiss as was often his custom and ended the call. If he hadn't heard from her by 4 pm, he'd have to call Eric and Tanya and cancel. It would be a shame; he'd been looking forward to dinner with them both. Still, there'd be other times.

The next best thing he could do was arrange for a bouquet of fresh flowers to be delivered around 3.30 pm, so he telephone-ordered a large bunch of pale pink roses from the shop he usually used. He smiled to himself. It wasn't usually Bethany on the receiving end of his gifts. Without realising he was doing it, he readjusted his crotch. Lee had his fun time. He didn't regard it as an affair, and that's how he reconciled it in his mind. The younger man got what he wanted, and so did he. Taking him a gift occasionally was simply Lee's way of saying 'thanks' without insulting him. He coughed lightly to distract himself from his thoughts, crossed his legs, and pulled himself back up to the desk in one fluid movement. At that moment, his office door opened, and his PA filled the doorway.

"The boardroom is ready now, everyone is seated and waiting," she announced with efficiency and grace. Jean had been part of the bank's staff since decimalisation it seemed, though really it was only about thirty years, not nearly fifty. With her hair neatly knotted in a plait pinned close to her head, she looked like Miss Moneypenny. With her look, it was apt that she worked in a bank, though he never teased his PA like James Bond teased M's.

"Thanks, Jean, I'm on my way. Listen, can you give me a nudge at 4 pm? I need to call home, and this meeting could see me carried away never to return." He smiled as he said the last couple of words and then added, "And I need to be out of here no later than 4.30." He gathered papers and his pen from his desk and shuffled everything into a pile ready to go.

"Something nice on for the weekend?" she enquired.

"Dinner with friends tonight, that's all, but Bethany wasn't well when I left, and she's not answering now so I'm assuming she's sleeping."

"Rest is always best. I hope she feels better soon. Please give her my regards." There was a gentleness in her words.

Lee moved towards the door, papers in hand. "Thank you, I will. Right, interrupt at four then."

"I will, Mr Meady," she said in a light sing-song voice. Always as bright as a freshly bloomed sunflower, she spread just enough of her pleasantness without cloying.

For the next two hours, he concentrated on the group of men and women in front of him, and when Jean entered the room with a fake message for him, he quickly ducked out and made the call. Bethany answered and gushed her thanks for the exquisite flowers. He was delighted she was feeling much better.

"I'll be leaving here in about half an hour, so I'll be home in plenty of time. Are you sure you're okay for dinner tonight?" He ladled concern on his words, and Bethany laughed a little at his attempt to sound like a caring nurse.

"A little tired and fuzzy but I'm sure a hot shower will wake me up. I'll see you when you get home. Drive carefully."

"Right, yes. I'll finish up here and be on my way. And Bethany?"

"Yes?"

"I'm glad you're feeling better." He blew a kiss, listened for a return one, then ended the call.

CHAPTER 16

Butcher
Friday afternoon

Following a spot of lunch, Ron and Felix left the pub around 1 pm. Barry, as he was now calling himself, had left them soon after Felix had arrived, having seen a female acquaintance standing at the bar that he wanted to catch up with. When Ron and Felix had walked out, the two were looking cosy together. Barry moving on suited Ron down to the ground since he was anxious to know how his son knew the man. It was also an opportune time to breathe without the fetid halitosis seeping out from behind stained teeth. Apparently their paths had crossed about a year ago, when one of Barry's customers had used Felix for financing the new documents for himself and his young wife. Felix had found himself finalising the purchase because the husband had ended up in hospital with a kidney stone and the young woman had made contact with him. Long story short, Felix had got further involved so the transaction could continue, as she couldn't drive and hand over the cash.

"I wouldn't have thought he'd pull anything with a mouth like that. Someone should give him some hygiene pointers," Ron said as they carried on along the pavement. He was parked a little way off and pulled out his vape pen. Vanilla drifted on the air, and Felix wafted the haze away, not impressed with its sickliness.

"I don't think the kind he usually goes for has any say in the matter anyway, if you understand," Felix added. "He likes 'em young. Too young. Weirdo."

Ron grimaced. "You should report the nonce, that ain't right," he said, shaking his head.

"That's not going to be either of us, now, is it? Come on, Dad, we liaise with the cops when they come calling, not the other way around. Anyway, they need to catch him at it, in the right place, else there's nothing to charge him with."

"His breath would be a start. And he's bound to have a computer full of evidence. Anyway, you seem to know a lot about him, I thought you only met him a year or so ago?"

"Yeah, but he talks, brags a bit. He's obviously stupid. Anyway, back to our documents problem. My gut says he's not trustworthy, which is one reason I hadn't approached him myself. But I have to admit, it's a top job he's done, on his own at any rate. I'd say better than our current supplier." Felix raised a cigarette pack to his mouth, caught a filter tip between his teeth, and removed the whole thing from the packet. A silver lighter clicked open and lit it. Grey-blue smoke wafted lightly around his head, overcoming the vanilla instantly.

"Do you have any other options up your jumper?"

"None, no. But I'm working on it. Anyway, I'll give him a call later and set one up. Give him a trial, like I said, though I'm not convinced about him holding his mouth as tight shut as we're accustomed to."

"Well, he's kept himself out of prison thus far, so he must be clever enough to keep the important stuff quiet."

"It's his own skin he's looking after, that's why." They were back at Ron's car, which was sitting gleaming wet after the rain had finally stopped. He moved his index finger through the moisture on the roof as Felix finished off what he was saying. As a young boy, he'd always been fascinated with water, and as one of life's little luxuries, watering the garden on a warm summer evening was right up there in the pleasure chest. He found it almost mesmerising, therapeutic even, and he rubbed his wet finger against his dry thumb, feeling the water's softness. He turned his attention back to Felix. "You on your way home too, or have you something on?"

"I've a couple of late-payers to pay a visit to as it were," he said, half-smiling at his own choice of words. "Which reminds me, how did you get on first thing? Have you still got the knack? Want to do these two for me?"

"I have, and no, I don't. That's your domain, not mine. Anyway, if it's that young mum with the dank hair and spots again, I thought you had an arrangement? Not that payment in kind pays for your beer. Plus, it's not good business sense."

"It's not me that goes there, not my type. Gez pays the visit and gives the equivalent owed money to the kitty. I think he enjoys that part of his job role. Suits them both really."

Ron could only shake his head. "Didn't do that in my day. But then I'd met your mother early on." The two men fell silent as memories of Lyn lingered in their heads. Both had doted on the woman. With her firm ways and soft heart, she held the balance in their household like a spirit level – perfectly. Ron had slipped a miniature level inside her coffin, their own private joke shared to the grave.

Felix broke the silence. "I'll be back later then," he said abruptly, turning to walk back to his own car, which was parked behind the pub.

"You out tonight?" Ron called.

"No. I fancy a night with the telly and a six pack," he shouted, waving a hand in the air. Felix still lived at home with his dad, though the huge detached property they shared meant they could go almost all week without actually bumping into one another. Ron at one end, Felix at the other. Felix had even added a small kitchen for his own use, which he found handy when entertaining. He liked to keep his private life just that, private. His latest lover was a married man, and while his father had a broad mind for many things, Felix was still living his life firmly in the closet. If word got around to the rest of the crew, he doubted they'd still see him the same way. They weren't open-minded enough to risk it, and Felix didn't want to fall out with his father either. Since his mother had gone, his dad was his guiding force, a friend, mentor, and all he had to look up to. He was keen to keep it that way.

Ron watched his son head back to where he'd parked his own vehicle, grateful for the short chat they'd just had. The two of them shared the same passion for smart cars, a shining, bright red Range Rover was his son's pride and joy. It was about time the lad settled down, Ron thought, got himself a girlfriend. He'd seen precious little activity on that front in recent months. Or was it years? Still, he enjoyed knowing the boy wasn't staying far away from him, there was a comfort in that of an evening. He turned back to his own car, shaking his head at Barry Cribbins and his lack of dental hygiene.

CHAPTER 17

The crime scene
Friday afternoon

Dr Faye Mitchell had been the pathologist on more of Amanda and Jack's cases than they cared to remember. She was part of the furniture in many respects, a member of the extended team even though she was not officially employed by the police. Some years back, budget cuts and restructuring had seen forensics and pathology services go from being publicly funded to being contracted out to private companies. Long gone were the days when a DNA test was done as part of an investigation. Now, the cost of that same test was weighed against whether it would do any good.

When they got to the old lady's house, Faye was sitting in her car waiting for them. Jack pulled up behind her and lightly honked his horn. It obviously made her jump, judging from how her shoulders rose and then sunk quickly at the sound.

"Are you trying to bug her?" Amanda asked, opening her door and stepping on to the pavement. Jack followed, and Faye opened her door to join them. As her golden blonde head entered the frame, her eyes caught Jack's, and they weren't exactly smiling. She wrinkled her mouth in a silent reprimand, and the three headed towards the front door with nothing more than a polite 'afternoon' from her. Jack let Amanda take the lead since it was her case and she was actually the boss – it was easy to forget at times. He took up the rear as the three of them entered the hallway.

The temperature inside was on a par with yesterday, and he rubbed his arms against the chill. Even with his own jacket on, he felt the cold on his face and was reminded of the elderly lady they'd found lying naked in the lounge. The three of them filed into the room and took in the scene again. Everything was how it had been only yesterday, although Nelly Raven was now on a trolley back at the mortuary. Faye pulled a sheet from the file in her hands and read.

"No prints found."

"Must have worn gloves," Amanda offered.

"And the temperature, when we found her yesterday, was eight degrees in here."

Amanda looked at Jack and shrugged her shoulders, both likely guessing where the statements were heading.

"Yes," they said in unison. Following Faye out of the room where the woman's body had been found, they headed to the kitchen. The tin of baked beans, stale bread, marmalade, knife, and tin opener were exactly as they had been yesterday. Jack noticed Faye looking at the tin of beans closely, the fragments of peeling label still dangling down the side like tiny tassels.

"Apparently," Amanda started. "The neighbour thought Nelly was losing her mind a bit, and I wondered if perhaps, in her confusion, she tried to open the tin with the carving knife instead of the tin opener. The marks on the label look like they've been scratched at, perhaps by a thin blade."

Jack stared at Amanda. That was exactly what he'd been thinking only yesterday. The management course hadn't worked if she was nicking his ideas to impress the doctor. Faye turned to Amanda, registering what she was telling her.

"Well done, you, Amanda. Because I'm wondering the exact same thing." There was a coolness in her words, almost as cool as the old kitchen, and Jack wondered if she herself might thaw out anytime soon. She wasn't usually so icy, not with Amanda at any rate. He made a mental note, don't make her jump in future.

"Well, I don't think you'll find a burglar in this instance," she announced, standing up fully, authority and knowledge on her shoulders. A big announcement was about to be delivered.

"Then how do you explain the mess, the upturned books, photos scattered everywhere? Not to mention her being naked?" Amanda sounded confused because she was.

"I think we'll find our only culprit, in this instance, is the cold," Faye said. "Nelly Raven simply died of hypothermia."

"It's not *that* cold," added Jack incredulously. "Really? At eight degrees?"

"It doesn't need to be any colder, particularly if there's a strong draught to increase the chill even further. A common misconception, I'm afraid. It's the vulnerable, young or old, that can die indoors and do. It's about the body's core temperature. If it falls below around twenty-six degrees Celsius, death will almost certainly follow, and I think that's what's happened here. Plus, it fits with what you are saying about her mental state. She may not have been capable of turning the heater on, may not have been aware it was so cold. And sometimes hypothermia can add to an apathy that affects one's willingness to eat or look after one's own hygiene. Like depression."

Amanda wasn't entirely convinced and asked, "But what about all the mess in the lounge? Are you saying it was part of her confusion?"

"Yes."

"And the fact she was found naked, under the table? How can that be part of it?"

"It happens often. Hypothermia survivors say they felt hot despite the cold and so strip off their clothes, making matters worse. They are convinced it's what they should do. And Nelly

Raven had a classic case of hide-and-die syndrome, so she hid under the table. Again, it's common for victims to pull furniture over or hide under things, as Nelly did." The room fell silent as all three digested what had likely happened. Faye started back towards the front door. "I needed to check because hypothermia can be tricky to diagnose. The dead are cold anyway, and dying of cold looks fairly similar. But looking back over the scene, the beans tin, for instance, it all fits."

"We need to find the son," said Jack. "His poor mother in effect died of neglect is what you're saying, isn't it?"

"I'm afraid so, yes. Self-neglect really. Had someone taken an interest in her wellbeing, had things not got to this state, she likely would still be here today." It was a desperately sad state of affairs. "At least the neighbour popped along yesterday, or else who knows how long she could've been lying there. It's pitiful."

"Thanks, Faye. We'll find the family. Maybe they'll care," said Amanda.

"And maybe they won't," said Jack. "What a sorry state to die in," he added, shaking his head in disbelief.

CHAPTER 18

The police station
Friday afternoon

Back at the station, Jack relayed to Raj and the rest of the team that they were no longer looking for an intruder in the previous evening's case. Nelly Raven had died of hypothermia with precipitating dementia. That is what would be recorded in the coroner's report, though Jack threw in his own thoughts. "Self-neglect because no one looked out for their old mum," he added bitterly. "What type of person does that, eh? Ignores their own flesh and blood, letting them freeze to death naked and alone and likely frightened." The room was deathly quiet while Jack finished his rant, all eyes to the ground as if they too were guilty of such an atrocity. Clearly upset, nobody had anything to add, the show all Jack's own. He finished off by suggesting everyone give their mum and dad a call before they did anything else; he wished his own mum was still around for him to be able to do so. When his sermon was finally over, he grabbed his car keys and headed out towards the back entrance without another word, leaving the team in stunned

silence. Amanda knew it was better to leave him when he was
upset, and since he clearly was, she let him have his space. Not one
to slack off from work, he'd be back later when he'd cooled off and
got his head back in the right place. She stood and walked over to
the window. From a particular spot, she could just make out the
staff car park exit, and she watched Jack's car pull out on to the
busy road below. Where he'd be headed, she had no idea, but wherever it was, she hoped he'd be back in a better mood.

There was almost steam coming from Jack's ears as he drove
towards the pub. He wasn't a drinker, but he'd always found the
gentle background chatter and clinking of glasses somewhat therapeutic, as he did his music. Now he knew how to operate hands
free, he directed Siri to play his 'thinking' playlist, and ELO joined
him en route. 'Sweet Talkin' Woman', the next song queued, filled
the confines of his car. It took a few moments for his shoulders to
relax and for him to gently mumble along to the words he knew so
well. Jack knew each and every song ELO had ever recorded and
played them regularly, particularly if something was on his mind.
Nelly Raven's senseless death inhabited that space now. It was times
like these that he missed his wife, Janine, more than life itself. She'd
have known how to comfort him, as she had through so many cases
that had saddened him over the years. She'd been his strength when
he'd felt weak, and even though she'd been gone about seven years,
it often felt like only yesterday. Recently, Vivian, a woman he'd
known for most of his policing career, had come back into his life.
They'd been dating for a couple of months and Jack was getting
fond of her, but they didn't yet have the same emotional connection
he and Janine had had. Would they ever? Still, he was enjoying her
company.

He pulled into the pub car park and wandered inside. It hadn't
occurred to him where he was actually driving to. Almost on
autopilot, he'd made his way subconsciously to the old Baskerville.
He'd always know it as such, no matter which fancy brewery took it

over and turned it into an eatery. He nodded to the barman, pointed to London Pride, and waited for his beer to be pulled. A burly, tattooed arm deposited the tall glass on the bar, and Jack handed a note over. Change appeared by his elbow, but he left it where it was – maybe he'd hang around for another. Taking a long swig, he savoured the malty taste and thought about his Janine again. Why had the old woman's neglect case bothered him so much, and why was he thinking about Janine at the same time? He'd not neglected her. Quite the opposite, in fact. No one could have predicted such a ravenous cancer making its home in her body, and he'd stayed alongside her to the bitter and uncomfortable end. He drank from his glass, keeping his eyes to himself, hunched over the bar like a man with problems. A deep male voice broke into his thoughts, "Another pint?" it asked. Jack raised his eyes to meet the barman's and nodded. As an afterthought, he called, "And a sandwich of some description to go with it, please." He'd need something to soak the beer up with. It wasn't usual for Jack to drink early afternoon, not like old policing days. He'd find himself dozing off to sleep in another hour and, at that thought, let a yawn escape his body. The next pint sat next to his almost empty glass, and he watched the foam settle while he thought about finding Nelly Raven's son. Remembering the neighbour had given him a telephone number, he found it in his phone, called, and waited for it to connect – again. Was this the right time and place to have such a conversation? Particularly while he was feeling both angry and maudlin? Was he in danger of giving the individual a piece of his mind? He didn't even know the man's name, nor where he lived – a mobile number could mean anywhere, literally. He needn't have worried. The phone rang out without going to voicemail. Again. He hung up and tossed his phone on to the bar, letting it bounce and clatter along for a couple of feet.

"You'll be breaking that," the barman said, setting a beef sandwich down. "A bad day is it?"

"It appears to be, yes. Well, a sad one actually."

"Sorry to hear that. A pint will do you good then." And then he was gone, off to serve another customer waiting nearby. Paying no attention to anyone else's world other than his own, he ate his lunch in silence and drank the second pint to halfway down before deciding he'd had enough. Booze was not the answer. Stifling a belch, he nipped into the gents and then headed back out to his car.

At least the rain had stopped.

CHAPTER 19

Banker

Friday evening

Right on time. It was coming up to 5.30 pm when Lee Meady pulled up at his electric gates, which slowly opened their arms for him. Tiny smooth pebbles crunched under his tyres as he parked his gleaming red Jaguar by the front door. Since they were dining out later, there was little point in putting it in the garage. Under the pale creaminess of the outdoor wall lanterns, the metallic red of the sleek vehicle looked as inviting as a glass of mulled wine.

His warm breath billowed as it mixed with the coldness of the early evening, forming tiny clouds that evaporated as quickly as they were formed. It was only a handful of steps to the front porch where he slipped his key in the lock to enter. A warming atmosphere greeted him as he made his way through to the back of the house and their bright, open-plan, glass box of a kitchen where they both spent a good deal of their time. A fire burned in the corner where two giant soft sofas invited you to sink into them. It was the best place to sit and read, snuggled up, particularly when snow was falling on the other side of the windowpanes. They'd often joked their formal lounge was a complete waste of space since no one ever used the room. Bethany called a greeting from 'her' sofa, swinging her legs off at the same time.

"Great timing," she said, standing up fully and pecking Lee on the cheek. The pale pink roses he'd sent filled two vases and were set on the coffee table along with the book she had been reading. A faint perfume lingered around them.

"And how are you feeling? Better?"

"Much better, thanks. A little droopy, but at least my headache has shifted. I took your advice and stayed home."

Lee glanced at the roses and sniffed. "I can smell perfume, and not your usual."

"It's the roses. Aren't they stunning? And their perfume is so pretty. I wondered if the florist had perhaps sprayed them with something. Only, commercial roses hardly ever smell of anything." Lee watched as Bethany poured herself a glass of water. "Can I get you a drink?"

"I'll head up and shower first, I think. I'm driving, so I'll save my glass for dinner," he said, smiling.

"I'll pour you a small wine, dinner will be ages yet," she said, opening the fridge, retrieving a bottle of white, and pouring him a half glass. "You've plenty of time yet. Sit and relax a while, and tell me about your day," she instructed casually, heading back towards the comfort of the sofa. The glow from the flames reflected on the hearth tiles giving the illusion it was on fire. A comforting warmth wrapped around them both, and Lee felt his cheeks turning pink from the heat. He rested back and closed his eyes for a moment, savouring the comfort he felt as he started to unwind at the end of a rather long week.

"Penny for them," Bethany said gently. She'd been watching him relax, his facial muscles beginning to slacken.

"Oh, I was just thinking it's a shame to be going out. We've got everything we need right here. Warmth, wine, each other." His eyes were still firmly closed and were turning as pink as his cheeks were.

"But no dinner cooked," she teased.

"Takeaway can be ordered." He let the words linger.

"We'll enjoy it when we get there."

"I know. But I'm enjoying this too," he said, sounding sleepy.

Bethany joined him on his sofa and lay her head and shoulders across his lap. She looked up at him. He was a handsome man, the start of grey peeking through his dark brown hair, like minute threads of wavy silver cotton at his temples. They had a relationship many envied; maybe it had something to do with not having the stress of rearing children. It wasn't everyone's ideal, but it suited Lee and Bethany. Their downtime was theirs to do with as they pleased. It was a shame Lee spent his the way he often did, though he'd no idea she knew about his secret. Bethany had considered leaving him then thought better of it. She gave him a friendly nudge with the palm of her hand.

"Come on, before we both fall asleep."

"Hmm?"

"See what I mean? You'll be fast asleep if I leave you so come on, let's go and shower," she said, removing herself from the sofa.

Eric and Tanya were always good fun, though Lee had no clue who the other two guests would be. Usually, he'd look forward to the serendipity of it all. Great food, scintillating conversation, and a decent brandy at the end of it all. But tonight he was tired and given the chance would most certainly take a rain check, though it was too late to back out now. Lee knocked back the last mouthful of his wine and slipped his shoes on. Examining himself in the full-length mirror, he pulled his stomach in a little and turned to one side to appraise himself. Bethany's hand seemed to appear from nowhere, and she turned him towards her.

"As handsome as ever, Mr Meady," she said, smiling, and she led him from the room and back downstairs.

"I've got my phone so you needn't bother taking yours," she said, slipping hers into her bag. "Ready?"

"Ready."

It was to be a night they'd never forget.

CHAPTER 20

Baker

Friday evening

Back in Croydon, Kit Morris was watching TV with his young family around him, though he wasn't actually concentrating on what was being said. Worried that Jakub had agreed to get two sets of car keys for him over the weekend, he wondered when and how it all might happen. And, indeed, whether he himself had been idiotic in asking. If something went wrong, the lad would likely drop him in it to save himself, as most people would, unless they were protecting a loved one. Kit most certainly didn't fall into that category.

He glanced across at his two young girls who were watching the movie mesmerised, their sweet faces absorbed with the action on the screen, barely blinking in case they missed something. He'd do anything for those two, protect them no matter what, and he knew their mother, Natalie, would too. Idly, he wondered what she'd say about the state of their finances currently, at the predicament he'd put them in and about what he'd set in motion to sort it all out, had she known about any of it. While he'd reconciled it in his own head as taking back something that was rightfully theirs, he knew this wasn't entirely true. Still, he couldn't think of a safer way to get £20,000 back in the tin. The banks had made that plenty clear. He remembered the customer that morning, the one that worked for one of the bigger banks. Unwisely, Kit had told him he was expanding when in fact he hadn't even got number two off the ground, never mind any others. He'd amazed himself with his unnecessary fabrication, but the man had been taken by his product. Maybe it was worth a try. £20,000 to him would be small change, true, but as a family business, he had little collateral to offer, which was why he'd hit a dead end in the first place. No one wanted the risk. He was up to his limit all round. Natalie glanced over at him, gave him a questioning look, and mouthed, "You okay?" Kit stood, forcing a weak smile in return.

"Does anyone want anything?" he asked. "Hot chocolate? Another wine, Natalie?" It was the distraction from his thoughts he needed, and she nodded her approval. His daughters chorused a "Yes, please," two rosy faces glowing, allowed to stay up a little later than usual and drink hot chocolate before bed. At seven and eight years old, they were easily satisfied with the smaller things he could provide for them, but he knew all too well that come their teenage years, the pressure to provide would ramp up somewhat. He'd be ready.

"Two hot chocolates coming up."

"Make that three, please, scrap the wine," Natalie added, unwrapping a Quality Street and slipping it into her mouth. He watched her chew for a moment, smiled with satisfaction at his three girls and prepared to make their hot drinks.

Rain dashed against the back door and kitchen window. It was a foul night outside, and the small room was cool as he waited for the milk to boil. As the first of the tiny bubbles formed on the surface he glanced at the clock on the cooker. It was 8 pm. Early yet, there'd be no way Jakub could have, or would have, been able to retrieve the keys. Would he wait for Darrel to go to bed? Go out, perhaps? Do it first thing? Kit had no clue, and it was best it stayed that way.

He poured the warm milk into four mugs and topped the girls' with tiny marshmallows, leaving a teaspoon in each. While it was bedtime and the sugar not conducive to a peaceful night's sleep, it was Saturday tomorrow. The treat would be welcome, and they could stay in bed another hour if they wished. Natalie would likely welcome the lie in too. Having placed the four mugs on a tray, he headed back to the movie and handed out the drinks. The credits were starting to roll. Apparently he'd missed the end and the volume had been turned down.

"Is that rain I can hear?" enquired Natalie.

"It's bucketing down actually," he said, making himself comfortable again. Natalie tossed him a Quality Street.

The girls chattered quietly and sipped their drinks, slipping half-melted marshmallows off their spoons and letting the sticky goodness melt in their mouths. Back to the small things. With the females in his life occupied, it was the perfect time for a text to land without being noticed. Kit glanced at it with interest. Jakub texted like he spoke: *got them.*

Kit could almost hear Jakub's deep monotone as he read the text again. The lad had worked fast, perhaps too fast since now he had to take care of his own part quickly. If Darrel, his old partner and current driver of the car, managed to get a replacement set of keys quickly, the exercise would have been a waste of time. And a pointless risk. He thought for a moment before texting a reply. Whatever he decided to do, he didn't want to wait any longer for the keys. He glanced again at his family. The girls would be heading to bed soon, but Natalie would be suspicious. Kit thought quickly – a problem at the bakery. He quickly tapped a reply to Jakub and gave an outward groan, just enough to convince Natalie something urgent needed attention.

"What is it?" she enquired.

"Nothing to worry about, but I need to nip back to the bakery. Apparently there's a window open, and I don't want to risk an intruder. Or a rat for that matter." He stood ready to get his coat from the hall cupboard. "I'll only be a few minutes; I'll be back before you go to sleep." He bent to kiss each daughter in turn. "But I'll say goodnight to you now, since you definitely will be in bed when I get back." The two groaned. No child liked being told the day was over.

"Are you safe to drive?" Natalie asked. "How many glasses of wine have you had? It's pouring down out there, you can't walk."

"I'll be fine, it's only around the corner." He bent to peck her on the cheek. "Back shortly." And he was gone. Rain pelted his jacket as he dashed from the front door to the driver's side of the car and slipped in. It was nights like this that he was glad he hadn't a dog to walk – unlike his neighbour who was returning back up the road, head down against the weather. The dog beside him would need more than a towel-dry. Not wishing to hang around for pleasantries, he set off towards the bakery to meet Jakub. He hoped the lad had found a coat from somewhere, or else he'd be as drenched as the dog. But then Jakub slipped from his mind. If he was going to get his car back soon, he needed to come up with a plan rapidly.

CHAPTER 21

Baker

Friday evening

As Kit had suspected, Jakub didn't have a coat and was soaked to the skin, his black hoody no match for the torrential rain that was still falling. As he pulled up behind the bakery, the lad stepped into the light, cigarette burning between his lips. The orange glow matched the sodium street lamp that cast its subdued hue over the rear of the empty space. Empty but for Kit and Jakub. Kit pulled his hood up and made the dash across to where Jakub was sheltering. In the odd light, his pale complexion looked like something from a Stephen King movie, his eyes seeming to have sunk back into his head. Had he taken something, perhaps?

"I wasn't expecting them so quickly," Kit said, holding his hand out for the keys.

"Me neither. Took opportunity." Jakub moved nervously from one foot to the other, or was he cold? He handed two sets of keys over, and Kit slipped them in his pocket.

"Over to me, eh?"

A nod. "Good night for it. Car on drive."

"Right. Thanks." Kit was playing for time, wondering what to do. Jakub must have read his mind.

"I know a place. Safe garage. Another hundred."

Kit took another moment to think. What options did he have to store it himself? Particularly since it would soon be reported missing. He could hardly leave it parked outside his own home.

"Deal. You drive it?" he asked, offering back one set of keys. Jakub stared at them.

Another nod. It looked like he was going to steal the car for him after all.

It wasn't optimal, but with little time or experience to dwell on such matters, Kit had to act. That meant giving Jakub a lift in his soaking clothes, and he'd told Natalie he'd only be a minute.

"I need to take care of something first." He fumbled for his bakery keys and unlocked the back door. An alarm warning beeped in the near distance and stopped when Kit entered the correct code. In the tiny office-cum-storeroom, he pulled out his gym bag and opened it. Tracksuit bottoms, sweatshirt, and an old cap were passed to Jakub who understood immediately he needed to get changed.

"Best I can do. They are clean." He added as an afterthought: "At least they're dry."

Jakub wasn't shy, slipping his own soaked clothes off where he stood, though leaving his tatty boxers in place.

Kit reached back into his bag to see if his shorts were there and handed them over. "Your underpants are soaked, use the shorts."

Not wanting to hang around to watch, he squeezed his way past Jakub and out of the small space, giving the lad some privacy. He sent a quick text to Natalie that he could be a while, the window was being uncooperative. When Jakub finally emerged in dry clothes that were a tad on the large side, Kit offered him a carrier bag for his wet things. With an old cap pulled down low over his eyes, Jakub could have been anyone from a rapper to a street dweller.

"Ready?" Kit asked.

A nod.

Having locked the place up again, they jogged back to Kit's car and almost threw themselves inside. Rain hurled down like from a fireman's hose, the windscreen a blur on the outside. There was no sense in driving for a moment, visibility was atrocious.

"I guess we should discuss what should happen next," Kit said, feeling a little uneasy now he was part of a crime.

"Drop me off, I drive to garage. Walk home."

That was it? The master plan? It sounded simple enough.

"Right. Okay." There was nothing to add but Kit couldn't help wondering if it should have been a little more complicated than that. Could it work?

"You said earlier, 'good night for it.' What did you mean?"

"Everyone in houses. No one looking."

Kit remembered his neighbour dragging his dishevelled dog home; he hadn't seen another soul out since. The rain bouncing off the windscreen appeared to be losing its pressure, so Kit started the engine to clear the mist that had settled on the inside. Heat from their bodies mixed with the moisture in the air made the car look like it contained two lovers, not two work colleagues preparing for a late-evening theft. The blast from the fan clearing the glass made conversation impossible, so the men sat in silence until visibility was good enough to move off. Finally, Kit pulled out of the small car park and headed to an address he knew well. He hoped Darrel and his neighbours were safely tucked away behind thick curtains, their televisions making the only sound they would hear until Jakub and himself were away and clear.

By the time they'd turned down the relevant street, the rain had almost ceased, which was fortuitous for Jakub since he had a short walk from where Kit had parked up. The last thing Kit wanted was his own car spotted outside Darrel's house so he'd opted to stay a good fifty metres back. They could see the car from their vantage point, Kit's property just waiting to be taken home. Indoor lights up and down the street were few and far between, residents taking an early night. Kit noticed his mouth had become dry, and he struggled to add moisture before he spoke, so his words seemed to stick.

"I'll turn around so I'm ready to follow you, okay?"

Jakub nodded, stepped out, and closed the passenger door gently. Kit figured the lad had done this before; he wasn't dumb, he wouldn't raise attention. As Jakub hurried along the footpath, looking almost ghostlike under the street lamps, Kit turned his own vehicle around ready for the off. He watched via the rear-view mirror as Jakub deftly slipped inside the car. The engine started in an instant. Almost silently, the car reversed on to the street and headed his way. Kit fell in behind, and at the end of the street, Jakub finally turned his headlights on. "Smart lad," he said to himself, grinning. "What a dark horse you are."

After ten minutes of backstreets, Jakub eventually pulled up at an ancient lock-up with Kit right behind him. All was quiet. Perfect. Quickly, Jakub slipped from the car, unlocked the roller door, and eased the Audi inside. A moment later, he was at Kit's window offering the keys back. Two dark marbles caught his own eyes, and Kit nodded his thanks. Without another word, the lad took off at a slow jog, and Kit watched him go. With the nerves he'd felt earlier now dissipated, Kit knew he'd done the right thing in taking the car.

It was his after all.

CHAPTER 22

Banker
Friday night

Bethany had had enough of pretending she was up for socialising. Although her migraine had gone, the niggly space it always left behind, the dull nauseating ache that took another day to vanish completely, lingered annoyingly. She'd drunk water for most of the night, figuring it would help her head stay clear, and particularly after taking such heavy painkillers earlier, she'd thought it safest. Whatever Lee had given her that morning had knocked her out cold; she hardly remembered getting back into bed, but apparently she had. She watched Lee regurgitating one of his stories, one she'd heard many times, for the other two guests, a solicitor and a barrister, Blake and Maxine.

Bethany finally poured herself a long glass of Pinot Grigio in a last-ditch attempt to try and enjoy herself and dull the pain of the present conversation. Even Tanya's vet stories were hardly getting a look in tonight. It was legal, legal, and more legal. How much longer could she hold on before finally succumbing and falling asleep on the bathroom floor upstairs? Surely then, someone might miss her, go looking, and take her home. She should have declined the invitation earlier when she'd had the chance, but she hadn't wanted to appear rude. After all, having guests for dinner took effort, and Tanya had obviously had her Wonder Woman bracelets on to create the meal they'd just consumed. How the hell she'd managed it after a full day at work, Bethany couldn't understand. Maybe she'd had outside help. Bethany rubbed both sides of her temples simultaneously and wondered about the bathroom floor; it sounded comfortable.

"Coffee, anyone?" Eric asked, standing like the good host he had been all evening. He was the type of person that everyone got along with, an amusing man to be around. He had a deep-pink face, a permanent smile, and eyes that twinkled mischievously, though one was in fact glass. His party trick was to tap his wine glass against the hard surface of the fake one, the light clanking it created causing amusement. It certainly made an impression on people. To Bethany's knowledge, he'd never actually removed the fake eye in the company of guests, and she hoped it stayed that way, but he was a nice enough man and always great company. A chorus of "Yes, please," went up around the table from everyone save herself.

"Bethany? Would you like coffee?"

It took a moment for her to realise he'd directly asked her a question and, a little foggy, she apologised and asked him to repeat it.

"Coffee?" he tried again.

"Sorry, Eric. No, thank you."

"Are you feeling all right?" Lee asked, rubbing her shoulder gently. He sounded concerned.

"Not too good again, actually," she said, placing her napkin on top of the table. She'd been fiddling with it, deep in thought. "I'm sorry everyone, but I had a nasty migraine this morning, and I fear I should be home in bed before it comes back with a vengeance." She stood to leave, expecting Lee to say something further, though he didn't. She glanced across at him, willing him to stand, give her a sign they could go home. Nothing came. She tried a different tactic: "Why don't I take the car, and when you're ready, call a taxi?" she enquired. "Stay and enjoy yourself. I'm fine, I just need my bed, that's all."

Tanya sent her a sympathetic look – at least someone was showing a little concern – and stood to wish her goodnight with a light hug. Finally, Lee stood and found his tongue.

"I'll come with you then," he said, smiling. The rest of his face said otherwise.

Grateful, she thanked her hosts and the two other guests, and together Lee and Bethany headed towards the front door, Tanya on their heels. Lee handed her the car keys.

"You've had less to drink," he said.

It was the last thing Bethany felt like doing, but it seemed she had no choice. Plus, she'd been willing to drive herself only a moment ago – what was the difference?

The difference was his manner.

Following quick air-kisses all round, they stepped out into the rain and dashed to their car. Lights flashed and the car unlocked itself; Lee took the passenger's seat, and Bethany worked to demist the windscreen. A moment or two later, they pulled out of the driveway in silence, waving a quick 'thank you' to Tanya, who was standing in the doorway. In her rear-view mirror, Bethany watched the woman head back inside and close the door.

The tension inside the car was palpable. Even though it was only a short journey home, Bethany couldn't wait to get there before an argument ensued. No sooner had the thought entered her mind, than Lee started with a comment to kick the match off with.

"Just when I was starting to relax."

She waited for the follow-up, the tension building around her.

And Lee flipped into the unlikeable man he became after a drink or two: "Why did you come if you weren't feeling great? Eh? Those guests are highly influential people, and we won't get to know them any further because *we* had to head home because *you've* got a headache!" There it was, the crux of the matter laid bare. Lee was feeling let down and pissed, and the two didn't play nicely with each other. Even with her headache gaining momentum thanks to the atmosphere between them, there was no way she was going to sit meekly and let him berate her like a child.

"I went because you wouldn't have gone there on your own! You know I've been unwell today; I took the day off work. You sent me flowers, remember? So don't go blaming me for *my* lousy headache spoiling *your* evening. It's spoiled mine as well you know."

"You didn't want to go! Something about dissecting a case or a cat corpse, if I remember rightly? Hell, Bethany, next time do us both a favour and stay home."

"Next time I might just do that. But that won't be right either, will it? There's no sense from you when you're pissed, and that's all this is." She was shouting now, as rain lashed against the windscreen. The wipers automatically increased their speed, fighting to keep the view clear. They were no match for the ferocity of water descending on the car.

"I'm not pissed! I'm angry. At you."

"Angry at what exactly, a headache?" she shouted back, turning his way while she delivered the words with force. With no real light in the car and a lack of street lamps along the back road, his silhouette was barely visible.

"For being selfish."

"For... Really? You think *I'm* being selfish?" Incredulity laced her words as she put a space between each one, still watching his outline intently. But there was no chance of him answering her question as she turned back to face the road. Instead it was Lee's scream that filled her sore head.

"Bethany!"

CHAPTER 23

A party
Friday night

By 11 pm, Melody was ready to leave for the party of the century. It was being hosted by a friend-of-a-friend whose parents were overseas for a fortnight, and it had taken her five days to prepare for it. Outfits had been in and out of her wardrobe, dancing the hokey-cokey, and her mother had borne the brunt each day as she'd moaned that she had 'nothing to wear'.

Melody Holden was well known as the life and soul of the party, and that's exactly why she was invited to so many. She was a typical Insta-babe: all long, expertly blonded hair, oversized brows, pouty lips, and an all-year-round showroom tan. As a local minor celebrity, she was working hard on taking her brand to the next level, though she was yet to decide whether actress or singer was the way to go. In the meantime, her mission was simple: be in all the right places and get noticed. 'Meloden', as she liked to be known, particularly online, spent a small fortune on looking the part and at age nineteen had already run up her uncle's credit card bill with minor procedures at the beauty clinic. Not that Ron Butcher minded. Until Felix settled and had children of his own, Melody was the youngest in the family, the baby he cherished and had indulged since birth.

However, it was about time he stopped paying for her every whim and forced her to make her own way in life. Doling out for her as he did was not going to do her any favours in the long run, and he needed to take the stabiliser wheels off long before they broke off. Even though Melody was his sister's girl, he'd always felt more like her father than her uncle. Plus, his sister had never married and so appreciated Ron as a male presence in her daughter's life. He knew many thought of Melody as a spoiled brat, but that didn't stop him doting.

"Don't wait up!" she called as she trotted out of the front door on heels as thin as knitting needles. Her Uber was waiting just by the front porch, and the driver was standing there with a giant umbrella open so she could avoid the rain that was still falling. He escorted her dutifully from the porch, and she teetered her way to the rear car door, which he opened. In one practised move, she glided on to the back seat, and he closed the door. Her toes were wet but her hair, the important thing, thankfully was still intact. As they set off, Melody pulled out her phone and took a series of photos of herself, each one a little sultrier than the last. When she was satisfied with her efforts, she chose the best, added a caption, and the all-important #tag, and posted it to her thousands of followers. While she didn't have the Kardashians' following, at close to 400,000 she was popular enough. For now. Within moments, tiny hearts filled her screen as people 'liked' it and left their fawning comments. It made her smile.

Melody was meeting her current boyfriend at the party. He lived with his parents a few doors down from the venue, and at twenty-five he too should have been making his own way and not living in the granny flat out the back. But with everything he needed right there, what was the sense in moving out into a tiny two-up two-down and forking out for utilities? She hoped they'd make their relationship more permanent sometime soon but despite her dropping mighty hints at getting engaged, he'd remained oblivious. Or he was ignoring them. And she wasn't going to propose herself. What if he turned her down?

As they pulled up at the front awning, she checked her hair and lipstick one last time. The place was set up like it was Oscars night, complete with narrow carpet and temporary canvas to protect those arriving or leaving from the elements. Melody turned on her brightest smile and expertly stepped out of the car, showing just the right amount of tanned thigh. A flashlight took her by surprise. She hadn't noticed a photographer, and she took the opportunity to linger ever so slightly so another shot could be taken. Satisfied, she sauntered to the front door and slipped inside.

Dance music was throbbing, though no one was actually dancing yet. Chatter and laughter fought to be heard over the music as girls posed with drinks and young men ogled. Melody scanned the room to see who of note had arrived already and, most importantly, whether Luke was among them. She searched faces and returned exaggerated smiles as people reacted to seeing her, but there was no sign of him in the main room or the kitchen. The rear patio doors were wide open, and Melody peered out to the covered area in case he was having a cigarette – she hoped not, he was supposed to be giving it up – but he wasn't there either. Thinking he must still be on his way, she decided to find the loo and check on her hair. She walked gracefully back to the main room and headed off up the stairs. Partygoers lined the staircase, chatting and drinking, and she stepped over feet and glasses, picking her way through in designer shoes. A line of closed doors greeted her on the spacious landing, and she wondered which might be the toilet and figured that, like many houses, it was probably at the end of the hallway, the other doors leading to bedrooms. She headed, then, straight for the last one and grabbed the handle to see if it was locked, and since it wasn't, she felt inside for the light switch before going in.

As bright light illuminated the room, it became quite apparent where Luke was. Obviously startled at both the sudden blaze and being caught with his trousers around his ankles, Luke screamed in horror at a redhead bent over the dressing table.

"I thought you'd locked the door!"

They weren't the words Melody had been expecting to hear from Luke's mouth, but then she hadn't been expecting to find him in such a compromising position. She couldn't get out of there fast enough. With a mixture of sheer embarrassment and heartbreak, she roughly pushed her way back down the stairs, stepping on anything and everything on her descent. Angry voices called after her, but Melody didn't hear them, the rush of pain the only sound in her ears as tears gathered and burst like the storm clouds in the sky above. Fighting to breathe, she headed straight out the front door, caught her footing and one skinny heel snapped off dramatically. It was too much to cope with. Crying in earnest now, she bent to remove both shoes before heading out into the rain barefoot. Within moments she was soaked, her skimpy dress no match for the weather. Melody was in a hell all of her own, and she walked, sobbing, along the road back towards home, not thinking about the distance. Nothing in her head was computing, the space taken up with one vision only: Luke with another woman. She rubbed her eyes, but rather than dislodging the photo so fully developed in her mind, all she achieved were black, panda eyes from smudged mascara.

Wandering aimlessly in the dark, the only thing that stopped her tears was the car that slammed into her slender body, tossing it awkwardly through the air and dumping her into the ditch.

The torrential rain did its absolute best to wash away her smudged mascara, but panda eyes were the least of her problems as Melody Holden lay unconscious in the wet grass.

CHAPTER 24

Banker
Friday night, around midnight

Bethany was inconsolable, a quivering wreck. She'd seen someone, a woman, she thought, at the last second before the car had somersaulted her over the front bonnet and off to the side. Given the speed they were going and the force with which they'd hit her, Bethany doubted she'd still be alive. Amid Bethany's screams and floods of tears, it was Lee that took the calmer approach. He stepped outside to check on the woman. Even over the rain bouncing down, he could hear the hysterics coming from inside the vehicle. They broke an otherwise silent dark night as he tried to concentrate on what to do next. The woman was lying on her stomach, face to the side, and from the small amount of light available from the vehicle's rear lights, he could see she was only young. Her dress had ridden up to her buttocks. One leg stuck out at an awkward angle. There were no signs of movement from the woman as he fought inside his head for what to do next.

If he touched her neck to check for a pulse, he risked leaving his

DNA behind. If he moved any closer, he risked leaving footprints, a trace of himself or his clothing. There was little he could do for the woman who looked peacefully asleep, eyes closed. Soaked to the skin, he hurriedly made his decision and headed around to the driver's seat. Bethany had quietened a little but was still in a state of shock, staring straight ahead as if frozen to the spot. He pushed her shoulder roughly.

"Move over."

Bethany didn't respond.

"Bethany, move over. Come on, we need to get out of here," he said urgently. "Shift over!" Maybe it was the force of his words or another shove, but Bethany finally moved over, and Lee took up the driver's seat. He took charge, that's what he did best. A hit-and-run out in the middle of nowhere on a Friday night wasn't going to be blamed on Bethany or Lee Meady, and with the rain falling in torrents as it had been, any evidence of their vehicle's involvement would likely be washed away anyway. Plus, he didn't want the hassle that would come with reporting it. Bethany had been driving and had had a drink. Likely she wouldn't be over the limit, but add to that the painkiller she'd had that morning... well, he knew how alcohol and those pills worked together from experience. There was no point in getting involved. What was the woman doing out there anyway? Even if she'd seen anything, what would there be to tell? A dark car in a dark lane? There was nothing to tie them to the accident.

It was ironic really, hit-and-run had been the topic of conversation over dinner from the woman guest, Maxine. A barrister close to retirement, she'd spoken of a past case that she'd worked on and the sentencing boundaries for leaving the scene versus staying and reporting it and being found over the limit. The law and its penalty, or lack of, almost encouraged the driver to run once they'd hit. Stay, and you'd find yourself with a hefty prison sentence for reckless driving. It seemed the law favoured the lowlife. He wasn't going to allow Bethany to go to prison for fourteen years. No way.

Lee pulled up outside their home and helped a shaking Bethany from the car and inside. Her hair was damp from sweat and plastered to her head and face, but tears had finally ceased leaving black streaks down both cheeks. He eased her on to a kitchen chair and poured a brandy for them both.

"It will help you settle," he said, holding the glass out for her. When she didn't take it, he pressed it to her lips as if feeding a child with a spoon. "Open. Drink. You'll feel better soon."

Reluctantly, Bethany took the cut glass from him and took a sip and, feeling the warmth fill her stomach, tipped the rest back, swallowing it all down in one. She gasped at the fire as it flowed, and she jiggled the glass, a sign for a refill. Lee obliged, topping his own up at the same time. As Bethany sat numb, Lee paced up and down, working through what could happen next.

"Nobody saw us, we never passed another vehicle. Add that to the weather conditions, and there's no way anyone would put us anywhere near there or think we could have had anything to do with it. We could have gone the other way around, the more obvious route, but we didn't. We took the back roads, but no one needs know that, and why would they be asking questions anyway?" He was talking to the room rather than Bethany and not looking for answers or input, merely emptying his head and sorting through possibilities. Bethany stayed silent, deep in thoughts of her own. When Lee had finished his sermon, she finally spoke.

"Did I kill her, do you think?" she asked, almost inaudible. Red eyes, their lids smudged with black, looked up at him from her chair. She looked pitiful.

"I don't know." His words were quiet, calm even, as he added, "What was she doing in the road anyway? It's her own fault. I bet she was drunk, staggering home."

His words triggered something in Bethany, and she gathered strength from her glass. "Do you think that matters, Lee? That she was drunk? Because I don't. I've just hit a woman and left her lying at the side of the road." Bethany was gaining in momentum and spirit as she found the words to describe what she'd done. "I may have killed her for heaven's sake, and all you can say is she was likely drunk? Like that makes everything all right again?" Her eyes flared as she made her way over to him, glass still in her hand. "I could be done for murder, and we fled the scene because you thought it best! What sort of man are you?"

His eyes bulged. His mouth contorted. "One that's trying to sort out your damn mess, that's what sort of man I am," he snarled back directly in her face. "You heard that woman at dinner – six months and a few points for hit-and-run and up to fourteen years for drunk driving if you've killed her. Tell me Bethany, which option would you like to choose?"

"But she may not be dead. We could have helped her!"

"And you'd be sitting in a police cell instead of here, in your own home," he said with arms spread wide in gesture. "Tell me again, which would you prefer? I know which one I'd choose. So, if you're that bothered, call the police and tell them what *you've* done, but leave me out of it." He slammed his empty glass down hard on the coffee table. Glancing back at it, he saw a crack now ran down one side. He picked the glass back up and threw it at the fireplace where it smashed into tiny pieces that skittered around the room. Bethany jumped at the sound, her nerves already shredded. She watched him head towards the door.

"Where are you going?"

"To bed. I've had enough for tonight, thanks. Goodnight," he said as he stormed from the room, his words laced with sarcasm and anger, the 'goodnight' firm and unfriendly.

Bethany chose not to say anything further and watched him go. Her own glass was still in her hand, and she reached for the decanter to refill then sat back to think. At least with Lee out of the room, she had space for her own thoughts now she'd simmered down a little. What the hell should she do? She certainly didn't fancy prison time, but as the wind beat the rain against the full glass windows, she couldn't help but think of the woman lying cold and drenched at the side of the road.

For her sake, Bethany hoped she was already dead.

CHAPTER 25

A dog walker
Saturday morning

It didn't matter who stopped to help her, as long as someone did. That someone didn't find her until daybreak the following morning. Like most members of the public that stumbled across bodies, the elderly man who discovered Melody was a dog walker. As he caught up with his two retrievers that were making a fuss over something, he gasped. Blonde hair almost covered her badly bruised face, and it was hard to tell what was dirt and what was the deep, earthy brown of dry blood. She looked like she'd been severely beaten and tossed to the side of the road. Realising what he was looking at, he stepped into the ditch and, with trembling fingers, checked for a pulse on her neck. It was faint, but he was sure it was still there.

The girl was still alive, but only just, and he knew she wouldn't hang on for long. No matter what had happened for her to be in the ditch in the first place, a long and cold night outside in the rain would have only added to the young woman's problems, and he feared she might already have hypothermia. He reached for his phone and called for the police and an ambulance. Then he took his own thick coat off and laid it over her body. He hoped he wasn't disturbing any evidence by doing so, but there was no way he was going to do nothing for her. Another layer in an attempt to provide some warmth was all he could offer. Preservation of life was the main concern right then.

Ten minutes later, the familiar sound of the ambulance's siren filled the quiet back road, and he prepared to flag it down. No sooner had it stopped than he informed the first responder what he'd found and what he knew so far. A retired army veteran himself, he'd been part of a medical team during the first Gulf War and so knew quite how serious her situation could be, and that she was likely tapping rapidly on death's door.

"We'll take it from here, thanks," the woman medic said as the back door was flung open and the stretcher wheeled out. Her colleague was already at the spot where Melody lay, making early assessments and calling out for equipment. The dog walker could only watch on as the crew worked on her body. Eventually, they carefully strapped her back and neck with splints and loaded her on to the stretcher. It seemed an eternity before they were able to get her into the ambulance and finally set off, leaving the man to give his details to the police constable that had arrived in the meantime. She was still alive, that was the main thing. No, he'd no idea who she was.

The constable walked on further down the road and spotted what he assumed was Melody's bag in the hedgerow, shoulder strap snapped and dangling aimlessly from the prickly branches. The officer collected it easily and slipped it into an evidence bag, just in case. At this point, they didn't know quite what they were dealing with, and any evidence needed to be preserved. Another officer placed tape around the area and took initial photographs with his phone. The woman was alive now, but that could always change, she was obviously in a very bad way. The dog walker was thanked and told to go home. There was nothing more he could do.

Once at the hospital, it was discovered that Melody's pelvis had been broken in two places, and scans revealed a brain haemorrhage. Her broken arm and leg were the least of her problems as they prepared her for surgery. It would be several hours before the surgeon would be able to tell the waiting constable anything further about their mystery woman's prognosis.

Melody's bag had contained her learner's driving licence, as well as credit cards and other female paraphernalia, so the constable had alerted a family member that there had been an accident. From her injuries, it appeared she had been hit by a car.

Ron Butcher paced up and down in the family waiting area of Croydon University Hospital. His sister, Teresa, was occupying her mind with the cuticles of each finger, which had barely been visible in the first place. Her right knee jigged up and down like a nervous junky in need of a fix. She looked haggard and ill. Ron wondered about his sister's demeanour, but now was not the time to ask. Maybe when this was all over... Instead, he opened his mouth to suggest coffee and thought better of it.

"Tea?"

"Whiskey," she said without looking at him. Direct and not helpful.

"It's not even lunchtime. Tea?"

"Fine," she snapped back. The knee jigged.

Ron took the opportunity to stretch his legs for a while and vape outside the main entrance. He knew they'd call him if there was anything to report. After his vanilla fix, he purchased two teas and took them back to the waiting area where there was still no news, and Teresa's knee carried on jigging up and down. He handed her tea over and sat with his head bowed.

He wasn't a religious man, but Ron took a moment and prayed for his Melody to pull through. He prayed for her to receive the strength she needed to fight, and he prayed that the person who did this to his sweet young niece experienced a pain like no other as he slowly dismantled them, both physically and mentally.

He pulled his phone out and made a call.

CHAPTER 26

A café in Croydon
Saturday morning

Jack was enjoying poached eggs and a side of streaky bacon at a café on the outskirts of town, the *Daily Mail* folded in half in front of him. A pot of tea sat waiting to be poured as he chewed and read at the same time. It was a sad state of affairs – youth stabbing figures were climbing out of control and something had to be done. Politicians, police, and the general public could all agree on that one it seemed, yet knife attacks continued to dominate the news. Thugs were getting younger, nothing more than kids really. The worst he did as a youngster was throw stones. He wouldn't want to be fourteen in the current climate. Shaking his head in dismay at the state of his local world, he turned the page in search of a little lighter reading. He was interrupted by his phone ringing out. Not recognising the mobile number, he was tempted to let it go to voicemail, but being a detective, he rarely did so, day off or not.

"DC Jack Rutherford."

"Jack. You still sound the same as you did when you were a

teenager," the voice said. Jack tried to place where he knew it from, searching his memory banks rapidly. Bingo.

"Ron Butcher. Are you not in prison yet?" Jack said, laughing, a tease carefully laid along a legitimate question.

"I'm a businessman, same as thousands of others around these parts. All above board, like. You should know that," he quipped, though his voice sounded stronger than he likely felt.

"I guess they'll get you for tax evasion or perjury one day, eh? Make something stick?"

"Now, now, Jack. There's no need to be like that."

"Well, I know I don't remember you ever in the history of ever calling my phone about anything, and I doubt you want to confess something, so what's up?"

"Smart man, Jack."

"I find it useful with my job," he chuckled. "So, tell me what's up before my tea goes cold."

"Can we meet?"

"I'm sat in a café right now if you want to come over. Where are you?"

"University Hospital." That stopped Jack asking anything else.

"Well, since my pot's almost gone cold already, I'll meet you in the café inside. I'll be there in ten, and you're buying."

"I'll be waiting." And then Ron was gone. Jack sat back for a moment and pondered. Ron Butcher didn't call for a chat, and he shied away from any involvement with the police, so why the sudden call on a Saturday morning? And after so many years of keeping the law at arm's length. A detective as your friend was not common in Ron Butcher's trade. Jack looked back at the remaining bacon and eggs and snatched the slice of toast. Grabbing his jacket, he made his way back to his car chewing and headed over to the hospital to get some answers.

It had been a while, several years in fact, since he'd last seen the Ron Butcher, and from memory, the man hadn't looked too good back then. Idly, Jack wondered if he'd have put any weight on his pipe-cleaner-thin frame; a strong wind and he would have been blown into the bushes back in the day. Jack glanced down at his own stomach that was now rolling over his belt somewhat uncomfortably. Since Mrs Stewart had started cooking meals for him, he'd piled a few pounds on. Maybe it was time to omit the bacon from his otherwise healthy poached eggs. Starting the engine, he said to himself, "Maybe in the spring. Too bloody cold to live on rabbit food in October."

By the time he'd found a parking space, Jack wondered if Ron would still be waiting or would have given up and left, but he was pleased to see the man had stayed put. Sitting at a corner table, almost bent over double, he was barely recognizable until he pulled his head back up. Deep sunken eyes focused on him, and Jack couldn't help but think how ill the man looked. Perhaps he should stay for some tests himself after their little tea party. But he wasn't going to voice his thoughts on that one. Not to Ron Butcher.

"Ron?"

"Thanks for coming, Jack," he said, fixing his gaze on him. Weak, pale blue eyes searched Jack's. "Your tea will arrive shortly." Jack smiled at the man's forward thinking and his somewhat unconventional ways; he'd obviously given his instructions for its delivery after their call. Sure enough, a fresh pot of tea was soon set down in front of him along with a thick cup and saucer. Jack picked it up and gazed at it.

"I wish cafés would give you a proper teacup with your tea and not a coffee cup. There's a difference. They are different beverages," Jack moaned.

Ron shook his head gently in mild amusement. "Finally, someone that thinks the same – on that at least. Drives me potty." Jack poured a little but, curling his nose up at the anaemic colour, set the pot back down to let the tea brew a while longer.

"So, what's troubling Ron?"

"My young niece is lying upstairs in ICU, critical. They say she might not make it."

"Ah, Ron. I'm sad to hear it. What happened?"

"Hit-and-run apparently. Broken bones and a brain bleed.

They've drilled a hole in her skull to relieve the pressure, and she's in an induced coma while she fights." Ron's voice caught, and he tried to ride the choke out before carrying on. "Last night. She left to go to a party at about 11 pm and somewhere along the way got mowed down. She's been lying in a wet ditch along a lonely back road, all alone in the dark, since then." A moment passed before he could continue, "My poor, sweet Melody. She's only a baby, only nineteen, with all her life ahead of her." Jack could hear the despair in the man's voice and wasn't surprised to see the tears rise in Ron's eyes, but being a tough man, he wouldn't be seen to let them spill over. He pulled out a clean handkerchief and wiped them away.

"How can I help?"

Clearing his throat, he said, "I want to be kept informed, and I know you're the decent kind. You were always the good lad, back when we were lads."

Jack thought for a moment. "Without sounding rude, Ron, you'll already have someone on the 'inside' as you put it. What else can I do they can't?" A spy, Jack was never going to be.

"You always had compassion, Jack. A soft spot. A kind heart. I need someone on the inside that understands the torment of losing a loved one. I'm not looking for details you can't tell me, but I want to know all I can about how the investigation is going and when you get close. I'm not asking you for sensitive information."

"I don't even know if I'll be working on Melody's case, no one has contacted me as yet. I might be no use to you at all."

"I hear you. But you can get yourself on the case, right? For me?" It wasn't a threat, but it felt close. Jack sighed heavily; it wasn't a position he wanted to be put in. Ron and Jack went way back, but they were never the best of pals back then, and they weren't now either. And since Jack represented the law, they each sat at opposite ends of the football pitch for their game of life.

"I can't promise anything, but I'll find out who's on it. I'll see what I can do." Jack reached across and touched Ron's elbow gently. "I hope with all my heart she pulls through for you, Ron. I wouldn't wish the experience of losing someone you love on my worst enemy."

Ron looked directly into Jack's eyes. "Thanks, Jack. I know you mean that. I remember meeting your Janine once. Lovely lady, she was. I was sorry to hear of her passing."

"I didn't realise you'd ever met her." It was unwelcome news to Jack.

"I stopped one day, her car had broken down somewhere, and I happened to be driving by. We chatted a while. I put two and two together."

Jack looked on as Ron talked, searching old memory banks for a recollection, remembering his wife with the deep fondness he'd always felt for her. It didn't matter about the past event now, she was gone. Jack stood to leave.

"The number you called me from, is that the best to reach you on? How long will it be live?"

Jack thought he saw a glimmer of a smile, but it passed so quickly he couldn't be sure.

"It's good for a while."

"I'll call you when I can."

He made his way back to the main entrance then thought better of it. Turning around, he headed straight upstairs to intensive care. He may as well find out what he could while he was in the building.

CHAPTER 27

The hospital
Saturday morning

Jack half expected a private guard, supplied and paid for by Ron, waiting on the young woman's door, but there was no one to be seen. It wasn't like she was a target, at least it didn't seem likely at this stage, because otherwise Ron would have said something, and a street battle would likely ensue. Still, the man was hurting, and perhaps the incident was too fresh to think about retaliation, if there was to be any. As long as she was alive, and long may she remain so, there would hopefully be no violence in response. Jack flashed his warrant card at a surly-looking nurse who decided she'd head on over and have a word.

"She's not able to speak right now. Induced coma," she said in a harsh whisper, as if her words could wake Melody. She had all the hallmarks of a mother hen, and if it had been his own niece or family member lying there, he would have wanted her to be exactly the same.

"Thanks. Yes, I realise that, I've just been talking to her uncle downstairs. Not good, eh?"

She shook her head. "The next couple of days are crucial for her. We can't do anything else now. Her battle is all her own."

Jack gazed down at the battered-and-bruised face, a bandage wrapped around most of her head. The blonde hair that he could see was grimy with dirt from a night in the ditch, and her arm was set in a plaster cast. Machines did their jobs, but Melody's eyes stayed firmly shut. Jack had seen many accident victims in his time, and it never got any easier. She was someone's daughter, friend. Niece.

"Have my colleagues been in as yet, while she's in this state?"

"Only briefly. I sent them away. No point in hanging around yet." Her tone told him he should take the hint and do the same.

"Right then, I'll be off too." He handed her his card, "I'd appreciate being kept informed of events, please," he said, smiling in an attempt to defrost the icicles of her demeanour. She was obviously being protective, but she needn't be so with him. He'd been in ICUs countless times and knew the way things worked. At least she glanced at his card before slipping it into her pocket.

"I'll be off then." Jack slowly ambled back out into the corridor and leant against the cold wall for a moment to think. He fiddled with the right side of his moustache, a habit that helped him focus. Looking down at the battered-and-bruised face of a nineteen-year-old, he'd been instantly reminded of a young girl he used to know, Mary, who would be about a year older than Melody now. It could well have been her lying in that bed, left for dead after the coward that hit her fled the scene. What sort of a mongrel does that? Likely a drunk on a Friday night, that's who. He pushed himself off the wall and headed back to his car, wondering why he was again feeling maudlin. There was the old woman who'd died of neglect, all on her own, and now young Melody, left for dead on her own, her life now hanging by a thread. Life wasn't fair, people weren't fair, and both situations could have been avoided if those responsible had done the right thing to prevent it. He needed to be on Melody's case. His day off could wait until later.

Ron was still sitting where Jack had left him when he passed the café on the way out. He'd be there a good deal longer yet by what the nurse upstairs had said, and no number of cups of tea would help the girl fight her battle. There was little else for Ron to do until she woke up. Idly, he wondered what Amanda was doing on her day off. Since she was no longer spending time with Ruth, perhaps she'd welcome the distraction from boredom and give him a hand. He placed the call and waited, dashing through heavy drizzle as he headed for his car, which was some way away. When she answered, he was puffed out of breath. And rather damp.

"It's a good job I know it's you, Jack, because it's been a while since I've had a heavy breather," she quipped. Unlocking his car, he slithered inside, a wet hand holding his phone to his ear. By the time he'd pulled the door shut, he was covered in a fine wet sheen. He wiped himself down as best he could with his sleeve, took a deep breath to catch his wind, and exhaled loudly.

"Jack, what are you actually doing right now? Or shouldn't I ask?"

"Funny. I've been running. Too old for it." Another deep breath.

"You've started running? This I've got to see!" she said, laughing.

"Don't be a smart arse. Running to the car in the rain. That sort of running. Anyway, can we get away from my lack of fitness for a moment?"

"If we have to. Though it is rather amusing, the vision of you in short shorts, gasping for breath. Maybe I should join you. We can gasp together."

"Perhaps not, though you might want to join me in something else. Cancel your plans, we've got work to do."

"No plans to cancel."

"I figured. Meet me in the office in ten."

"I'll be there in thirty. I'm not at home."

"Sounds promising..."

"Jack..." she said warningly.

"Sorry. That was insensitive. I'll get sustenance for coffee time, breakfast disintegrated on me."

"You going to fill me in beforehand?"

"Another case of human disregard to sort out. I'll tell you more when I see you. And, Amanda?"

"What?"

"Drive safely, eh."

CHAPTER 28

Baker

Saturday morning

Kit hadn't slept a great deal. He'd tossed and turned about his own late-night antics and whether he'd done the right thing, particularly about involving Jakub. But the lad had turned out to be a little darker than he'd originally thought, and that had been a useful trait. Jakub's access to an old lock-up and his willingness to not only break in for the keys, but then drive the car away himself had astonished Kit. He'd often wondered about the lad's background and how he'd come to be in the UK, but since he was an individual that kept himself to himself, he'd never actually found out. Even at his interview, he'd been the silent type, but Kit had seen something in him and had taken a chance. His workmanship and work ethic couldn't be faulted, and he'd passed his probationary period easily. The rest of the team, including Kit, had reasoned he preferred to get on with his work and was not interested in idle conversation, and they'd all long given up trying to wheedle anything from him. It turned out he had skills beyond making bread rolls.

And so, at his usual 4 am, Kit had made his way into work and started mixing, attempting to leave his conscience behind. By six, his first customers had started arriving, and by nine, he was taking a coffee break of his own. As usual on a Saturday, they'd be run off their feet come ten o'clock, and it wouldn't stop again until well after lunch, so it was now or never. For a change of scenery, he took a spot in the window, a mug of coffee and a pastry at hand, and settled down to peruse the outside world.

Sitting there, it dawned on him that Ron, a creature of habit, had not been in that morning. Since he could count on one hand how many days Ron had missed, Kit knew it was highly unusual. Perhaps he wasn't feeling too good. Kit hoped the man was all right. He hadn't been looking well of recent, and Kit had put it down to a hidden illness. Maybe he was actually diabetic? The amount of sugar the man ate would not be conducive to healthy insulin levels and his body could be finding it hard to deal with the effects. Perhaps he'd be back in on Monday. Kit would be neighbourly and enquire after his health then.

Ron wasn't his main concern. Getting new ownership documents and avoiding any police involvement were the main items on his agenda, and possibly finding a new location to store the vehicle. He doubted it could stay in the lock-up for the next couple of weeks until he'd squared things and preferably sold it on. To get it through an auction though, he needed the correct paperwork. A private sale would need the same for that matter. He needed to get moving but how? With everything happening so quickly, he hadn't had the chance to plan any of it out, and the last thing he wanted was for it all to fall apart. He'd be in trouble and likely Jakub would too, but what was his next move? He bit into his pastry, not really tasting it, and felt his phone buzz in his pocket. It was a text from Darrel. He was good at adding up.

Car theft? Really?

The three words slapped him in the gut with a thump. He wasn't expecting Darrel to contact him, not so soon. Damn! He knew the car was gone and already suspected him. Had he reported his suspicions? Would the police come marching in shortly? With the text, he could only do one thing: act dumb.

What's happened?

He waited.

My car and two sets of keys stolen. Where are they?

No idea. Nothing to do with me. Tell the police.

I have. Expect a visit. Prick.

It was a risk encouraging that particular course of action, but an innocent man would have advised the same and that meant he should to. He hated lying, and he seemed to be doing more and more of it of late. Only last night he'd lied to Natalie as he'd slipped out.

Well, Kit doubted the police would be in a rush to chat to him over a car gone missing; they'd be busy with more important issues on a Saturday morning, like the drunks in the overnight holding cells for one. He hoped so anyway. No sooner had the thought entered his head than a uniformed officer entered the shop and glanced around.

"Here we go," Kit said under his breath as he approached the counter to serve the young man. He looked like he'd finished Hendon Police College only last week, his pale complexion identical to that of Jakub. Kit half expected him to stutter nervously but, to his surprise, the officer's voice was as strong and deep as his own. Maybe he'd misjudged the man.

"Morning, I'm looking for Kit Morris."

"That's me, I'm Kit. What can I do for you?"

"Is there somewhere I can ask you a few questions, Mr Morris?" Kit heard the front door open as another customer entered. He motioned to Jakub to serve while he escorted the young constable towards the back office-cum-storeroom. There was just enough room for two chairs if the door stayed open.

"A bit tight for space," Kit offered as explanation. "Or we could go outside if you prefer? It's not raining."

"Here's fine." The two sat and Kit waited patiently, doing his damnedest to look neither concerned nor guilty. He hoped the constable wasn't trained to spot nervous body language at this stage in his career, as Kit would be in handcuffs in the following ten minutes if he was.

It was as he expected. A car had been stolen, as had the keys. It was his ex-business partner, and he'd suggested Kit as the first person to chat to. All Kit could do was repeat that it was nothing to do with him. He hadn't taken the keys or the car. There was no lie there. He'd managed to stay calm and focused and had told the truth to the officer. He was glad he'd not been asked if he'd seen the car or knew where it was hidden – that would have been a different story entirely. Ten minutes later it was all over, and the constable headed off as peacefully as he'd entered. Breathing a slow sigh of relief, Kit watched him stop outside to chat to an older man who placed a friendly arm on the officer's, spoke a few words, smiled, and then headed inside.

Jack had doughnuts to buy.

CHAPTER 29

The crime scene
Saturday morning

On a rain-ridden back road, Dr Faye Mitchell and her team worked the area where Melody had been found. At least the rain had stopped for a time, and a weak autumn sunshine was even squeezing itself out through slim chinks in the clouds. But by the depth of grey of those gathering in the distance, it wouldn't be long before the heavens opened once more. Autumn and winter could be cold and wet in the UK, but then so could spring and summer.

Amanda and Jack had consumed morning coffee while he'd filled her in on his conversation with Ron Butcher. She'd raised her eyebrows at the man initially calling Jack and again at the man's request that his old pal investigate and keep him updated. Amanda had had the same thought as Jack, that the man would already have someone on the inside. Still, his request made her nervous.

"I'm glad we don't have to deal with his crap directly, and I'm not happy about you being his 'inside man'," Amanda said as they approached the scene and parked up a little way up the road. They got out and stood watching.

"Me neither. We might go back a good few years, but we were never best mates, far from it. We both know he'll have his own snout in the station, maybe even higher up. He hasn't stayed out of prison for this long without help. I bet he could get a lot more info going his normal route."

"You just watch your back with him, okay? I don't trust the weasel."

Jack nodded his understanding then took another look at the area and decided to get his wellington boots from the car. He'd only yesterday polished his work shoes, and the thought of picking mud off them and doing the job over didn't thrill him. He glanced at Amanda's footwear as he slipped each foot in turn into a boot. As usual, her highly polished Docs stared back at him. He pointed at them, "Do you wear those things all weekend too?"

"You invited me into the office, remember?"

"Yeah, but it's not really a workday is it? More a little snooping. Just thought you might wear something a little more casual, like. For a change."

Ignoring his comment, she frowned at him from under her eyebrows. Even though she'd started an evening exercise class, she hadn't made it common knowledge within the team. With so much empty time to fill, she actually found herself enjoying it. She'd splashed out and bought a new pair of trainers to sweeten her own deal, an incentive.

Since the weather was somewhat inclement, a white, gazebo-style tent had been erected to keep the area and workers as dry as possible. Liveried vehicles and scene technicians filled the surrounding space making it look like the proverbial hive of activity. Amanda and Jack made their way forward then watched the goings on for a moment before trying to attract the doctor's attention.

"There seems to be a lot of fuss for a conventional hit-and-run, don't you think?" asked Amanda. "Is that Butcher's influence already?"

"Beats me. Maybe because young Melody's prognosis isn't too bright."

When Faye eventually looked up, she nodded by way of greeting and carried on with her work uninterrupted. Nothing and no one broke into her professional zone until she allowed them to, neither mentally nor physically. Amanda and Jack knew to wait. They also knew she'd say precious little until she had all the information at hand, and the two detectives knew there'd be scant at the scene. There rarely was with a hit-and-run. With no body to examine, Amanda wondered why the doctor was even in attendance. *Silent Witness* was not how real policing and crime scene investigation went: pathologists rarely left the mortuary in reality, though Faye was often needed to pronounce a death. Amanda had seen many dead bodies and knew exactly what one looked like, but it was always down to a doctor to name it, a police officer not being qualified to do so. Still, she wondered about her presence. Jack must have read her thoughts.

"Maybe Butcher's knobbly fingers reach to high-up places?" asked Jack.

"I'd say you're right. Odd, don't you think?"

"Not much surprises me any more." Then, after a beat: "Actually, one thing does," he added quietly. He turned, an almost squashed smile on his mouth and his eyes almost begging. He couldn't have looked more like a caring father if he'd tried.

"Now is definitely not the time," Amanda said warningly, walking forward and not waiting for permission from anyone to slip under the taped area. Jack was left silently cursing himself for pushing it with her – not the time or the place. It wasn't his intention to bug her, though he might have done just that, but he wanted Amanda and Ruth to sort through their differences and get back to normal, pronto.

He wandered over but kept a slight distance from his partner, concentrating on what was going on around him instead. Plastic cones with numbers, though there were only a handful, highlighted debris. Jack scanned the area, looking all around. Green fields, scattered houses, and long stretches of road. In the dark and wet of a Friday evening, there would have been no witnesses to the tragic event, and that meant every tiny piece of anything they found could be useful. Finally, Faye made her way over to Amanda, and Jack moved in closer to listen and offer his thoughts if needed.

"Morning," she said formally. No matter the scene or situation, Faye Mitchell rarely cracked a smile. "There's rather little to tell you or see I'm afraid. No footprints and no tyre marks, so the driver didn't brake before hitting the victim. Could be the young woman was in the road but unseen somehow."

"Headlights would have highlighted someone, surely?" said Amanda.

"Depends on the conditions. It was bouncing down most of the night. Any news on her state as yet?"

"She's in an induced coma for now, to give her brain a chance to heal. Jack popped in earlier but there's nothing to do or see."

"Are you on the case then?"

"Not officially, no. Ron Butcher called Jack earlier, she's his niece."

Faye twigged her meaning quickly and rolled her eyes. "That explains it then, the friends in higher places." She turned back to the scene. "Money buys all sorts of things, particularly large donations to causes." Her sarcasm didn't go unnoticed. "I wonder what I should do for a little cash injection for the lab."

It wasn't a question that needed an answer so neither detective spoke. And smut was not Faye's thing.

"Let's hope we can get something of use from her belongings. They should be at the lab by now," Faye said, checking her watch. "I'm done here now so I may as well head back. I'll let you know what I find. Let's hope we have something before Butcher gets angsty."

After one last look around, Amanda and Jack headed back to the car as spots of rain began to fall once again.

CHAPTER 30

Banker
Saturday lunchtime

It wasn't like Bethany to lie in bed. Normally she was up early, out for a morning walk or jog, or attending to chores like other people did on a Saturday. But today was different. Her head thumped like a jackhammer, not from a migraine returning but from the amount of brandy she'd drunk the previous evening. And all the crying. After Lee had stormed out, she'd stayed up for another couple of hours on her own, just sitting on the sofa drinking, listening to the rain pounding on the windows, and wondering about the woman lying unconscious in the ditch. She hoped she wasn't cold, and that her senseless state would save her from discomfort – and memories.

Light twinkled in through the bedroom windows, reflecting off her dressing-table mirror and dazzling her, then catching another shiny object, a watch maybe, so it twinkled on the ceiling. She watched the movement as it came and went with the sun peeking out from behind a cloud. For the moment it wasn't raining, and she hoped it would stay that way. She turned over on to her side and groaned at it all. Her eyes stung from crying and felt swollen half shut.

Had anyone found the woman yet or was she still lying there? She hoped they had, that she was in hospital getting help for her injuries, that she was warm.

Bethany had almost got out of bed earlier but had pretended to still be asleep when Lee had popped upstairs to look in on her. It had been too soon to speak to him. She didn't want any more of his stupid, selfish diatribe that he'd delivered the previous night. Drink and Lee never mixed well. She had heard him moving around downstairs so knew he was home, that he hadn't gone out anywhere. Most likely, he was sitting with a morning pot of coffee, newspaper in front of him, glasses on, reading.

As if she hadn't smashed into a young woman and left her to die.

While she'd been downstairs alone drinking, she hadn't come up with a solution to the problem. Lee had been right on one thing, it was a case of own up and get up to fourteen years if the woman died or stay quiet and hope for the best. When the accident became public knowledge, a hit-and-run, she hoped none of the other dinner guests would wonder about their possible involvement and connect any dots. And if they did? She'd find the strength to deny any involvement. Why would they have driven that way home? It wasn't the shortest route.

Bethany could hear footsteps approaching and instinctively turned away from the door as it creaked open slightly. She knew Lee would be in the room, staring down at her, but she kept her eyes closed, trying to hide behind her lids, hoping the bed covers would protect her, like a child might hide away from a monster. His presence revolted her.

"Are you awake, Bethany?" Lee asked in almost a whisper. What should she do? Carry on pretending or stir gently as if waking for the first time? He tried again. "Bethany, would you like a cup of tea?"

She couldn't lie there forever; it was time to make a move, so she gently rolled over to meet his gaze. She wondered what she looked like, eyes red and puffy, the swelling not gone down any. Did it matter really?

"Morning, or should I say lunchtime?" he said in his sing-song voice like nothing had happened. He was obviously feeling better, unlike herself.

"What time is it?" she asked, as though she had no clue. It was more for something to say, something to keep away from the subject she knew they'd have to talk about further at some point.

"It's almost lunchtime, almost twelve. How are you feeling?" A polite smile caressed his lips. He was a completely different animal from the one he'd been only a few hours ago, but that was Lee. He was like a chameleon adapting and changing on a whim.

"I'll get up," she said, struggling as pain shot through her temple. Her hand went to it in an instant and she winced in agony.

"I'll bring you some tea and painkillers, stay there," he instructed.

Closing her eyes against the pounding, she attempted a proper sitting position to rest back on the headboard. There was no point trying to get out of bed for a moment. Her head was swimming and her stomach rolled like the wave machine at the swimming pool. She grimaced. It was all her own making.

It was all her fault.

A moment later Lee returned and set a cup and saucer down on the bedside table and made himself comfortable on the edge of the bed.

"I'm glad you're awake. I've had a quick look to see what I can find online, what reports are around yet, and it appears a young woman has been found, but that's all I can tell you for now. They won't know anything about her at the moment, so we'll just have to wait and see."

"I feel appalling," she said. He reached out his hand and put it on hers, squeezing it gently. Bethany tried not to wince at his touch.

"You don't look it, my darling," he said, smiling. "You'll feel better when you've had your painkillers and had something to eat so I suggest, when you're ready, we get some fresh air and take a walk in the park. Just try and relax. We can't *do* anything, so let's just get on with our lives and see what happens, eh?" He leaned forward, touched the stray hairs that were in danger of slipping over her eye and moved them gently back, tucking them behind her ear. The gesture felt loving, like the man she married. Where had he gone?

It was a pity he hadn't been the caring man last night when another woman had needed him most.

CHAPTER 31

Baker

Saturday afternoon

It was generally quiet in the bakery late on a Saturday afternoon, particularly if it was wet and cold. Rivulets of water ran slowly down the pane of glass as Kit watched the outside world scuttle by. He yawned. It had been a good deal later than he'd intended when he finally got to bed, slipping between the covers as silently and gently as he could so as not to wake Natalie. With only a groan from her lips, he felt sure she'd no clue just how late he'd been. Wired, he'd lain awake for another hour or so before finally dropping off, only to be woken three hours later by his alarm. He felt bone-tired and several cups of stronger than usual coffee didn't appear to have made much of a dent. A visit from the police had risen his adrenalin levels, which had in turn left him feeling further depleted not long after the officer left.

Was he in the clear? Or was it just the start? Time would assist him there. He sensed Jakub nearby and turned to meet the lad's gaze. As usual, he looked like death warmed up. He should spend some of his illicitly earned money on proper food and a coat instead of whatever he did spend his earnings on.

"Are you looking for me?" Kit enquired wearily. He cleared his throat and repeated himself with a little more vigour.

"Need to move it. Another lock-up."

Kit hastily pulled the sleeve of Jakub's shirt before anxiously whispering, "Not so loud." Then: "Why, what's happened?"

"Space needed. I have another one. Two minutes away."

Kit groaned. He didn't need the hassle right now, if ever, but if it had to be moved, so be it. "When?"

"When we close, two hours."

It wasn't ideal. First off, it would be only just dark and they could be seen. Secondly, it was a risk he hadn't expected to have to take. He'd hoped to move it himself in a couple of days, once he'd found somewhere of his own, something a little more in his control. It wasn't to be.

"Damn it."

"No problem, I say we have other place."

It was easy for Jakub all right. It wasn't him the police already had in their sights. "Okay, we'll do it then. Have you got the door keys for the lock-up?"

"Of course."

Kit's phone buzzed in his pocket, distracting him for a moment. He slipped his hand in to retrieve it then thought better of it. He'd wait.

"I'll meet you there. We can't be seen to go together."

Jakub nodded and sauntered back to his work, leaving Kit to fish his phone out. It wasn't a person he wanted to hear from; it was Darrel once more.

24 hours to return it before things get messy.

Really? Messy? Who the hell did Darrel think he was, the local mafia? He sounded stupid and childish in his behaviour.

I don't have it. Nothing to return. It was partially true.

Bullshit. 24 hours.

Did Darrel suspect or did he know? Perhaps he'd seen Kit's car parked up the road, peeked out from behind his bedroom curtains maybe. It was plausible. And worrying. But why the time constraint? And why was his ex-business partner behaving like a local thug? A customer entering jolted him back and focused him on serving her. Jakub and Elizabeth had disappeared, likely out the back taking a break. Kit greeted the elderly woman as cheerily as he could, completed her order and, with a forced smile, watched her leave again, one of the last loaves peeking out of her trolley bag. He hoped it wouldn't get damp.

By the end of the day, he was dithering from anxiety, wandering from room to room, checking the time on his phone every two minutes. After he'd said goodnight to the others, he headed off towards his own home to retrieve a set of car keys from where he'd hidden them. Just in case.

No one would look inside a bag of hamster food. If they had, they'd have found a small plastic tub with keys in it. Even though the hamster belonged to his girls, he himself allocated the feed and so knew the keys would stay untouched for the time being. He opened it and picked a set out. Natalie had heard him come in and was standing behind him in the porch area.

"If you're hungry, I can make you a sandwich, you don't have to eat Hammy's dinner," she mused. He had time to place the right mask on before turning around. He couldn't have looked any more guilty if he'd tried but attempted to brush it off comically.

"Darn it, you caught me. Now you know my dirty little secret," he said, pretending to lick his fingers clean for her amusement. Just at that moment, both his girls entered the tiny space to see what was going on. Hamming it up, literally, he took on the role of 'hamster-food-eating human' to the shrieks and delight of the three girls in his life. But he had little time for playing. He made his excuses to leave on a short errand, assuring them he'd be back in an hour.

More lies.

He'd also have to find another place to hide the keys.

CHAPTER 32

Butcher
Saturday afternoon

Felix pulled his Range Rover into the car park and found a spot under a tree. It wasn't ideal, but hospital parking spaces were as rare as blue steak. He could only hope the birds didn't shit all over it while he was inside with his dad and aunt. There'd been no change in Melody, but at least she was still with them, her body continuing to fight. He quickly sent a text to Ron:

Need a coffee bringing up? Anything?

The reply pinged through as he approached the main entrance.

Nothing thanks.

Felix called at the small shop and purchased a balloon on a ribbon. The big yellow bear was the only one that didn't have 'congratulations it's a girl/boy' painted on it. At least when Melody woke up, it might make her smile. With the balloon and a small bouquet of flowers, he headed up to the ICU. Ron and Teresa were standing just outside the ward door, chatting quietly, his aunt looking as fidgety as ever. Both looked at his gifts, and Ron rolled his eyes at him.

"What?" Felix whined like a teenager, "What's wrong with flowers and a bear? They're to make her feel better, when she comes too."

"I doubt they'll let you take them in there though, it's not a regular ward," Ron said, pointing over his shoulder with his thumb.

"Maybe not, but they can keep them for her, in the nurse office."

Felix pressed his forehead against the door, trying to peer in through the tiny glass window to the ward beyond. He could see a nurse in the distance walking back his way, no doubt having just checked on a patient. She was almost back at the nurse's station when she quickly turned on her heels and started running. Another two nurses bolted out and followed suit, though Felix couldn't see where they'd gone, what they were attending to.

"Looks like something's going on in there," Felix said casually. "Three nurses have all just legged it across the ward, to the right. I wonder what's happening?"

Ron twigged what his son had just said. "On the right you say?"

"Yeah, why?" Ron pushed passed him and pressed the buzzer to open the door.

"Shift! Because Melody's room is on the right, that's why!" he shouted, catching his sister's attention too. With all nurses away from their station, there was nobody to respond to the doorbell and Ron, Teresa, and Felix were left thumping their fists on the glass.

It would do no good. Finally, after a hell of a lot of shouting and banging, a sour-faced nurse approached. Her expression said she was about to deliver the berating of a lifetime, but she hardly had a word out of her mouth before the three had pushed their way passed her and raced into the ward, her stern words ringing in their ears. Melody's room was indeed over to the right. It was Ron that noticed the difference first.

The blinds were closed, the door shut.

He slowed to a crawl at the realisation. The nurse that had let them in caught up with them all, her face now wearing sympathy.

Ron spoke first.

"Has she gone?" he asked quietly.

"Are you next of kin?"

"No, I am," Teresa said, walking forward. "But he is family."

"Why don't we go into my office?" she said to her. "It's a bit more private there." They left Ron and Felix glancing at each other, fearing the worst. It was only a moment before the ward sister delivered the blow.

"I am sorry to inform you, but Melody passed away a few moments ago."

Teresa's wail could be heard at the other end of the ward as she screamed a long drawn out 'no'. It was one of the most harrowing sounds Ron had ever heard. With the worst confirmed now, he went to comfort his distraught sister, wrapping his arms around her, letting her sob and wail on his shoulder. He'd grieve in a moment, when it was his turn. Right now, his sister needed his strength. Felix stood in the doorway, his head dropped low. The balloon felt stupid now. The ribbon was still in his hand and he wanted to smash it into a wall, burst it loudly, but the ward was not the place to do so. As if he could read his son's mind, Ron shook his head lightly. His boy understood. When Teresa's initial emotions had finally eased a little, Ron passed her a handful of tissues from a box on the desk and moved to Felix to comfort him for a moment. Nobody said a word. Nobody needed to. Finally, as Ron pulled away from Felix, the two men sent a silent message to each other, one that both of them fully understood.

Whoever had taken their girl would pay with their own life.

CHAPTER 33

Amanda and Jack
Saturday afternoon

Amanda and Jack were almost back at the station when the call
came in from Ron. Instinctively, Jack remembered the number
from earlier and knew who it was. He glanced across at Amanda
before accepting the call. He knew what was coming as Ron's voice
filled the car, but he'd hear it from the man himself.

"What's the news, Ron?"

"She's gone, Jack. She's gone."

Jack sighed heavily, "I'm sorry to hear that, truly I am."

"Well, you know me, Jack, I won't let this lie. How do we get
you on the case? Because I know that you, like me, will hunt down
whoever did this to my girl. I'll not rest until they're found, and god
help them if it's me that finds them first." His words hung heavy
with malice. Nobody spoke while they each considered what Ron
had threatened. After a moment's silence, he carried on, "I know I
sound like an old movie but, on my life, I'll not stop until I find
them. You've been warned."

Jack didn't doubt Ron's intentions for one second, and glancing across at Amanda, he knew she felt the same.

"I'll make the call, do what I can, Ron," said Jack, "because this changes things dramatically."

"And don't forget about our conversation earlier," Ron said. "Keep me informed with how things are progressing, okay?"

Jack ignored the question. "Before you go, Ron," Jack said. "Don't go and do anything stupid and make things worse. Leave this to us, yes?"

It was worth a try, though Jack knew he'd be ignored.

Again, a silence filled the car while he waited for some sort of response. When it finally came, a cool voice said, "I'll wait to hear from you, Jack," before the line went dead.

Both Amanda and Jack knew that the man would not heed the advice, that he'd do his own thing as he had done over all the years they had known him – though thankfully neither had ever had to deal with him directly.

"I suppose we should call the boss," said Amanda, changing the subject slightly. "Now we've got a death on our hands he needs to know that we're working on it."

"Agreed. We should let Faye know as well that there will be a body heading over to her team."

"On it," said Amanda.

Jack listened as she made the call back to base to DI Rick Black, who was relatively new to the station, and updated him on what had happened. Black had come down from Manchester for promotion and was someone they'd worked with on a prescription drug ring in the past. The man had been on a fast-track training course and had since done his time and exams, ending up working in Croydon as part of their team. He had replaced DI Dupin who had unceremoniously left some weeks back when it had become apparent that he'd well and truly screwed up on a case. Not to mention that, off duty, he had been involved in an altercation with a man who had later died. As it eventually transpired, it had been an unlucky, freak-of-nature event and nothing to do with the punches thrown. Still, it had led to new scrutiny of his involvement in cases from way back, and when investigators found evidence of corruption, DI Dupin had no choice but to leave. It was sad when the man had been on the force for so long, but his own actions were his downfall – something that could have been avoided. Pension lost. Wife likely lost. Life as he once knew it changed forever. People made tough choices, often the wrong ones, and DI Dupin had done just that.

Jack imagined DI Rick Black on the other end of the phone. At a full 6'4" the dark-haired man that looked like Buddy Holly's double was a striking figure. If DI Black wore winkle-pickers, they wouldn't look more appropriate on the feet of any other man. He also had a penchant for wearing nice suits. Being tall and athletic in build, he made everybody in the squad room feel overweight – largely because they were. It was early days for the man, but so far Jack had taken a liking to him, as had Amanda. He hoped it would stay that way, he quite fancied a drive in the guy's Mustang one weekend, a car he kept just for pleasure. So far Black seemed like a decent sort – hard-working, fair, and incredibly energetic. He likely ran to keep in shape.

Amanda finishing her call dragged him back from thinking about DI Black and all that he was. Naturally, the team had given the man a nickname – Buddy.

"What does Buddy have to say then?" Jack suspected Black had heard the nickname before, though to his knowledge it had not actually been said to the man's face. There was time yet.

"He says carry on. And to watch Ron obviously."

"Duh, didn't think of that," he said, putting his own dopey voice on.

"I'll tell Faye to expect a body, though she may already know."

Jack watched as she chose the number and hit call. The one-sided conversation was short because most of them were with the woman of few words.

With the relevant parties informed, Jack glanced at the clock on the dashboard. Half his breakfast had been left on the plate back at the café earlier, and even though he'd had a doughnut, his stomach was screaming lunch. He turned to Amanda.

"What do you fancy to eat?"

His food intake was the main reason he'd never compete with DI Black, or Raj for that matter, on the athletic-body front.

CHAPTER 34

Amanda and Jack
Saturday afternoon

Amanda and Jack pulled into McDonald's and found a parking space. She hated the drive-through, too risky for potential mess in your lap, and preferred to sit at a table, though sitting inside opposite Jack, the odds weren't much better mess-wise. She watched as brown grease made a slow trickle down Jack's chin before he wiped it with a serviette. A skinny fry followed and had to be concertinaed up into his mouth. She smiled inwardly at the action – it was something she did herself, but then didn't everyone do that with Stringfellow fries?

"What have you got planned this afternoon then, Jack?" she enquired.

"Well, I had planned on going to the bowling club for a practice session, but with all this rain it might be a bit soggy. How about you?" Another fry was concertinaed up, following the last one.

"Not much. I find myself at a loose end at weekends now."

Jack looked across the table at her from under his eyebrows, giving her a fatherly look. She instantly knew what he meant.

"Don't push it, Jack," she said again. "You've tried a couple of times today, just leave it be. Or we'll end up falling out too," she warned.

"But it's so senseless. Are you even talking to one another?"

"Nothing to talk about really."

"But you two are meant for each other. Why can't you work through it?"

"It's not that simple, Jack. Aside from losing trust in her, the whole thing caused so much hassle back at the station too. I mean, I know everybody knows about my sexuality, but still, I didn't need the ridicule, and I certainly didn't need people to suspect that I was in on it all along. I take great pride in my work, and to have people doubt my integrity hurt just as much as her broken trust. There is no way I knew about that body. I investigated that landscaper's disappearance with you, if you remember. And I was more convinced than you that something was going on in that house." She concertinaed a fry of her own and chewed it so slowly she wondered if she'd ever swallow it. She carried on: "At the time, we had nothing to go on, no body. It was just a disappearance, a man gone AWOL. Neither of us could have known back then."

Amanda picked up her burger and took another bite, careful not to let grease dribble, and the two sat quietly with their own thoughts until the sound of Jack's phone buzzing broke the tension. She watched as he pulled it out of his jacket pocket, read the text, and nodded gently with satisfaction at the content.

"What is it?" she enquired.

"It's the phone number for the next of kin for Nelly Raven. The number the neighbour gave kept ringing out, so I've been waiting for another one to call now uniform have notified next of kin."

"I wonder what went wrong with their relationship?" she asked. "The fact that the son has left his mother seemingly without support. I wondered perhaps if he doesn't live anywhere near or if they've had a falling out maybe."

"Well, I guess you can't pick your family members," Jack said in a sing-song voice. "Maybe we'll find out eventually. I just hope somebody attends her funeral." Thinking as he ate, he added, "I hope someone attends *my* funeral too," he said, lifting his eyes fully to meet Amanda's. "I'd hate to be buried with no one in the chapel. No one to say a few words over me or sing a song or two. How about you?"

"I've no family, so there won't be many to miss me. And since I'm not planning on going anytime soon, not until I get into my eighties or nineties, I've got a bit of time to make some new friends for the occasion. Though since I've just lost one, I'm officially in a deficit." She tried a weak smile that lasted all of a split second.

"Have you picked your songs or chosen what you want at your funeral?"

"A bit premature aren't you, Jack?"

"Not really. We could each depart this earth tomorrow, and it would be handy if someone knew what you wanted beforehand. Is it in your will? Mine's all written down, every last detail, including the egg sandwiches."

"Really? I haven't given it much thought," she said. "Like I say, I hope it's a good long way off yet."

"Don't be so sure. In our job we both know death can take a person at any time, it can't be scheduled, except by suicide, so we can only plan to get to the age we want to. Look at poor young Melody, a slip of a girl at nineteen, minding her own business and now she's gone. And Nelly Raven, gone. I can't believe you don't have a will sorted, Amanda. That's crazy and not like you, you're usually so well organised."

"I'm not sure I can cope with your cheery conversation," she said sarcastically.

"A funeral doesn't have to be maudlin. Mine won't be at any rate," he carried on, undeterred. "At least whoever is in the chapel with me will know the words to 'Morning has Broken'. There'll be no half-hearted singing to that one," he said triumphantly.

"Can we change the subject, please?"

But Jack was on a roll. "There's just so much death around at the moment, don't you think? The old lady and Melody, both at different times in their life, both taken for different reasons, both quite unexpected, both leaving families behind to mourn. Well, Melody has anyway; we don't know yet about Nelly Raven's family."

From Amanda's face, Jack could tell she'd heard enough and took the hint. He wiped his mouth and fingers with his serviette, screwed up his paper wrappers into a ball and, when Amanda had finally finished her meal, took their rubbish to the bin.

Weak lunchtime sunshine filtered through the building's smeared glass, revealing fingerprints and possible DNA traces for half of Croydon's inhabitants. He wondered what the son's story was, why he was not in his mother's life any more, or not close enough to know that she'd been ill and needed help.

But he wanted to speak to the son anyway, for reasons of his own.

CHAPTER 35

Baker

Saturday afternoon

Kit hated being furtive. Hiding things and lying to his family didn't sit well, it wasn't something he or Natalie did, and he certainly brought his young family up to be honest and truthful at all times. If they were ever in trouble, say something, he could help. He wished he had that support from someone right now, someone to tell his side of the story to, someone with whom he could share the madness he'd undertaken. He was confident, though, that they'd tell him to stop.

From his spot parked a little way along from the lock-up, he watched Jakub saunter towards him, hoody up over his head, hands stuffed in his jeans pockets, looking like any other pale, nondescript youth with trousers hanging too far below their boxer shorts. What was that even all about? When Jakub was almost at the garage entrance, Kit slipped out of his seat and joined him. Unlocked, the roller door screeched and groaned as metal rubbed against metal, slowly revealing the Audi parked quietly inside.

"Shouldn't we swap the plates or something?"

"Not far, no need."

Kit shrugged his understanding.

"You drive. I open next door."

"Why don't you drive this and I'll follow then give you a lift back? We'll both have to walk if we go your way."

"No driving. Like walking."

Kit glanced at Jakub. He couldn't exactly push him into it, the lad was doing him a favour after all. He took the key back from Jakub's outstretched hand and reluctantly opened the driver's side. Starting the engine, he eased out of the lock-up and idled as the roller door screeched and groaned its way back down behind him once more. When Jakub was seated, he waited for directions. It felt good to be back behind the wheel of his old car, particularly as he still owned two-thirds of it. He revved the engine like he was in an action movie and about to give the bad guys a run for their money. All he needed was a tattoo on his forearm and a bandana around his head, and he'd be all set. Jakub sensed his warped enthusiasm, the dark dots of his eyes telling Kit to calm down, it wasn't a game. Eventually they moved forward casually. Directions came from a silent passenger using hand signals. Kit followed the lad's instructions, turning a series of lefts and rights around streets, each of which looked as rundown as the last, until they eventually pulled up at another set of lock-ups that looked much the same as the one they'd just left. Jakub signalled the unit, and they pulled up ready to drive in. Graffiti tags covered each door, the layers of sprayed haphazard words, symbols, and lettering, as each kid left their mark on top of the previous, made no sense. Jakub searched his pockets for the keys and another roller door opened, though somewhat more quietly than the last one. The storage area itself was empty save for what looked like a tarpaulin sheet rolled up at the far end. Kit drove in and parked up. He turned to look at the rest of the car, his car. Darrel had looked after it at least, the interior as immaculate as Kit himself had kept it, which could be difficult with a family. He rubbed his hand along the leather back seat and smiled at memories of what he and Natalie had been up to there in previous times.

It was time to go, get back home, and Jakub was waiting patiently. He hoped he could find his way back to his car; he had no doubt Jakub would get home easily enough. One more time, he ran his fingers over the bodywork as he neared the boot and flicked the key fob to open it, the lid rising mechanically. He peered inside casually. All appeared to be in order, but something prickled at the hairs on his neck.

Sure, Darrel wanted 'his' car back, but the last message seemed at odds with the man he'd known for so long.

24 hours to return it before things get messy.

He lifted the false carpet and peered into where the spare wheel lay. It all looked normal, unused, and fastened in place. He scanned the area anyway and, apart from a first aid kit and a jack, it was empty. Still something prickled. Jakub called out to him, they had to leave. But Kit wasn't satisfied, he wanted to see what was in the hollow of the wheel, the side he couldn't see. It took him only a couple of seconds to free the spare and lift it out.

"Oh shit, Darrel. What have you got yourself into?"

There was never any mistaking what a tightly wrapped bundle of £100 notes was ever going to be. Though Kit wasn't a budgeting expert, he knew the cash wasn't Darrel's summer holiday savings account; there had to be a good few grand laid out in front of him. A large envelope stared at him, and he picked it up and peered inside. It held a passport, driver's licence, birth certificate, and other basic identification documents.

Kit looked at the photo on the passport. It was Darrel's face.

But not Darrel's name.

Fake ID documents. Was the man planning on doing a runner? Kit felt Jakub at his shoulder and heard the slight intake of breath as he too realised what he was looking at. The reason Darrel had made the threat.

Things could get messy.

Kit slipped the envelope and tyre back in place and closed the lid.

"Not a word to anyone, do you understand?" Kit warned. A nod from Jakub. There was no point in removing it now – where would he take it to? Not the hamster feed bag, that was for sure. He needed time. The two men closed up, said brief goodbyes, and went their separate ways.

Kit gave himself until he'd walked back to his vehicle to decide what to do next. While he had trusted Jakub up to now, with this new and rather more delicate secret to keep, he wasn't so convinced. The young man could surely do with the cash himself. That gave him another thought: could he keep the cash for *himself* and give the car back somehow? Abandon it? The documents would be of no use or concern to a chance car thief. But then Darrel would still be suspicious and might come after him. He couldn't just give the wad back to Darrel without admitting it was him that had the vehicle. Perhaps he could use it as a bargaining chip?

Either way, he had to decide what to do and fast. But by the time he'd arrived back at his car, he still didn't have the answer. He slipped inside and pulled away slowly, headed home.

The motorcyclist parked silently in the shadows of the dingy street started his engine and pulled out as Kit drove off. There was no point in following, he knew just where the driver was going.

CHAPTER 36

The mortuary
Saturday afternoon

Dr Faye Mitchell preferred to undertake weekend post-mortems as bodies were brought in, rather than leave them for Monday morning. She hated the fact they might feel they'd been waiting for her to finish her 'time off' – they needed their own closure. Plus, as someone who's current love interest lived out of the area, her weekends weren't normally filled with gardening or other hobbies. They'd only been dating a handful of weeks and it was early days. So far, those days were turning out to be all good ones, and Dr Kevin Douglas, a pathologist himself, was turning out to be quite a catch.

At four o'clock on Saturday afternoon, she took delivery of Melody Holden's badly bruised and broken body. Gazing down at the young woman's face, she tutted to herself softly. What a waste of life, one that had hardly got going.

"Let's get her X-rayed and photographed first off," she said to Val, her mortuary assistant, who nodded and moved away to get the necessary equipment ready. A student hovered nearby, eager to learn and happy to help wherever possible. Looking about the same age as the victim lying in front of them, Orson had jumped at the chance to attend the post-mortem on a Saturday afternoon. Crystal Palace were probably going to lose anyway, and there was always the recorded game to watch later. He was proving to be an asset to have around despite his youth.

Orson flitted about taking pictures of his own while Val did the official ones. Once Faye was satisfied, they removed Melody's gown and began a thorough surface search, describing for the recorder everything witnessed that was noteworthy. The list was a long one, with every bruise and every scratch measured and recorded. When Faye came to open Melody's chest cavity and remove her organs, she wasn't expecting to find anything out of the norm. It had been her head wound that had caused her death, but still, a post-mortem would confirm it. Or not. While the heart had stopped beating, it wasn't necessarily the cause of a person's demise.

When each organ had been inspected, weighed, and logged, everything was put neatly back inside a bag and inserted back into the cavity. There was little point sewing each organ back in position, and nothing could be disposed of, but they carefully closed the body up for when the family took over. With her chest stitched back up and the crown of her skull back in place, Melody was settled back in a chilled cabinet for the next chapter of her death.

There was nothing unexpected in Faye's findings. Whoever had hit Melody with their vehicle had killed her when her brain bled out some hours later. Perhaps if they'd stopped, called for help, and Melody had been given the treatment she'd so desperately needed, she'd still be alive now. It was a coward's act.

While Orson scrubbed the trolley and sink down and cleaned away, Faye took a look at Melody's sparse belongings. Her bag, containing a few items for an evening out, including her ever-present phone, her clothing, and her footwear. Judging by the heels on the strappy sandals and scratches on the undersides of her feet, she'd been walking on the road barefoot for some time.

There was little else to go on. The objects laid out in front of her could have been any young woman's. Faye picked up each item of clothing in turn and carefully examined it, but there was nothing of interest. The dress had a small amount of blood on it that was likely Melody's own. Faye put it to one side to get a sample from anyway. Melody's main injuries, including her fatal injury, had been of the internal variety – apart from severe scrapes to her arms and legs, which she'd likely sustained on landing.

Her belt, however, gave Faye pause. She used her magnifying glass to check the metal buckle, and sure enough, there were tiny particles of what looked, at first glance, like paint. Faye was never one to get excited – the paint could have been from an event nothing to do with the hit-and-run – but it was a start, it was something to go on. She took a tiny sample and placed it in a sterile pot for further examination by the lab later. They'd be able to tell what sort of paint it was and the colour code. If it was paint transferred from the vehicle that hit her, it would narrow the search for the driver down drastically. She was hopeful. Orson hovered nearby, waiting for a break in her concentration.

"Find something?" he asked, peering a little closer.

"I'm hoping so. Paint. I'm thinking the buckle here may have got caught somewhere on the car bonnet, or maybe the wing, and transferred." She kept her gaze on the buckle rather than turning to speak with him.

"Want me to take it over and see who's in to deal with it?"

Always the helpful one.

"Please. You might need to use your charm," she said, finally lifting her eyes to meet his young face. Even though he was in med school, he looked about eighteen. No doubt he'd still look eighteen on his wedding day; some people were blessed with youthful looks.

He grinned. "Always do," he said and took the pot away to see what he could do, leaving Faye to finalise her notes. She dialled Amanda to tell her what she'd found.

Amanda and Jack had split and gone back to their respective

homes. There was little more they could do for the moment. There was no CCTV footage for the back lane because there were no cameras. The only thing they could look at was what travelled up a particular road that led to the back road, from an area that was actually surveyed. Hopefully there'd be a camera close enough, but with so many cars entering at the estimated time they were working to, they'd need to narrow it down somehow. They needed a clue to follow.

Amanda was sitting in her lounge with a mug of tea, flipping through the weekend supplement. Landscapes' 'Einstein A Go-Go' ringtone interrupted her. She had one set for everyone that called her regularly so she knew who it was long before she reached her phone. 'Einstein' was the obvious choice for the doctor.

"Hi Faye. Some news?"

"Afternoon, Amanda, and I'm hoping so. We might have some red paint on the victim's belt buckle. Orson has taken it to get tested so hopefully we'll know later, but it may be Monday. I thought if it was car paint, it would help narrow the search. The cause of death is as we expected, so no change there."

"Thanks, Faye. Paint colour and type will be helpful. Thanks for doing the post-mortem so quickly; this could be the lead we need in the absence of much else."

"Also, the victim was knocked down from behind, not from the front. Out on that dark back road in that rain, the driver may not have seen her."

"They'd have felt her though and could have stopped. She might still be alive and in hospital then and not in the chiller," added Amanda pointedly.

"I'm not defending their actions, Amanda, far from it. And I agree, they'd have felt the impact, and if she went over the bonnet, likely seen Melody. The front wing, maybe not so much, they'd have been concentrating on driving and visibility was low. Those are just my thoughts."

"I know, I didn't mean to imply anything, but cases like this are so senseless, I get a bit worked up." Amanda paused then gave a heavy sigh and, changing the subject, asked, "No Kevin this weekend?"

"No, unfortunately for me. How about you, hot date tonight?"

Silence replaced their conversation while Amanda wondered what to say.

Faye took over immediately with an apology. "Damn, that was insensitive. Sorry, Amanda, I didn't mean to..."

"It's fine, don't worry. I've been with Jack most of the day, and he's not given up pushing for the most part. It seems everyone wants me to either move on or forgive and make up."

"You'll do what's right for you in the end. It'll all come together, you'll see. Life's train has its own destination in mind, and you're a passenger too."

"Well to answer your question, no hot date, no. Not unless you count a takeaway Vindaloo for one, that could be hot," Amanda said, adding a light chuckle. It was the best she could muster.

"Well enjoy it, and I'll let you know when I have some news."

Amanda sat back to digest the call. A car colour would help. She only hoped it belonged to a niche make and model and not a damn Ford Fiesta.

CHAPTER 37

Baker
Saturday evening

Kit was enjoying a game of Trivial Pursuit with his family when there was a knock on the door. From the thumping, it sounded urgent. Natalie looked up in surprise and said, "Whoever could that be? They've got a bee in their bonnet about something."

"I'll go," said Kit. As he opened the door, he had to admit it was odd on a Saturday evening. The outside light that had been triggered by movement shone down on a familiar face, but within that split second Kit barely saw the fist that headed straight for his jawline. The punch landed and knocked him back into the hallway. In a moment, the man was on top of him, lashing out and hurling abuse. With all the commotion going on, it was Natalie that came out of the lounge first and, recognising the intruder, tried her best to intervene and cool things down. Darrel had made his visit known by barging his way in and throwing the first punch. Natalie screamed at him to calm down and to get the hell off her husband. Two children's faces appeared around the lounge door and started screaming, "Daddy! Daddy!" Their presence did the trick, and the lashing out finally stopped. Darrel stood and glared down at Kit.

"I knew you'd be behind it," he spat, satisfied.

As Kit struggled to get up off the floor, he rubbed his chin. Natalie gave him a hand, letting Darrel cool down a little. She nudged the door shut with her foot and turned back to Darrel.

"What the hell are you doing, Darrel?" she screamed at him.

"Why don't you ask your husband what he's been doing? That will answer your question," he said sarcastically.

"What's he talking about?" she asked, turning to Kit and ushering the two girls back into the lounge at the same time.

Kit knew exactly what it was his ex-business partner was talking about. He just wondered how he'd found out. This intrusion was a long way from a couple of threatening texts. Turning up on his doorstep and smacking him one was another level. Doing so while his family were present was a low move, and he wondered just how much the man knew.

"Kit?" Natalie tried again.

He decided to go for act dumb and see what transpired.

"I have no idea, Natalie."

"Like hell you haven't," snarled Darrel. "The small matter of my car?"

"What about your car? I've told you I'm not involved with that. How many times do I need to tell you I haven't taken your car!"

"Maybe this will remind you," Darrel said, pulling his fist back for another go. Natalie screamed as another punch headed for Kit's head, and she tried to intervene by putting herself between the two men. Kit kept his balance and the punch never landed, but he was intent on delivering one of his own. He lurched forward at Darrel, but it was Natalie's scream that stopped him.

"If you two don't stop scrapping, I'm calling the police!" she said.

"That's probably a good idea under the circumstances," Darrel said. "Since it's your husband that stole my car."

"I haven't stolen your car. How many more times? I haven't taken it!"

"You damn well have and I know it, and I also know that it's in a lock-up on Howard Road. I saw you there. You moved the car today, you parked it in the garage."

That stopped Kit in his tracks. How did the man know so much? And then it dawned on him. Somebody had likely followed him, someone that suspected him. He wondered for a second if Jakub had anything to do with it or if it was all his own making. He hadn't noticed anybody, but then he hadn't been looking for anybody either.

"It's not your car though, is it? Kit said. "You only ever paid one payment; you still owe me two more."

"That's your stupid fault. You signed the documents over to me so the car's legally mine, and I want it back."

Kit wondered whether to mention what he knew was in the boot, hidden under the tyre, particularly with Natalie present. Could he use this as his bargaining chip? After all, Darrel knew that he'd got the car, but did he know *he* knew about the documents and the cash in the boot? If Kit took the money for himself, he'd have Darrel banging on his door again. But perhaps he could keep the car and leave the money and documents for Darrel; they were of no use to him, and Kit was hardly a criminal himself. It had been a badly thought out plan, one that was now backfiring loudly on him.

"Kit?" questioned Natalie. "Is that true? Did you take the car?"

"Officially, no, I didn't take the car."

Darrel scoffed. "Technicalities. Someone took it for you. You've got it, and I want it back – along with the two sets of car keys, please."

"Well, you're not getting it back, because I'm two-thirds owner. It's mine."

"Right then, I'm phoning the police since you just admitted you've got it," said Darrel, pulling his phone out to make the call.

Kit hastily wondered what to do. Should he say anything? He didn't really need the cops involved in this, but would they be even interested? Surely it was a civil matter. Given the guy never paid for it, was it really a police thing? But stealing it back most certainly was. Could he chance it?

"Go ahead," said Kit flippantly, "dial. I don't care. It's Saturday night. They've probably got more important things to do, like getting drunks off the street, than finding your stolen car. Though I expect they'd be more interested in what was inside the boot," Kit said with a smirk.

That stopped Darrel in his tracks.

CHAPTER 38

Baker
Saturday evening

It was neither Darrel nor Kit that called the police. A next-door neighbour, who'd overheard the commotion going on next door, was the culprit. While Darrel was thinking about Kit's final comment, uniformed officers were parking up outside and heading to the front door. It was Natalie that saw the blue flashing light over the shoulders of the two angry men that were too busy sparring with each other to notice. She inwardly groaned. From what she understood, Kit had in fact taken the car but, by his revelation, there was something in the boot a good deal more precious to Darrel than the car itself. She had no idea what that might be though. Knuckles rapped on the glass door and everyone stood froze to the spot.

"I have to open it," said Natalie. "You two made enough noise to wake the dead between you. No wonder someone called the police. Why don't you both back off and go wait in the lounge? In fact, no, don't do that, the girls are in there. Go down to the kitchen. I'll see if I can sort this out."

After waiting a moment for the men to leave, Natalie opened the front door. Kit glanced over his shoulder to see two uniformed officers stood on the outside step and hoped Natalie could get rid of them. As the officers introduced themselves, Kit could just about hear that they'd been called by a neighbour, something about a disturbance. Natalie tried to pacify them by saying all was well. It was a misunderstanding between two friends, and they were sorting it out.

"Are you sure, madam? Only, people don't normally call the police for a heated discussion. There were reports of screaming and crashing. I think we should take a closer look."

"I'm sorry you've had a wasted journey officer, but really there's nothing going on. Everything is fine here." The uniformed officer looked doubtful, and Natalie smiled her confirmation, anxiously waiting to close the door. Just when she thought they were about to leave, shouting erupted again at the back of the house. She glanced at the two officers and took a deep breath, opening the door wide for them to enter.

There was no point in pretending any more. If the men couldn't keep it quiet for five minutes, they deserved a talking to from the law.

Perhaps it was a good thing the officers had persisted because the two hotheads were quite clearly still going at it and hard. 'Documents', 'car', and 'cash' were words she caught flying through the air, and she wondered how they all fitted together. What the hell had they been up to? She followed the two uniformed officers to find out. By the time the three of them reached the kitchen, punches were again being thrown and connecting. A chair clattered to the floor. Things were getting ugly rather than better, and Natalie wisely let the police take over.

There had been a time when the two men had been close friends, but looking at them now, they were two wild animals that had hated each other from birth. Blood ran down Kit's nose from where a punch had landed and he was threatening Darrel with a chair when the three walked in. Taking one look at the scene in front of them, the officers each grabbed a man to separate them and calm things down. Heavy breathing filled the room as hormones raged over who was the bigger man. Natalie looked on, bewildered and upset that it had come to this. Whatever it was, something had gone terribly wrong in their relationship, and she was anxious to find out for herself just what that was. After formal introductions to both Kit and Darrel, one of the officers took charge to find out what the argument was about. Darrel screamed the first answer.

"He stole my car, and I know where it is!"

Petulant adult.

Kit was somewhat surprised at the outburst given what was in the boot, but tempers were running high and Darrel was obviously not thinking straight. Was he stupid enough to forget what it contained when it had been mentioned just minutes earlier?

"Is that true?" asked the officer, turning to Kit, who had simmered down somewhat.

"The opposite actually. It's my car. Darrel never paid for it fully. Therefore, it's still mine."

"Whose name is the car registered in?" the officer asked.

"Mine," said Darrel smugly.

"Where is the car now?" asked the officer.

Kit wasn't going to say but Darrel was: "It's in a lock-up on Howard Road, I watched him drive it in there today. I know he's got it, and I want it back."

The officer turned to Kit again. There was no getting away from it now, they could check the lock-up and find it. But maybe he could use what was in the boot to his advantage somehow. There wasn't much time to think about how and he made his decision in a flash.

"Yes, it's in the lock-up. And while you're there, you might want to check the contents of the boot, specifically under the spare tyre. You might be more interested in that than me taking my own property back." Kit's smugness far outweighed his former friend's.

Darrel lunged forward and shouted, "I'll get you for this, Kit Morris!"

It was Kit's turn to be cocky, and he pushed his button again: "Check under the wheel and see what's there," he taunted.

Anger raged in Darrel's eyes and sweat glistened on his forehead from his temper. "I'll have you for this," shouted Darrel nastily, realising finally what information was now in the room. Given how the man's eyes blazed, Kit had no doubt that he would.

"What's in the boot that we might be interested in?" the officer asked Kit.

"Why don't you ask Darrel? He says he's owner of the car. It's all his."

The officer turned to Darrel, asked the same question, and waited. Darrel glared, no doubt wondering how much to tell, how much he could get away with. He played for time.

"He's bluffing. There's nothing in the boot. He's just trying to take the pressure off himself."

"Rubbish," said Kit. "You'll find cash and documents – false ID documents to be precise."

Natalie's gasp was audible. She'd been stood in the kitchen, arms folded, listening and watching as the night's events unfolded before her between two men she thought she knew. Rage fired up again on Darrel's face and he lunged forward, trying to reach Kit, fist at the ready. He knew damn well that he'd be in trouble.

"How can you explain around £20,000 in cash and false documents, Darrel?" he sneered provokingly. "I know I'd love to hear the answer to that one."

As Darrel struggled to retaliate and attack Kit, the officer asking the questions decided what would happen next.

It was no surprise then that both men ended up in handcuffs and were carted away unceremoniously. They could each spend the night in a cell, but not before they'd answered a few more questions at the station.

It would be a night Natalie would never forget.

CHAPTER 39

Baker

Saturday night

Kit found himself alone in a cold police cell with nothing more than a plastic-covered mattress and a thin blanket. Darrel was likely further down the hallway in a cell of his own. Not that he cared much about what happened to his one-time friend, not now. They'd both been dragged in to cool off, and he was grateful he wasn't sharing lodgings with a drunk, or anyone else for that matter. He lay gazing up at the ceiling with not much more than the outside street lamp for light. While the tiny concrete room had an orangey glow, it didn't feel warming. He'd been there for a couple of hours and had largely been left alone, but he knew come morning he'd have to answer more questions. There was no point in denying he'd taken the car; he was bang to rights. His prints were on it. He had the keys. Darrel had seen him park it and knew where it was. So, what was the point in denying it? He might as well get the whole sorry mess over with and move on. He was more annoyed at himself that he'd let Natalie down again.

It wasn't his first offence, unfortunately, as he'd been done for being drunk and disorderly some years back. Not long after he'd met Natalie, he'd ended up in a punch-up after a bloke in a bar had been a nuisance to her, and Kit had stepped in to help her out. The trouble was, he'd had a few to drink himself, and that had resulted in his first night lying in a cell.

Now he just hoped he'd be let out on bail in the morning. He didn't care much what happened to Darrel; he was still too angry with him. But their history together didn't stop him wondering what his former friend would be thinking about as he lay on his own plastic mattress. Just where the hell did he get those documents from in the first place, and what were they for? The police would want to know. Would Darrel grass that person up to save his own skin? Kit figured it depended on who that person was, probably someone from the more sinister side of society that lurked about in the underworld not the common world. But that was for Darrel to worry about. Kit just wanted to get out of his cell in the morning, take any punishment, and get on with his life. He had a business to run and a family to provide for.

Would he be charged? Depending on how everything transpired after questioning, he may have to stay in for the weekend until the magistrates' court opened on Monday, though hoped it wouldn't come to that. If it did, there was the small matter of representation to worry about. With no funds to pay anyone, he'd have no option but to have the duty solicitor or do it himself. Kit shuddered as he lay there thinking about it. He'd had the experience of a duty solicitor last time, and while he hadn't had to do any prison time, the kid that represented him hadn't been much use either. He'd got Kit off on luck alone; there hadn't been too much savvy in the young man's head. He'd shaken with nerves like a tree in an earthquake – never a good omen.

Maybe Kit could do a better job on his own, and maybe, just maybe, he wouldn't need to worry about it at all. If Darrel got shitty about the car and wanted to press charges, he could make Kit's life a tad more difficult. Being released without charge was all Kit could hope for.

In a cell right next door, Darrel was running through his own thoughts about what would happen next. His fake documents were going to be of police interest. Even though the UK and Europe virtually had open borders, the authorities still liked to know who they had in their midst and took fake documents seriously. He hadn't been planning on running anyway, but he was planning on setting up a new identity for certain business transactions. Darrel's main concern was how much to tell the police when he was interviewed. Come the morning, when his solicitor would be present, they'd have a good go at him. It wasn't like he'd stolen a packet of cigarettes. Carrying forged documents was never good in anybody's book, and when his wife and family found out, how was he going to explain what his plans were to them? Or maybe, just maybe, the police didn't really give a toss about him and would be more interested to find out about the supplier? Maybe he could bargain, give the name of the person, and escape prosecution himself. That sounded the best option, leaving him to look after his family. But what about when that person found out he'd dobbed them in? He didn't want to be on the receiving end of that particular person's anger. Or put his family at risk. Darrel went around and around in circles with his options. First offence or not, he was in trouble, and for now, the plan was cool off and think it through.

And Kit, did he even care about him?

He did once.

CHAPTER 40

Banker
Saturday night

Bethany lay awake in her own private hell, sleep eluding her, though she at least had sheets and a quilt. The Saturday evening news had reported a hit-and-run case on a quiet back road out of town where a young woman had been found. Due to her substantial injuries, she'd later died in Croydon's University Hospital earlier in the day. Police were appealing for anyone that saw anything that could help them identify the driver to please come forward.

Bethany Meady had killed someone.

She'd gasped at the television report, and as the newsreader had run through the few known details, Lee had finally comforted her by putting his arm around her shoulder, assuring her with useless words that everything would be all right. Nobody could link them to the scene, and the rain would have rinsed any evidence of their involvement away hours ago. They were both safe.

Lying next to him now, Bethany tried to steady her breathing by listening to his, her chest rising and falling gently in time with his own, like a pianist might use a metronome to keep the timing of a piece. But her chest felt restricted, and she eventually gave up trying to stay in tune with his rhythm and let her own ragged breathing be. Moisture glazed her neck and cleavage, and she pushed the covers down, willing the cooler air in the room to cool her anxiety away. But her arms grew cold quickly, and she pulled the sheet up close, hoping the single thin layer would be a satisfactory in-between. How the hell Lee could sleep, she'd no idea, but evidently he could. She knew she'd be wiped out in the morning. Two restless nights in a row didn't bode well for a restful Sunday. Plus, there was work on Monday to get through. After taking Friday off with a migraine, there was no way she could wangle another day off so soon. Maybe the monotony of her job would help keep her mind off things, maybe work would be a good thing. But she couldn't fester in worry tomorrow. She'd keep herself busy some-how; it was the only way to get through it.

She glanced over at the clock. Green digital numbers grinned back at her. It was 3.30 am, well and truly too early to get up, though having lain there for well over an hour already, Bethany knew persevering any longer was pointless. Silently, she found her robe and slippers then left the room to head downstairs. Lee wouldn't even realise she'd gone thanks to the several brandies he'd had just after dinner, not to mention the bottle of red he'd consumed with his meal. She'd picked at her food and declined any more than the one glass of wine, choosing to stay clear-headed. Perhaps she should have done the opposite and got drunk. At least her brain would have been addled for a while, and like Lee, she could have slept it off peacefully.

The kitchen was filled with a pale grey light that streamed in from the moon and through the glass ceiling until a cloud floated by and darkened everything again. Bethany looked up. The charcoal sky directly above offered a glimpse at occasional stars before more cloud re-covered them and plunged the room into total darkness. It must be windy, she thought, with the clouds moving on quickly and the changes in light repeating in the kitchen. A bush scratched at a nearby window, attracting her attention. Was autumn always going to be wet and wild? Would they ever have a clear day for a change? The thought depressed her for a moment. Then, as the moon peeked out again, she caught a glimpse of a set of keys on the work-top. They were her own. She reached for them and held them close to her chest, the sharp metal edges digging into her skin as she urged them closer, leaving an impression. Since the accident a little over twenty-four hours ago, she hadn't been back behind the wheel, there'd been little need with Lee taking over everything.

An idea idled in her head. The hall cupboard housed all kinds of footwear, and she quickly found a pair of old boots and slipped them on. Pulling her robe belt tighter around her waist, she opened the front door and silently headed to her car. She sat inside it and waited a beat. For lights upstairs maybe? For divine intervention? For courage and strength, perhaps? Without turning the headlights on, she pulled out of the driveway and headed out towards Tanya and Eric's house, where they'd been for dinner Friday night – was it only that long ago?

It felt a little weird being out so late and dressed in her robe, but something pulled at her conscience, telling her to go back to where the young woman had been hit.

That she'd hit. That she'd killed.

Moonlight steered the way and tears sneaked down Bethany's soundless face as she drove. The road was deserted, nobody else out in the middle of the night, not on this quiet back road, nobody to accompany her thoughts. It wasn't long before she was at the spot where she'd hit the woman. She stopped on the road as there was no real need to pull over, and without torrential rain beating the car, visibility was somewhat clearer. Not that there was much to see: damp tarmac, a grassy ditch, a hedgerow. Police crime-scene tape caught the wind and billowed like blue-and-white streamers. It was her gut that encouraged her to get out of the vehicle. A strong breeze whipped at the edges of her robe, flicking the fabric back-wards and forwards around her bare legs like fleecy flags caught on their flagpoles. She stepped forward towards the ditch and bent down, touching the grass long since bent over under the weight of its own length and wet from recent rain. She caressed it, stroked it, as if the motion soothed her aching soul. Fresh tears slipped off her jawline and on to the ground, never to be seen again.

"I'm so sorry," she wept out loud. "So very, very sorry."

Bethany looked up to the sky before releasing a long-strangled howl of pain to the heavens. Perhaps she should have been stronger at the time, stood up to Lee and reported the incident, but he'd been adamant they kept quiet, and the prospect of fourteen years in prison had helped on that score. Could she now cope with their actions? Her actions?

Guilt gnawed away at her insides. She wasn't so sure.

CHAPTER 41

Banker

Sunday morning

Bethany eventually arrived home and crawled back into bed just before 4.30 am. Lee hadn't bothered stirring. If he was aware that she'd even left, he didn't show it. Her hair was damp from the moist air blowing outside, her eyes as swollen as they had been for the last twenty-four hours. If she could sleep, get some rest, she might feel better in the morning, but she knew deep down that was never going to happen and lay waiting patiently for dawn to come.

Somewhere along the way she must've dozed off because when she finally opened her eyes daylight was peeking through a crack in the curtains, and Lee was no longer beside her. Trying to tune into her surroundings, she heard music playing downstairs, just lightly in the background, and wondered what time it was. Her eyes were sore and gritty as she rolled over to check the clock – it read 9 am. At least she'd had a few hours, though she could hardly term it rest. What would today bring? Exhaustion racked her body, but there was no point in staying in bed maudlin over events, and so she decided instead to go downstairs and make a start on the day. She had to get her head together, she had to make herself feel better, because she was struggling to cope with the alternative. Maybe her solo journey during the night would have done some good, just to revisit, to say sorry, to cleanse her system, and refocus her mind. She hoped so. The smell of coffee greeted her as she opened the kitchen door, and Lee turned instinctively, a broad smile on his face.

"Morning, sunshine," he said brightly.

"Morning," she replied, though not filled with quite the same energy, or the warm rays.

"I thought I'd let you sleep," he said. "You looked so peaceful lying there. I'm making toast. Would you like some?"

"Please," she said, grateful, and sat down at the kitchen counter. Lee placed coffee in front of her, and she took a long sip, keeping her eyes low and away from her husband. Could she trust herself not to tell him where she'd been last night?

"I thought we'd get some fresh air," he said. "It will do us both good. And then I thought we might grab a spot of lunch somewhere nice, what do you say?"

Fresh air seemed to be Lee's alternative to a good, old-fashioned cup of tea. To the English, it cured or solved everything. If only it were that easy.

"Sounds good," she said, her voice somewhat flatter than Lee's more excitable tone.

"Oh, and before I forget," Lee said, "Tanya called a few moments ago. She has obviously heard, and she sounded terribly worried, but she wants to talk to you. I said you'd give her a call back. I couldn't not do really."

"That's all I need."

"You'll be fine. Just stick to the story. We didn't drive that way home and so we haven't seen anything, and yes, it's terrible. Simple."

Bethany wondered if she would have been able to be so matter-of-fact if it had been Lee driving. He'd been just as responsible as her in the car, even though she'd been the one behind the wheel, and yet he didn't seem to have a care in the world. He was the positive one for both of them. But was he the sensible one? It wasn't him dealing with what was climbing around the inside of her skull and the anxiety and pressure of it all. Internally, Bethany was being torn apart. Could she hold it all together? She picked up a piece of hot buttered toast and nibbled on the edge, not really wanting anything to eat but knowing she needed something since she'd hardly eaten anything at dinner. In fact, she'd hardly eaten anything since the accident, and if she carried on this way, she wouldn't have the strength to get through this. Food was her only fuel.

"Eat up then run and have a shower, and we'll get going," he said. "Oh, and ring Tanya back before we head out, get it out the way."

He made it sound so damn easy.

"That's my girl," he said, bending to give her a quick peck on the cheek before leaving her to finish her breakfast. When he'd left the room, she dragged over the newspaper he'd been reading, which had been hanging over the edge of the worktop. She flicked through the pages, looking at photographs to find something to capture her interest and distract her mind. She was almost halfway through when a small headline and photograph hit her. There was a picture of the nineteen-year-old woman, Melody Holden, who'd been tragically killed by a hit-and-run driver. She absorbed the scant details of the woman's short life then ran for the kitchen sink where she violently threw up her breakfast.

CHAPTER 42

Baker
Sunday morning

On the other side of town, Kit observed his own breakfast, which looked like it had been vomited on. Cereal, warm milk, polystyrene bowl, and a plastic spoon sat in front of him. If this was the start of things to come, heaven help him. Nobody had disturbed him through the night, no doubt to let him have his entitled eight hours' peace and quiet, but questioning would start soon enough, he was sure. He'd wait for the duty solicitor to roll up in his cheap polyester suit, though he was sure they were in no rush to do so on a Sunday morning. Kit could well be there a while yet. He took a couple of mouthfuls of the soggy cereal and let it slip down his throat, mainly to get something into his empty stomach and not because he wanted to eat what was on offer.

He thought back to events of the previous evening and, more importantly, Natalie and the girls. He hoped she wasn't too worried about him, had managed to settle herself last night. He'd hardly slept a wink. Too much noise on a Saturday night, with drunks and others coming and going, and doors clanking loudly, hadn't helped at all. Plus he'd been cold. The thin blanket hadn't offered much warmth, and he'd spent most of the night shivering. He'd asked for another but had been refused. One blanket was all you got so you didn't try to knot two together and hang yourself. It was a sad state of affairs for those that really were simply cold and had no intention of suicide.

It was all a total mess. He'd been trying to get back what was rightfully his own and didn't consider himself a car thief. Unfortunately, the police felt differently. He wondered about Darrel for a moment and if he was awake and eating his sorry cornflakes in a cell nearby. Perhaps he'd even gone home? Perhaps he'd given them what they needed and been released? Maybe he'd been the smart one, but how the hell had he got tied up in illegal documents anyway?

He could hear somebody outside his cell door and waited to see who it was. A uniformed officer put his head around the frame and informed him the duty solicitor was there. He was to escort Kit to an interview room where they could spend a moment or two and talk in private. Kit wondered what the solicitor would be like, but he doubted that he or she would be any better than his previous one. Any solicitor worth their salt worked in private practice, didn't they? Unless they were a junior, perhaps, like his last one had been.

As he entered the small interview room, his suspicions were confirmed. With a belly making his shirt buttons bulge, the sweaty-looking man was about retirement age. The balding individual started with a grin and an outstretched hand. With his positive grin, he reminded Kit of Bill Maynard, who played Greengrass in *Heartbeat*, and he wondered about the hand and how much moisture it might contain, whether he wanted it transferred on to his own skin. A fist bump or a high five didn't seem appropriate for the occasion though. He really had no option if this man was to help him. Their palms joined and Kit inwardly grimaced, he'd been correct in his summation. The balding, round man introduced himself.

"Ned Pickle," he said matter-of-factly.

"Kit Morris," he replied in the same way and took a seat. The uniformed officer left them alone, and Kit waited for Ned to begin.

"Right then, Kit Morris," he said, "why don't you tell me what's been going on and I'll see how I can help."

And so, he did. He left out Jakub but told the story of the car that was rightfully his, along with his plan to take it and what he'd found in the boot. He watched as Ned Pickle wrote it all down. He gave precious little away save for a few 'ums' and 'ahs'. Kit wondered what they meant.

"And you've been done for drunk and disorderly before, your only offence?"

"Yes, some years ago. Just got a fine and a slap on the wrist."

"Still," Ned said, "an offence recorded against you."

"Can that be a problem?"

"That rather depends on the magistrates, what they've had for breakfast, and whether they like you or not, it's that simple."

"I'll have to plead guilty, because all the evidence is there and I've said as much, but I want it known that I don't consider what I did stealing. It's my car still."

"I doubt the magistrates would be too interested in that, but you can try. But right now, we've got a few questions to get through with the detectives, and I reckon you'll be charged and released on police bail. Magistrates' in the morning. Have you got a solicitor?"

"Not yet. I haven't got the funds either. Do you think I need one for a first appearance?"

"You still need legal representation. What about legal aid? How much do you earn, more than £22,000?"

"You can't feed a family of four on £22,000, and yes, I do, I earn about £40,000. Why?"

"No legal aid for you then, you'll have to pay for your own representation."

"I can't afford a solicitor, I'm cash-strapped at the moment. My savings have all gone into my expansion plans for the business."

"That's the rules, I don't make them," he said dismissively, jotting notes down. "Just be thankful it's not a murder case, else you'd have to stomp up a great deal more yourself, though the legal-aid threshold is bit more for Crown court cases. But not much. Some have to sell their homes to pay for it all, and even if you're acquitted, you don't get it all back," he went on, seemingly enjoying delivering the bad news. "Some call it the innocence tax. But still, that's not you. Though with no legal aid or solicitor, I wouldn't recommend defending yourself. But hey ho, at least it's only theft of a car." Could the man be any more blasé about it?

"My car," Kit said, almost sulking.

"So you say, though the documents are in someone else's name and that makes it his car. Plus, the contents of the boot need explaining, yours or not. Anyway," he said, focusing on Kit, "are you ready to face some questions?"

"Let's get it over with. I want to get back home. Can you at least help me do that bit?"

"I'll try."

The words didn't fill Kit with comfort or optimism.

CHAPTER 43

Jack's house
Sunday morning

Jack was enjoying a Sunday morning lie-in with Vivian, his newish girlfriend, lying by his side. It was relatively early days in their relationship, but as old friends from the past, they hadn't felt like they needed to wait long before taking their liaison up a notch. Plus, age did that to you. Jack was not far off retiring and Vivian had already taken early retirement, so they didn't feel the need to conform and wait like two young lovers – if people even still did that these days. With Vivian a former sex worker whose services Jack had utilised occasionally after his beloved Janine died, their bodies were no strangers to each other. They had been close friends for a while previously, though had eventually lost touch, and only recently reignited their friendship just a few weeks back. Among those back at the station that knew he was dating an ex-sex worker, it had raised some eyebrows *and* gained him some brownie points, as well as some glaring jokes, all of which Jack took in his stride. Vivian was now out of the game and spent much of her free time helping the younger generation sex workers stay safe. Just like an office worker, they too had a health-and-safety code for their industry, and it was equally important that they were looked after. Being a sex worker didn't make them any less important. So far, Vivian's support was turning out to be a great move for both her and the people she spent time with. Jack's phone buzzed from the side of the bed and he groaned, as did Vivian.

"On a Sunday. That can only be one thing," said Jack as he prised himself away from her and reached over to check the screen. It was Amanda calling.

He pressed the phone to his ear. "What's so urgent on a Sunday morning?"

"Thought you might be interested to know Faye called again. It seems we have something to work on. The lab results are back on that paint from Melody Holden's buckle and it's Firenze red."

The line fell silent. Jack waited.

"Have I to drag it out of you this morning? Come on, Amanda, tell me a bit more."

Jack struggled to a sitting position as she filled him in. His mouth was parched, and he attempted to moisten it. "Apart from the fact it's red, what's it come from? Something helpful I hope."

"Well, the good news is it's not a Ford Fiesta, but it still could be a couple of cars, a Land Rover Discovery, a Range Rover, or a Jaguar. They each have Firenze-red models, so at least that narrows it down a bit. I don't know that I've seen many red Range Rovers or Jaguars about, do you?"

"Not that I recall, but here's a fact for you: you will do now, since you're looking for one. It's called your reticular activating system, but don't expect me to explain it for you, except it means you'll see them everywhere. There'll be hundreds of them."

"Useful to know. Thanks, Jack," she said sarcastically.

He sat quietly for a moment, something niggling at the back of his head.

"You still there, Jack?"

"Contemplating. How's this? If a car used the back road, it's bound to be a local, so that should narrow things down quite a bit for a start." He swung his legs out the bed and stood up to talk to Amanda properly, feeling a thrill of excitement that they might have something to work with. They needed some way of catching the coward that killed Melody Holden. He thought of Ron and wondered if he already knew about the paint, but he doubted it. Faye would never have leaked it.

"Right, okay, I'm on to it," said Jack with authority.

"Can you manage the office?" she asked. "See you there in an hour?"

"Right you are," he said before hanging up. But then a thought occurred to him, one that he needed the good doctor to answer. He dialled Faye and she picked up immediately.

"Just thinking," he said, without any further greeting or preamble. "Would you say that Melody's injuries were consistent with the higher-up Range-Rover-style vehicle or a lower-nosed Jaguar vehicle?" he asked. I'm just thinking a Firenze-red Land Rover, Range Rover, and Jaguar are built completely differently."

"And hello Jack," she started before answering his direct question. "Her injuries were to the lower part of her legs so the Jaguar is your best bet. The others are too high, I've checked ground clearances already. Sorry, I thought I'd mentioned that part to Amanda." Jack let the slip go and waited for her to carry on. "She was hit from behind. Had it been the higher-nosed vehicle, I'd expect the damage to be further up her legs. The majority was at the bottom half, mid-calf area, so I'd be looking at the Jaguar."

"Great, that narrows it down even more. Thanks," he said and was gone. Vivian had obviously overheard one side of the conversation and knew what it meant, that Jack would be going into work for the day.

"You get going then," she said encouragingly. "The sooner you go, the sooner you'll get back. How about I cook?"

Jack wasn't fond of Vivian's cooking, he much preferred Mrs Stewart's and wondered about when they shared more than their bodies and perhaps moved in together – how would he introduce

Mrs Stewart into the equation? It would be a threesome of a very different kind. Vivian might not appreciate another woman cooking and cleaning on her behalf. Then again, she absolutely might. He could hope.

"How about we go out? No need for you to go to a lot of trouble. You find us somewhere nice, somewhere new, and I'll be back as soon as I can."

"It's a deal. Come on then, you'd better get in the shower."

"Had I? I had one last night."

The knowing glance she gave him said it all. Jack eventually caught on. "Ah, I see. Yes, I'll go."

He was beginning to enjoy having someone in his life again and wondered if Vivian felt the same about him. An independent woman, she'd lived on her own for so long, her job dictating her life. Relationships were a disaster for her in the past, but things were different now she was retired.

As he stepped into the shower to wash away the previous evening's activities, he wondered how far they'd go together. And where Mrs Stewart might fit in.

CHAPTER 44

The police station
Sunday morning

By the time Jack had returned downstairs, Vivian had made him a bacon sandwich to go, wrapped in tinfoil, knowing full well he wouldn't hang around to eat it at home. He was like the dog with the proverbial bone, and that's what had made him a damn good detective over the years, and he continued to be so. She was proud of the man she was now dating and passed the sandwich to him along with a reusable cup filled with fresh coffee. It would keep him going until later. He gave her a lingering kiss, and she watched as he climbed into his car and drove away on a grey Sunday morning. At least it wasn't raining.

There was hardly any traffic out so early, and Jack slipped through the gates of the staff car park ten minutes later and found a space easily – only skeleton staff covered at the weekends. He could see Amanda's vehicle already there, and he entered through the back door, waving good morning at a couple of colleagues. Reaching the squad room, he found Amanda seated there already, nobody else about. He placed the tinfoil package down on his own desk and hung his jacket up.

"Do you want a coffee?"

"I've just had one, thanks," said Amanda, "but you've already got one, what's that in your other hand?"

"I don't like plastic cups. Coffee's got to be in a proper mug. She loves the recycle thing, and I haven't the heart to tell her."

"Why don't you just tip into a new mug then?" Amanda was intrigued at her friend's reasoning.

"Because it will be cold then. I'll just make another, it's easier."

"Right," she said, getting to her feet and heading for the coffee cupboard with him.

"I rang Faye back," said Jack. "I had a thought."

"You, thinking? Jack, you okay?" She smiled as she made fun of him.

"No need to be snarky," he said, "but the Firenze red is for a Range Rover Sport and the Jaguar, so we know which vehicles we're looking for, but we can narrow it down even further. So, I rang the doctor and asked her about Melody's injuries, how far up they were, because the Jag will be much lower at the front than the Sport will be, so it stands to reason."

"Ah, sorry, Jack, she did tell me," said Amanda, reaching for a pod and slipping it into the machine for Jack. A chug, chug, chug filled the space, as did the aroma of coffee.

"Not like you, Amanda," Jack said with a note of question in his voice. "Melody was hit from behind, remember, in the lower legs. So, we're looking for a Firenze-red Jaguar and likely a local since it was a back road."

"Agreed, and there can't be that many around Croydon, so that's where we make a start."

"I've seen one somewhere recently, though I can't for the life of me remember where. Red Jaguars tend to stick out a little bit more than your average car, particularly the nicer ones."

"Well, that doesn't mean it's *the* car, Jack. I'm sure we'll find plenty of them when we get searching."

"I know, but I hate coincidences. I just need to figure out where it was."

"Print the list of owners off," said Amanda, "then we'll split it in two and go through it, see if anything jumps out at us. Although, why would it at this stage?"

"Do you want half of my bacon sandwich?" Jack offered.

Amanda knew he didn't really want to share but couldn't very well sit there eating without offering her some.

"No thanks, Jack. I wouldn't want to take it away from you. I know how partial you are to a bacon sandwich."

Jack returned to his desk, generated a list of local vehicle owners with Firenze-red Jaguars, and printed it out. There didn't look to be too many names, which was a good thing, though they were only starting local. Could they be so lucky as to find something in this list? Deduction was part of detective work as well as the painstaking stuff, the boring stuff that had to be done. Combining an inquisitive brain and tenacity was the only way to solve crimes. He wandered back to his desk, grabbed a ruler and pencil, and started his way down the list to see if anything popped straight out at him. He was about halfway down when a name gave him cause to stop. He'd heard it before, though not recently. He searched his memory banks, trying to figure out where. The name was listed as FELBUT Enterprises. He quickly searched the database to see what he could find, and a moment later, the details were staring at him from the screen. Felix Butcher Enterprises.

"Well, what do you know?" he said.

"Have you found something?"

"Kind of."

"What does 'kind of' mean, Jack?"

"It seems Felix Butcher drives a Firenze-red Jaguar or is the owner of one anyway. He must like the colour; he's got the Range Rover too."

"Melody's cousin?"

"The very same," said Jack. "You don't think he could have done it, do you?"

"People do strange things in our line of work, you know that," she said in a sing-song voice. "We've got to check it out though, we've got to take a look at his car."

"Rather you than me," Jack said. "After meeting Ron at the hospital, I wouldn't want to be the one to say a member of his family was a suspect."

"Well, we have to check it out. I don't mind going, though he does know you so it probably would be better coming from you."

"Anything on your list?" he asked hopefully.

"Nothing so far, but then I'm not really expecting any names to jump out. That said, I'm going to go through the addresses and see who might have had cause to drive that road. Maybe they live that way."

"I'm doing the same and I'm nearly at the end of mine. Damn, I hope it isn't Ron's son. Or Ron himself? He wanted to be kept informed, if you remember. He could be using me to gage if we're getting close."

"Don't get carried away, Jack. Check the car out and see if there's any damage, because that buckle must have left a decent scratch at the very least."

"I'll carry on and see who else pops up as a possible. I hope for my sake it's someone else."

CHAPTER 45

Banker

Sunday morning

Lee found Bethany cleaning up her own vomit in the kitchen. He wondered what had gone on.

"Are you okay?" he asked.

"Do I look okay?" she snapped back, her face wearing her woes for the world to see.

"Why don't you go and have a lie down again? We can go out later."

"That won't change anything. She'll still be dead, and I'll still have killed her."

"No, it won't change anything, but the rest might help steady your nerves a little."

Bethany ignored his instruction, and her anxiety ramped up another notch. "There's a picture of her in the paper and an article. She was nineteen years old. Only nineteen, Lee. And I killed her. How do you expect me to feel? Sick to my stomach doesn't even get close." She rinsed the cloth she'd been using in the sink, turning her back on Lee.

"What are you suggesting, that you go to the police and confess? Will that make you feel better?" Lee forced his fingers through his hair as he paced up and down the glass box of a kitchen, trying to understand what she wanted from him. "We've both got to get through this," he said urgently. "No one can know what actually happened. You don't want to go to prison, do you? Because I certainly don't."

"Of course not! Of course I don't, but I *do* want to do the right thing," she said.

Lee stood directly in front of Bethany, his face beet red, his blood pressure likely through the glass roof above his head.

"And how will doing the right thing bring her back, eh?" he shouted in her face. "You're going to land yourself and me in a whole load of shit if you go blabbing, so you're going to have to get over it pretty damn quick. Keep your mouth shut and don't say anything to anybody. Understand?" Spittle flew from his mouth with the ferocity of his words. Bethany had never seen him so mad and for a moment she was stunned. Was he about to lash out, physically? Bethany dropped her eyes from his in submission. There was no need to reply to his questions, she'd heard him loud and clear. The back door slammed shut as he stormed out, where to, she'd no idea, she had more important things to concern herself with than an angry husband demanding his own way. Bethany took a long, deep breath to ease her own tension, then returned to cleaning the sink.

Lee needed to cool off before he said something he'd later regret – or worse. Outside in the garage, he figured he'd better take a closer look at the vehicle to see what damage there was, if any. With the shock of what Bethany had done taking over most of Saturday, it had completely slipped his mind that the car could well be damaged. With its high safety rating, Lee assumed the bonnet would have held up well and that it wouldn't be badly dented, but having never hit a human being at full force before, he'd no idea what to expect. He flicked the light switch on and walked around to the front of the car, to the passenger's side, where the impact had happened. He ran his hand over the smooth paintwork; it looked in good order. There was a slight dent but nothing major, and nothing that couldn't be explained away as the result of having bumped into something else. A panel beater would fix that easily enough. He moved his hand further up the bonnet, and that's when he felt, then saw, the scratch. Running his finger down the groove, he estimated it to be three or four inches in length. But it was there all the same – and deep.

"Dammit," he said, wincing.

He checked the rest of the front of the car over; there didn't appear to be anything obvious. The odd stone chip, but nothing more than the annoying scratch further up. Had it occurred during the accident? It likely had. Otherwise he would have noticed it before now, and how else would a scratch get halfway up his bonnet? It had to be from the woman. She must have been wearing something sharp, maybe her ring had caught it. He ran his fingers over it again, wondering if he could repair it himself, he'd seen the sprays on the television. It was worth a try, just to blend the colour back over it. He could probably get it fixed properly at a later date, but for now the scratch remover might just do the job, and he headed back to the kitchen to tell Bethany he was popping out.

"I need to take your car," he said, looking around for the key.

"Why don't you take your own?" she enquired.

"Not after Friday night. I don't want to be seen in it yet. I've just inspected it, and there's a nasty scratch on the front, so I'm going to go down to Halfords to get a repair kit. Until that scratch is gone – I've no idea if it came from the woman or not, but I'm assuming it did – it can just lay low for a while. We don't know if the police are already looking for it or not, so I'll use yours. Do you want to come? Fresh air might do you good," he said encouragingly, all signs of his earlier temper gone.

He could be nice at times.

"No thanks, I'll stay here, you go. I'll give Tanya a call back, I haven't spoken to her yet and she'll only ring again."

"Right, I won't be long. And remember, stay strong and admit nothing. Just carry on as you normally do, don't tell her anything."

Bethany watched him grab her keys from the kitchen work surface and leave. She was glad of some peace and quiet, a chance to be in the house without him breathing down her neck. No one intruding, no one pushing, telling her what to think, feel, or do. She wasn't stupid, but the constant rowing was beginning to drive her to the point of explosion.

Lee stood in Halfords browsing the scratch repair kits. There were quite a few to choose from, but in essence they all did the same thing. He felt a staff member hovering nearby.

"Can I help you, sir?" he enquired. He was young, pimply, and had a young man's body odour from too many hormones and not enough showers. Lee pitied anybody that shared the break room with him at lunchtime.

"I've just got a bit of a scratch on my car that I need to shift, do these sprays really work?"

"They do. They're all pretty much the same, but this one is popular," he said, handing Lee an aerosol. "Just squirt it on and gently rub around the edges with a nice soft cloth and your scratch will be gone in no time."

"Great, thanks," Lee said, and he headed over to the cashier to pay. As usual on a Sunday, he wasn't the only one looking to do a little work on his car, and there were several people in the queue in front of him. He stood waiting his turn and then heard a familiar voice behind him.

It was Eric. Damn!

He couldn't very well ignore him so he turned around to say hello.

"Morning, Eric, what brings you out here on a Sunday?" he said cheerfully.

"Probably the same as you, a little shopping," he said, waving screenwash at him. "What about you?"

Lee was not going to show off his item, but he was holding it in his hand for all to see so he couldn't really say he needed a new sponge. Eric looked at the aerosol.

"Oh, good stuff that," he said. "I've used it myself." And left it at that.

A cashier became free and Lee hurriedly said goodbye to Eric and headed over to pay. Close, he thought. Though why should Eric think anything out of the ordinary? He finalised his purchase and only breathed a sigh of relief when he got back to the car.

Lee Meady felt guilty because he was guilty.

CHAPTER 46

Banker

Sunday morning

As Lee walked from the store back to his car, he never saw Tanya sat in her own, waiting for Eric to return. She didn't see him either, her head buried in her phone, likely surfing a social media site or an email or some such. It was only when Eric got back in beside her and disturbed her train of thought that she found out Lee had been there.

"Did he see you?" Tanya enquired. "Did you chat?"

"Yes, I was stood behind him in the queue. He was buying some scratch-remover spray."

"That's a shame, a scratch on that nice new car of his."

"It could be for Bethany's car," said Eric as he started the engine and pulled away.

"I've just spoken to Bethany, actually," said Tanya. "She just returned my call."

"Oh, what did you want her for?"

"With the young woman that was killed, I wondered if they'd

gone that way home, the back way rather than the main road. Though on such a foul night it's not a road I'd like to drive down."

"I suppose not, I'd have gone the other way around too, better lighting on a night like that. So, did they? Did they go that way?"

"I asked and she said they went the other way around, the way you'd have gone. Anyway, I was just curious, there wouldn't have been much traffic and they may have seen something."

The car fell silent for a moment as Eric concentrated on exiting the car park and Tanya processed her thoughts.

"The poor girl's family, her parents. They know someone's responsible so it's not the end of the story. Not for them, not yet," she carried on. "Anyway, I was just curious if they'd seen anything." Changing tack, she said, "Come on, let's get to the garden centre before the temperature drops any more. It's getting chilly out already, and I'm hungry for lunch."

"Right you are," said Eric with a smile. But a picture of the scratch-repair aerosol he'd seen Lee with sat in front of his eyes as he made his way across to Wickham Road. He tried to shake it away, since apparently they'd not driven home that way that night.

But it wouldn't budge.

Back at the squad room, Amanda and Jack were hard at it, searching through the locals on the red Jaguar list. None of the names and addresses really made any sense with anything they already had, but then they didn't have much to go on at this stage, apart from the colour of the car. There were no obvious addresses that would take a route over that way but without knowing where everybody that owned a red Jaguar was headed on Friday night, there was no way to know who did and who didn't. It would be a big enough task to ask them all, though not impossible.

"Back to the CCTV cameras," said Amanda. "See which ones of these were out driving around Croydon roads in general on Friday night."

"I'll put the plate numbers into the ANPR, see if we can find their locations," Jack said, tapping away on his keyboard. "Let's hope so, though with only half a dozen cameras, it's not exactly going to solve our case in the next ten minutes. Bloody do-gooders and their privacy crap," Jack grunted. The public wanted it all ways – get crime off the streets, but don't look at me because it's not nice.

"Then we should drive up there again and see what businesses have external cameras pointing to the road, because we're not looking at a big time frame, only a few hours of the night. And even if two hundred cars went by, which I rather doubt at that hour, not many of them are likely to be red Jaguars."

"You're good at this, aren't you?" Jack said in play sarcasm.

"That's why I am the boss," she said sweetly.

"Come on then, grab your coat, I'll drive. The ANPR might have spewed something by the time we get back."

"And if we don't get anything from those cameras, is there a bus route up there?"

"I doubt it, but it's something else to check. Are you thinking of the bus's camera?"

"It's worth a try if we don't get anything from this," said Amanda.

"We should add the taxis too," said Jack. "Although the cameras in them tend to just be pointed into the back of the vehicle, but still, there may be something. We only need a Jag, even the slightest glimpse through a back window could give us a partial plate."

"Let's see what we get from the private cameras first. That's the most obvious place to try."

It wasn't long before they reached the start of the road where the town cameras finished, and it was down to private ones only. It wasn't an area that Jack or Amanda drove through very often; they had no reason to.

The road itself filtered out with almost single-track lanes going off in different directions into the green country areas of Surrey. The driver of the car could have come along any one of them, and there was not much to look at other than hedgerows and tarmac as they arrived at the place where Melody was found. They back-tracked, retracing their steps towards Croydon, looking again for possible camera spots. They counted three ancient, closed-down venues: an old-style mechanics' garage, a farm-type shop, and a small private welders'. Annoyingly, there was no petrol station chain with full-frame cameras, there were no city cameras, and there were no bus stops.

"It's not looking too promising," Amanda said as they turned around and drove back to the other end of the road, past the accident scene, and onwards. There was nothing further out that way either: horses, another small store that had closed down some years ago, and a handful of houses. More smaller roads split off in various directions. There was nothing else to see. Jack pulled over and left the car engine running, the heater keeping them warm.

"There's not much here," Jack said resignedly.

Amanda sat thinking for a moment. "Maybe there is," she said.

"What are you thinking? Because I can't see anything of use."

"I'm thinking horses are extremely valuable, and people that have valuable things like to protect them."

"I see what you're thinking," said Jack, smiling. "I like it. You're hoping that they might have their own private cameras watching over the animals? And there might be a little road coverage too."

"Yes," she said, pointing to a shed not far from the road. "And I would start right there."

CHAPTER 47

The stables
Sunday morning

Technology was a godsend in police work, with access to various databases and DNA records like never before. The UK currently has the largest DNA database in the world, but it wasn't DNA that helped Amanda and Jack right at that moment, it was good old-fashioned legwork. Amanda thinking about the horses had given them just the break they needed. Jack pulled into the driveway not far along from the shed and drove on past the stable block towards a house that couldn't be seen from the road. From the outside it looked like the owners were comfortably well off, the property surrounded by grassy fields and not another soul nearby. The only sound as they approached was the chatter of birds in the hedgerows. With Jack at her side, Amanda rapped on the front door, warrant card at the ready, and they waited for someone to come. A moment later, a middle-aged man stood before them. He was dressed in a dark checked flannel shirt and black jodhpurs that showed his trim hips off easily. From the look of his tight fair curls, which were flat on top and bushy at the sides, it appeared that he'd recently taken his cap off. Broken capillaries on red cheeks suggested he spent a lot of time outdoors in all weathers. He looked like he could do with some moisturiser on his skin.

"Hello," the man said casually.

"Hello, I'm DS Amanda Lacey, and this is my colleague DC Jack Rutherford. May we ask you couple of questions, please?"

"What's it about?" the man asked.

"Just some routine enquiries at the moment, sir," she said. "You may be aware, there was an accident, a hit-and-run, along this road a couple of nights ago. We're completing our investigations and I'm sure an officer has already been in touch and knocked on your door, but I noticed your horses."

"I did hear, yes. Sad state of affairs. An officer popped in earlier. What's it got to do with my horses?"

"I'm sure your horses are extremely valuable, and we figured that you might have security cameras. Perhaps one of those cameras would look out over the road somewhat, maybe pointed along your driveway entrance?"

"I see," he said. "Yes, I do have one pointing along the entranceway as it happens. You'd better come in."

Amanda glanced at Jack: finally, a break.

"Did you see anything on Friday night?" she asked, following the man inside.

"No, we were both tucked up in bed by ten. Slept through the whole thing, though that was a bit further up if I am correct?"

"Yes, a couple of miles further up, but we're anxious to look at anybody's camera footage that may have pictures of the road."

"So you've got a car in mind then? Something that you're looking for?"

"Can't really say much about an ongoing case, but I appreciate your help in this," Amanda said, closing his questions down without sounding rude.

They entered a small study area where an archaic computer sat on a desk in the corner. Amanda and Jack watched as the man brought the screen to life and found the relevant files from two nights ago.

"You're lucky it's only a couple of nights ago," he said. "This thing records over them after a week. It's a bit antiquated, I'm afraid, but it does the trick. The camera still works fine, although from memory it was a hell of a wet night. I hope there's enough clarity for you. Nasty business, leaving the scene. What sort of person does that?" he asked, shaking his head.

Amanda and Jack peered at the screen as he brought up Friday evening.

"What time are you looking for roughly?"

"Why don't you leave us to for a few minutes, and we'll have a look through, if you don't mind. I wouldn't want to keep you from what you're doing."

The man took the hint and said he'd be back shortly to see if they needed anything further.

Amanda sat at the controls, while Jack watched over her shoulder. Not many cars used the road that night, which was fortuitous, though it was difficult to see much in the wet weather anyway. The wind blew the camera somewhat, and the lens was covered in raindrops so everything had a starred effect, as if you were looking through a wet windscreen at lights coming toward you.

As each car approached, Amanda checked the time and made a note of what she could see, but it was closer to midnight that they were interested in – and the window of about four hours afterwards.

"Here comes another one," said Jack. The timestamp said 11.10 pm, and as the car approached, Amanda stilled it for more detail.

"Dammit," she said. "What sort of car is that? You can barely see it."

"I don't know, but I could tell you what car it's not," said Jack. "It's not one of those fancy SUV, four-wheel-drive affairs, it's something much lower. Can you make out the plate?"

"I can see two letters, perhaps. It's not clear enough."

Jack made a note of what they could see, and they fast-forwarded until the next car came along.

"That looks more promising," said Amanda. "The lights would be about the right sort of height and shape for what we're looking for. Definitely not a big car, but again, it's really difficult to make out the reg plate. What can you see?"

The two peered closely at the screen like they needed new reading glasses, noses wrinkled up as if that helped somehow.

"Just a partial," said Jack. "One, maybe two letters, but that's more promising, and it fits the time frame, but I'd say there's probably two people in that car. With little light and the raindrops on the lens, it's difficult to see isn't it?"

"At least it gives us something to go on. Let's watch for the next couple that come along." Amanda fast-forwarded on to the next car, which was some three hours later. As the vehicle approached, they could tell instantly it wasn't what they were looking for.

"Maybe a minibus?" Jack suggested.

"We may as well see what else is on the file," said Amanda, and she wound it forward. The last two vehicles appeared just as it was becoming dawn – way outside their time frame.

"We've got a couple to investigate," she said. "The right time, right sort of shape, and we've got partial plates to work with. So, let's go back to the station and see what they match up to."

There was a quick knock at the door and the homeowner popped his head around the frame. "Was it of any use?" he asked.

"Absolutely was. Thank you, you've been a great help," said Amanda. "We are going to need the footage though. Can you make a copy for us, please?"

Finally, something to add to in their search for a red Jaguar.

CHAPTER 48

Amanda and Jack
Sunday morning

As they drove, Jack couldn't wait to get back to the squad room and check his list. In the back of his mind, he really hoped it wasn't Felix's or Ron's car that was going to ping with the couple of letters that they could see, it would cause too much aggro. It had to be someone else, surely.

"Amanda, you're a genius for spotting that. Obviously uniform didn't think to ask when they were doing the house to house."

"It doesn't matter. We've found it now and have something else to work with. I think that last one we noted was the most promising, though it's a shame it wasn't clearer. I think there were two people in the car, in which case somebody is an accessory if they did in fact hit Melody Holden. Most hit-and-runs occur when someone just panics out on their own and leaves the scene, it's not often there's two or more involved. But let's see, we might be on the wrong track yet."

"Let's hope they're on that list, and let's hope they're local, and let's also hope they're in when we pay them a visit." Jack turned to Amanda and smiled. "Don't you love it when things come together?"

"I do," said Amanda, "though we still haven't got a great deal yet, Jack, so don't go getting too excited."

"I hear you, boss, but it would be nice to go back and tell Ron that we've got some news for him. Whatever his faults, he's still a human being. I just hope it's nothing to do with Felix."

"Knowing that man and where his knobbly fingers reach to, he's probably already at the house of the car owner as we speak," Amanda said sarcastically.

"He may well be, knowing some of the tactics he's used in the past. Taking the law into your own hands is not the way to get things sorted for the death of a loved one though."

"Try telling that to the local thugs," said Amanda.

"But we're jumping ahead again. We don't know anything yet. Hypothetical is just that: hypo and a bit thetical."

Amanda gave him a quizzical look. "Is thetical even a word?

"I've no idea, sounds impressive though. Google it."

Back inside, the first listing Jack headed for was the Butcher car. Thankfully it was negative for the two visible plate letters. He breathed an audible sigh of relief.

"It's not the Butcher's car," Jack shouted across to Amanda and carried on down his list in search of car plates that had the relevant letters. It was almost fifteen minutes later that Amanda's arm shot in the air.

"Bingo," she shouted.

"Got something then?"

"Yes, and it's the only one. How about you?"

"I've got one of the letters, but I can't get two letters in the same plate so mine is a blank. Who does the car belong to?"

"Lee Meady, and he lives on the Webb estate."

"Nice," said Jack. "Let's see if his phone pinged a tower during the drive, to add a bit more lead to our pencil. If we can put him at the scene with his phone, that will help with the lack of number plate for the CPS. I'll get it done, won't be a minute."

Amanda nodded, sat back, and stretched her back out. Her shoulders were tight knots from hunching over for far too long. She needed a massage.

Ruth used to...

Don't go there, Amanda.

"Right, fancy a drive in the country again?" asked Amanda. "Can't do much here just yet," she said, gathering her things once again. "Then, when we've paid him a visit, I'll need something to eat."

"I don't think there is a pub at the Webb estate – conservation area, isn't it?"

"No idea, Jack, that's your domain, useless information. Maybe you've got a fun fact to share on the area?"

"That's a bit harsh, isn't it?" Jack said as they walked at speed back down the corridor and out into the car park. Amanda's car beeped as the alarm turned off, and they slipped inside and headed once again out to the ring road.

Google was handy for accurate directions, and just before they got to the house in question, Amanda pulled in a few metres up the road to survey the area for a moment. Houses were set back nicely, secluded and private behind massive oak trees that generated shade in summer and provided a windbreak in winter. Ducks swam in a small pond on the village green. It was a beautiful, serene place to live for those that could afford it. Amanda pulled forward and on to the driveway of Lee and Bethany Meady's house.

"Well, would you look at that," said Jack slowly as they came to a stop. Parked at the front of the house was a shiny Firenze-red Jaguar, and someone was buffing it with a nice soft cloth.

"I guess lots of people clean their car on a Sunday," said Amanda.

"Particularly those that may have been involved in accident, wouldn't you say?"

"Jack, I'll do the talking, okay? You've already got the guy in handcuffs."

He grunted as they stepped out of the car, and the two approached the waiting individual. Lee Meady had an aerosol in one hand and a chamois leather in the other. Amanda presented her warrant card and introduced them, while Jack watched for a facial reaction. From the look of horror that crossed the man's telling face, Jack knew they were in the right place. What they needed to do now was discover who was behind the wheel two nights ago when the car that sat just in front of them slammed into the body of Melody Holden.

CHAPTER 49

Baker

Sunday morning

After spending most of the morning with the duty solicitor, Ned Pickle, being questioned in a stuffy interview room, Kit was glad to be going home, albeit having been charged and released on police bail. Since the documents in the boot of the car were obviously Darrel's, as was the cash, Kit was cleared of any involvement there. He'd been formally charged with car theft and had an appointment with the magistrates the following morning where he'd be processed along with the other riff-raff from the weekend.

He needed the hassle like he needed a hole in the head, but more importantly, he needed to apologise to Natalie and his girls for the upset he'd caused the previous night. Natalie was on her way to pick him up, and he could only hope she'd simmered down so they could talk properly and he could explain what'd been going on. It was time to come clean about what was happening with the business and just why and what he'd done with Darrel's car. Was it

Darrel's? The document said so, the police had said so, and the charge of car theft said so.

He was outside the police station waiting for Natalie to pull up out front. His clothes were dishevelled since he'd slept in them, stubble was sandy on his chin, and he smelled of dingy cell and his own sweat from the stress of it all, even though he'd shivered from cold most of the night. With all that and no real way of cleaning his teeth, he felt like and resembled hell warmed up. More concerned with his own situation, he'd no idea if Darrel was even still at the station. In fact, he wished he'd never set eyes on the man in the first place. If he hadn't, he wouldn't be here waiting to explain himself to his wife.

His thoughts drifted to the unfairness of it all. Darrel probably hadn't even spent the night at her Majesty's pleasure. No doubt his fancy solicitor had had him released on some technicality, so he'd be sitting down to a proper breakfast – quite the opposite to what Kit had experienced. Life wasn't fair. Here he was trying to provide a crust, quite literally, and make it on his own, building a steady legitimate business to provide for his small but growing family. Never had he done anything dodgy in all his life and taking back what he figured was rightly his own had landed him in a whole pile of trouble.

He and Darrel had once been close mates. Now they could barely stand the sight of one another, and he wondered where it would end for the man. Darrel had stashed illegal documents and cash in a car registered in his own name – surely he was in a lot worse trouble than Kit was.

Natalie pulled up, and he fastened himself into the passenger side, waiting to test the temperature of the atmosphere before saying a word. For a moment, his eyes met hers, and he waited to see if he was going to get a slap or a hug. Or something else.

"You look terrible," she said solemnly.

"I feel it. Can we go home and talk properly?"

Natalie pulled away from the kerb and drove them back. While they didn't drive in total silence, neither made mention of what had happened. Instead, they chatted about other, safer topics, Natalie informing him that she'd dropped the children at her mother's place to give them a little space.

"Do your parents know?"

"I didn't say anything. I just said we needed a bit of time to sort something out and asked would they take them for the day. I'll pick them up again at five."

"Thank you," he said. "I could do with the time to think," he said wearily "and perhaps catch up on some sleep. I'm back in work tomorrow, I hope."

"You'll feel better when you've cleaned up and had some rest," she said, and from her demeanour, Kit knew things were going to be okay. As they pulled up at home, Natalie tuned to Kit and said, "Get a shower and some sleep. We can talk when you wake up." A tense smile tried its best to light her face up but failed, and the two headed inside.

It was around 3 pm when Kit finally resurfaced, with his thoughts gathered in some sort of order in his head, ready to sit down with Natalie. They had two hours before the children arrived home, which was surely enough, he hoped. He was grateful for the fact that Natalie hadn't pushed him for information before he'd managed to rest up and think, but now there was no escaping it. She was owed and deserved a full explanation, and they sat around the small kitchen table together, back in the room where it had all gone so horribly wrong the previous night. Kit started at the beginning.

"I haven't told you too much Natalie," he started, "because I didn't want to worry you. The business needs money, and I saw an opportunity to get the car back and sell it on. When I sold Darrel the car, he only ever paid one of the three instalments, and I foolishly transferred the vehicle into his name, believing that he would pay up. He was a friend after all, as well as a business partner, we had history."

"And he never did," said Natalie.

"No, he didn't. And that was my first mistake. So, when the business needed some cash, I thought I'd get the car back. So, Jakub and I took it and parked it in a lock-up that he knew about."

"You involved Jakub? What was you thinking?" she asked incredulously.

Kit glanced across and the anger in her eyes died in an instant.

"I know, stupid mistake number two," said Kit. "Mistake number three was moving the car – we were seen, and that's how Darrel knew where it was. But I thought I had a bargaining chip, though I've used it now. In the boot was a bundle of cash and an envelope full of documents. Fake documents for a new identity for him. That's why he needed the car back so desperately, it probably wasn't the car itself, he just wanted what it contained. I've no idea what his plans are, nor do I really care."

Natalie reached out to Kit and brushed his cheek lightly with her hand.

"I'm so over this now," he carried on. "But I'm also very much in trouble, particularly with that drunk-and-disorderly charge from years ago. Remember?"

"I do, you fought for me that night," she said with a light smile. For Kit, it was hard not to grin at the memory too.

"That makes this charge not my first offence unfortunately, so I've got to be at the magistrates' court first thing in the morning and wait my turn. From what I saw of the duty solicitor, he didn't know his arse from his elbow, so with two out of two experiences being less than ideal, I'm better off trying to defend myself."

"I'll come with you," said Natalie.

"No, you're better off at work, it'll keep your mind off it. I'll be fine." Kit certainly didn't want Natalie to see him have his time in court; he was a proud man. "I'd prefer to do this on my own. I'll be nervous enough without worrying about you sat watching, if you don't mind."

Natalie nodded, she knew Kit well enough to know he'd feel

more comfortable without her presence, and she had
wishes, even if she didn't agree with them.

"Do you think you'll go to prison?" It was a question she
answering but was almost too scared to ask.

"I doubt it, but it depends on the magistrates. They've got the
power to give out the sentence, up to six months apparently, so it's
up to them. I can only hope for a decent set of individuals."

"What about this solicitor, Mr Pickle. You don't hold much
faith in him?"

"Hell no. Plus there's no money for another solicitor, and we
don't qualify for legal aid. All I can do is appeal to them as fellow
humans, tell the whole sorry story, and hope they've got some
heartstrings I can pull on."

"No, we need to do better than that, Kit Morris," she added,
finding confidence in their situation from somewhere. Her mind
was whirring, Kit could almost see it happening behind her beautiful eyes.

"What are you thinking?"

"Grab the laptop. We've got work to do." She was now in
control, taking over in Kit's hour or two of need. "I'll organise a
sleepover for the girls." She reached for her phone to call her
parents and a sudden energy filled the small kitchen.

"On a school night?"

"Yes. This is a hell of a lot more important than a maths lesson
missed."

He couldn't argue there.

CHAPTER 50

Amanda and Jack
Sunday afternoon

Jack believed in gut reaction, but he also needed hard facts behind
it to back it up. Just because you thought somebody looked guilty,
didn't mean they actually were, otherwise the prisons would be full
of people that looked a bit odd. Back in the early ages, looking
guilty had indeed been enough to throw a person in prison and
chuck away the key. No, the real criminals would then still be out
on the streets with their fancy Rolexes, fancy cars, and boyish good
looks, as a lot of them tended to have these days it seemed. When
he'd been a younger man in the force, criminals used to look like
gang members: scarred, wily, and generally up to no good. These
days, a variety of faces sat in front of him in interview rooms. He
suspected they'd be meeting Lee Meady in one soon enough. For
now, they approached the man on his driveway.

"Good afternoon, sir," Amanda started.

Once again, Amanda flashed her warrant card and introduced
them both while Jack watched on. He was good at noting the tells –

the little twitches, averted eyes – it was kind of like a hobby. All those little mannerisms, the person's body language, all added up as much as what the individual said, and they counted just as much too.

Lee Meady nodded back. "Afternoon," he finally replied, eyes searching both Amanda and Jack.

"She is a fine-looking car, lovely colour," Amanda glowed, tempted to run her fingertips over the bonnet to see how soft, how smooth it was, feel if there were any scratches there. "It is yours?" Nice and relaxed.

"Yes, I am the owner, Lee Meady. Can I help you both with something?"

"I can see you take good care of it, out here on a Sunday after-noon polishing it. But then I guess it's an investment. These cars don't come cheap, I'll bet. I imagine there's not many around Croy-don, that's for sure."

All the time, Jack was watching how Lee Meady interacted with his boss, what he said, what he didn't say. So far, he'd verbally said nothing much. His body told another story.

"We're making enquiries into an accident a couple of nights ago. Friday, in fact. What were you doing that night? Were you at home, perhaps?" Amanda asked innocently enough.

"No, I took my wife out for dinner, but she wasn't feeling too good, so we came home early." That was the truth.

"Nice. Where did you go? There's a couple of new places in town I'm dying to try." Amanda was all smiles.

"At a friend's place actually. Why, what's this all about?"

"Like I said, just some routine enquiries following up from an accident. What time did you get back home? If your wife wasn't feeling too good."

"It was around midnight, I believe, I don't know for sure. Again, what have I got to do with anything, have I done something wrong?"

"I wouldn't know yet, sir," Amanda said. "Do you think you've done something wrong?"

It was obvious to Jack, as he was watching, that the man was trying to hide the aerosol can behind his back rather than having it out front in his hands or on the tarmac. Jack took the opportunity to saunter casually to one side of the car and have a quick look to see what he was holding. He recognised the can, though couldn't place what the contents were actually for. Moving slightly closer, he remembered the brand and what it was used for. He'd wait for Amanda to finish her questions before maybe asking one of his own.

Amanda could see what Jack was up to and tried to look for herself without making it obvious, but she didn't really work like that. She preferred the more direct approach.

"What's that behind your back? What's in the can?" Amanda asked casually.

There was nowhere for Lee to go. It was obvious they were going to find out what it was that he was holding so he might as well just address it, which he did. Moving the can, he made light of it.

"Just car polish," he said nonchalantly.

Amanda could see exactly what it was and probed a little more. "Have you got some scratches? Now that is a shame on such a beautiful vehicle," she said, peering over the bonnet for a closer look.

"You know," he said, "I've a couple of stone chips, and this stuff just helps to keep everything looking smart. It's a valuable machine and cost me a fortune so I like to look after it."

"And does it work?" she enquired. "Because that's quite a scratch there," she said, pointing. "I'm not sure if that polish would do the trick on that one, might need a professional to take a look at it."

It was obvious Lee Meady didn't like where things were going and needed to stop the questions. He needed to cut it dead. "I'm sure you didn't come all the way out here to ask about my cleaning and scratch-removal capabilities," he said, ignoring the question and starting to look pressured and anxious to get rid of the two detectives. "So, if you have no more questions, I think we're about done here. I didn't see anything on Friday night so I don't see how I can help you any further." He turned to leave.

Amanda wasn't finished. "You said you were out on Friday night, got home around midnight. Can anyone verify that?"

"No, they can't since there's only the two of us here, myself and my wife. We were together. Now, I've told you we're done, so I suggest if you want to question me any further, we do so down at the station with my solicitor present." By the obvious colour change and strain developing on Lee Meady's face, he was getting annoyed.

Amanda looked at Jack, who still hadn't said anything but took over.

"Have you done something you need a solicitor for?" asked Jack. It was so clichéd, but it worked to rile a suspect up. Most people didn't understand how the police worked, what they tried on, what they were legally allowed to do, and what they were not legally allowed to do. They could push a little yet.

"I've done nothing wrong, but I don't want to be questioned outside my own house in the driveway casually. So, if you've got something that you formally want to ask me, like I said, I'm happy to come down to the station with my solicitor. Now, please, I'd like you to leave."

They had no choice now, they'd been told to leave, and unless they arrested him, that was the end of that.

The two turned ready to go when Jack pulled a Columbo moment as he liked to do. It always tickled him when the opportunity arose, and he wondered how many other detectives practised the same trick. It did actually work.

Pausing for a moment and turning, he called to Lee and asked, "Did your wife drive on Friday night, by chance?" It wasn't the verbal answer he was waiting for; it was to see the look on Lee's face when he realised they *both* might be in trouble.

And there it was, a mixture of 'oh shit' and defeat. Jack was quick to pick it up. Yes, they'd been out to dinner, that part was likely true, and he'd driven some of it.

But Lee Meady hadn't been the one driving home.

For now, they needed to get back to the station and gather more evidence to prove it before pulling the Meadys in for formal questioning.

Lee Meady never did answer the Columbo question that afternoon, not verbally, but casually walked away back towards his front door.

Both Amanda and Jack knew where to direct formal questions when the time came later.

His wife, Mrs Meady.

CHAPTER 51

Amanda and Jack
Sunday afternoon

Once Amanda and Jack were back in the car, they sat for a moment and chatted, waiting. It was their custom to watch the outside of someone's home for a moment or two after they'd visited them, and that's exactly what they did now. Not that there was anything obvious to see, but Amanda had lost count of the number of times something unexpected had happened when occupants thought the police had gone. The Meady's house, however, told them nothing. There was no shouting and banging, no screaming, nobody running from the back door. All was quiet. Amanda eventually started the engine, and they pulled away.

"Did you see his face?" Jack asked. "It was as obvious as balls on a bulldog. That man knows something." Amanda turned to Jack with questioning eyes and raised her brows. "Balls on a bulldog, really, Jack?"

"As is Meady's involvement. But anyway, you know what I'm trying to say."

"I do know what you're trying to say, Jack, and yes, I did notice his face and the colour draining from it. Particularly when we first pulled up and introduced ourselves."

"So, what do you think?" he asked. "Was he driving when they went out for dinner? They got back after midnight so the time would fit. We won't find his vehicle on CCTV cameras in town because he or she took the back way to wherever they were headed."

"We've got two letters of his registration plate on some extremely wet and grainy private CCTV camera footage that could be another Jag. And we've got him buffing out a scratch on his car that is nothing like the marks caused by the stone chips he was talking about. It was about three inches long – and deep."

"And they were out for dinner and driving home. Did you see his face when I asked him if he was driving?"

"I'm not blind, Jack. I'm a trained detective, remember? And yes, I did once again see his face. And no, I don't think he was driving at the time. So now we need to look at both of them. When we get back to the station, I suggest we do a background check on his wife before dragging one or both of them in for formal questioning. With a solicitor," she added for good measure.

"Sounds like a plan, but let's get some lunch first. My stomach thinks my throat's been cut." They were heading back into town, towards the station, and there was nothing open in the vicinity, nothing that he fancied anyway. Amanda's own stomach grumbled.

"Mrs Stewart's day off?"

"It's getting a bit awkward with Mrs Stewart when Vivian stays over, but no, I haven't seen her this morning."

"She doesn't approve then, when Vivian stays over?"

"Doesn't approve of Vivian full stop. Some people will always be a little judgemental, I suppose, given what her occupation used to be. Maybe she saw Vivian at that book-club man's house, her previous employer, I don't know. I don't like to think about her past occupation. While it doesn't concern me now, I don't like to be reminded of what she did before we became an item."

"I know what you mean about judgemental," said Amanda. "I got a lot of stick when I first joined the station, remember? My personal life raised eyebrows and snide comments, not to mention the jokes, but I was used to it by then, and it always dies away with time when something else tickles their small minds."

There wasn't much Jack could say to that but sympathise. "And then you got married..."

"I did," Amanda said with a sigh, a sigh that spoke volumes on its own. She missed Ruth terribly, and it was obvious to both in the car that the atmosphere had changed, like when you talk about death. Nobody spoke for a couple of minutes. Then:

"That reminds me," said Jack, perking up and changing the subject somewhat. "I never did get through to the old woman's next of kin." He pulled out his phone and searched for the number that had been texted to him earlier.

"What do you want to ring him for anyway?" Amanda asked. "I'm curious why you want to speak to them."

"I don't really know, if I'm honest. Nothing specific," said Jack, "but I'm kind of using it as an excuse to find out when the funeral will be. I think I might go."

"Really?"

"I wouldn't want no one to be at her funeral, and I would at least expect the next of kin to organise some sort of send-off for the old love. Another part of me is just curious who this callous person is that left her to die alone. Call it morbid interest."

"I'd have thought you had enough of that sort of stuff at work without going to the funerals of people you don't know, just so someone is there."

"I know, I don't quite understand it myself. But here's the thing, I'm going."

"Suit yourself," said Amanda, and the two drove in silence for the second time. When Jack was sure that the conversation was over, he clicked the call button on his phone to see if he'd be connected this time, but no joy.

"It's still just ringing out," he said to Amanda, who didn't need to respond. After maybe a dozen rings and no answer, Jack gave up.

"It's weird, most people at least have a voicemail on, this just rings out. I guess I'll try again later," he said and slipped the phone back in his pocket.

"What do you want for lunch then?" Amanda asked as they approached the town centre.

"Not McDonald's again, that's for sure. There'll be a café around the high-street area. You find somewhere to park, and I'll run and grab us a couple of sandwiches from one of them."

Jack running, she had to see. Moments later, she pulled up at the side of the road. He pointed in the distance, "Look, it's a Firenze-red Range Rover. I told you we'd see more of them now we're on the lookout. That's two today if you count Meady's Jag, and I'll bet we'll see another one later on, probably another one tomorrow. Just because we now notice them."

Amanda got out of the car and refrained from another eye roll. "I'll come with you and choose my own sandwich or else I'll end up with bacon and brown sauce if it's left to you."

"Seriously though, whose is that one, I wonder?" he said, looking across the street and making a mental note of the plate. Amanda was well ahead of him and not paying any attention.

Jack rushed to catch her up, and they headed inside the bakery.

CHAPTER 52

Banker

Sunday afternoon

While Amanda and Jack were busy choosing sandwiches in Dough Knots, Lee and Bethany were busy having yet another row. He'd gone back inside and, searching for his phone frantically, was interrupted by Bethany who wanted to know who the visitors had been. She'd heard a car pull up out the front. Lee didn't want to worry her, but things were moving faster than he'd anticipated. He filled her in.

"I can't believe they've been here already," she said, pacing up and down in the kitchen. "How the hell did they link it together so quickly? There was nobody out there that night, nothing."

"How the hell would I know!" said Lee, running his hands through his hair as he often did when he was stressed. "All I know is that they've been here and seen me polishing a scratch off the car, and they've already put two and two together. The only reason they could have come here would be because of the car itself. Somehow, they know that we were involved." He let it sink in with Bethany before carrying on. "This could get rather ugly extremely quickly."

"Do you think I don't know that?" Bethany said, whipping round. "I knew we should never have gone. I didn't feel well enough."

"Oh, give me a break," he said. "Whether you felt well or not is nothing to do with the accident that happened."

"We should have stopped! Lots of people have accidents at some time in their life, but we ran a woman over, and we never stopped to see if she was okay!"

"*You* ran a woman over," he corrected.

"Thanks a lot," she screamed, fire in her eyes. "That sounds like you're going to throw me under the bus already."

"I think there's enough people hit by vehicles for the time being, don't you?"

"Figure of speech. You know what I mean. Sounds like you've left me to it."

"I haven't left you to it. Stop being a drama queen. But *you* were driving." Lee tried to calm himself, his blood pressure threateningly high from yet another altercation. He needed a tablet. A couple of beats passed before he added, "We have to think about how to handle this, how to get out of it so that you don't end up in prison, and I don't either." He dropped down on to a soft chair and let the fabric fold round him like a soft blanket. It helped ease his tension and that in the room. Bethany toned her own stressed state down a notch and sat down beside him. Shouting at each other wasn't going to help.

Calmer, Bethany asked, "So, what do we do? Are they going to come back and charge us, either of us?"

"I don't know, but I agree they will come back. They won't be put off that easily. We need to get legal representation organised now, so we're ready."

"Then I guess the first person to ask would be Eric. He can point us in the right direction."

"That sounds sensible. I don't know if we need a criminal solicitor or what, or even how it all works. I've never been in a situation like this before, never needed a solicitor apart from when we've been buying a house."

"I guess we're about to find out, but how much do we tell him?"

"I guess we'll have to just go along with it and see. He'll ask the questions. We need to get our story straight though, because when we do end up down the police station or whatever the scenario is, we need to be ready. Neither of us is going to prison for this."

"What about that woman from Friday night, Maxine, wasn't she something to do with the courts?" Bethany asked.

"She's a barrister so I hope to God we don't actually need her. She works in the Crown court."

"But what about her husband, Blake. He was a solicitor?"

"Let's just ask Eric first and see. Maybe we need Blake, maybe we need Eric, maybe we need somebody else. I don't know, there's too much going on in my head at the moment, I can't think straight."

"I'll make some tea. You make the call. Perhaps we should go around there now?"

"Forget the tea. I think I need a whiskey," he said.

Lee stood for a moment and took a couple of deep breaths, massaging his head as though it was therapy or it somehow helped him think. He reached for his phone and dialled Eric's number.

"Lee," answered Eric cheerily. Twice in one day."

"Hello Eric," he said, sounding deflated, and then took a deep breath before he began. "I think I might need your professional expertise. We might have a situation and need legal advice."

"Okay, sounds intriguing. Do you want to come over?" Gone was chirpy Eric, replaced with a more business-like tone. Lee carried on.

"I think I might get called into the police station later on, and I'm going to need some help."

"In that case, if you're looking for professional help and advice on that score, I should come over to you. Does now suit?"

"Yes, then I'll tell you what's been going on."

"I'll be there shortly," Eric said and hung up. Lee wandered into the kitchen where Bethany was finishing off making tea for herself. "He's on his way over now. How much do you think we should tell him?"

"Well, he can't advise us properly unless we tell him everything."

"No, but I haven't been arrested yet, nor have you, so we've no idea how much the police know, and it doesn't seem right to admit killing someone to your friend or your solicitor unless you absolutely have to."

"Well, I don't think we have a choice. I think we need to tell the whole story and see what he suggests. He can't tell anyone anyway, it's confidential, remember. Though we could lose a friend over this."

"I think that's the least of our problems."

"Point taken. There's one thing for sure though," said Bethany. "They were pretty quick to find our car, so they've got evidence against us, we just don't know exactly what yet. I wouldn't be surprised if we don't get another knock on the door later on today, so the sooner we can talk this through the better."

"I agree. We'll tell Eric the whole story and take it from there."

CHAPTER 53

Banker

Sunday afternoon

Lee and Bethany stood in the doorway as Eric pulled into the driveway. They were on tenterhooks wondering quite what would happen once they admitted their involvement in the events of Friday night. The only problem that Lee could foresee was that Eric and Tanya had both seen Bethany drive them away from the house that night and so knew exactly who had been behind the wheel. Would that matter from a police point of view, would Eric and Tanya themselves be interviewed? Lee felt sure it could be a problem, but with no other avenues open to them, they had to seek advice somewhere. Maybe Eric could recommend somebody else, maybe the other chap Blake that had been at the meal. Or would they have the same problem with him too?

Since it was a Sunday, Eric was dressed casually in jeans and trainers that were at odds with the black leather briefcase he carried. He raised a hand in greeting as he approached them.

"Thanks for coming," Lee said, falling back into the hallway to let Eric through, and the duo made their way towards the kitchen at the back.

"Perhaps we're better at the table," suggested Eric, pointing as they entered the room, "since this sounds like quite a formal matter. I can tell by your faces something grave is up so why don't we have a cup of tea and get started?"

"Yes," said Bethany, who had joined them. "Let's get this over and done with." She busied herself finding a tray and filling it with mugs and a plate of biscuits, not that she felt like eating, and until she joined them, the two men made small talk. Last time Eric had been to their house, things had been somewhat more jovial, and as soon as the pot was filled with hot tea, Bethany took the tray over and joined in the chatter for a moment. When everyone had a drink in front of them, Eric took the lead.

"Let me just confirm that as long as you're my client, whatever you tell me is confidential; I can't say anything to anybody about anything that is said, so please speak freely. In fact, I need to know the whole story of whatever it is that quite clearly is troubling you both. Okay?"

Two heads nodded.

"Can I ask a question first?" Lee said.

"Of course, fire away," said Eric, sitting back in his chair and taking a sip from his mug.

"Before we tell you what's on our minds, what's happened, the police have already been round today and questioned me casually. But I know that they are going to come back because they've quite clearly got evidence of a crime that has been committed. But since you will be possibly interviewed as a witness in this case, and also because you're a friend, I don't know if you can actually represent us."

Eric nodded, slowly understanding Lee's words, but waited for them to percolate in his head while the answer came.

"Let me ask you this then. What sort of solicitor do you think you need before you tell me any more?"

"A criminal one. What's happened could land either of us in prison."

"Well, in that case, I'm not the one to represent you anyway, it's not my area of expertise. Blake, who was at dinner on Friday, however, is. He would be a better option, and if it does go to court, then Maxine is a barrister, so I would say he'd be a good place to start."

"So, should we tell you the story or not? Is it protected if you're not going to be the solicitor that represents us?"

"You better not tell me then, but this sounds serious."

"It is," said Bethany. "It's deadly serious."

"Let me make a call to Blake and see if he can come over. But, before I do that, there is something puzzling me."

"What's that?"

"You say I might be called in to be questioned as a witness. To what exactly? I'd like to be aware of it when the police call."

Bethany looked at Lee resignedly. "It's all going to come out soon enough."

Lee took the lead, the spokesman for the two. "They're going to want to know who was driving on Friday night when we left your place." There, he'd said it.

"I see, well Bethany was, wasn't she?"

"She was, yes."

"So, what's that got to do with anything? What did you do, ping someone's car?"

"We wouldn't be needing a criminal solicitor for pinging some-one's car," Bethany said coolly.

And then Eric understood immediately.

"Oh hell. Tell me you didn't," he said, pressing the palm of his hand to his forehead. "Tell me that person that got hit wasn't you."

Nobody said a word. They didn't need to.

"Then you are in a spot of bother." Eric stood up and paced the kitchen a little, the magnitude of what he now knew sinking in. Whatever he'd been thinking, he rapidly switched back to the question at hand. "From memory, on Friday night, Maxine and Blake stayed seated at the table as you two left, so they wouldn't have seen who actually got in the driver's seat. The police may still want to interview them though," he said, thinking.

"Well, even if they interview them, like you say, they didn't see anything. And since we only met them both that night, surely that should be okay for representation and not be a conflict of interest? That shouldn't cause a problem with the police?" Lee asked.

"Give me a moment to think about this one," said Eric.

"So, now you know," said Bethany. More as an afterthought, she added, "Not that we've actually admitted anything to you as a friend or as a legal representative, but are you obliged to tell the police that it was us?"

"Well, actually *now* you *have* admitted it to me," said Eric. "It's one holy mess."

CHAPTER 54

The police station
Sunday afternoon

Once back in the squad room, Amanda and Jack pored over the list of other red Jaguars and their registration plates to double-check whether they'd missed anything. Locally, there was no other Jag that fitted the bill. Nationally? That could be a possibility.

"If they were out for dinner, I wonder whose house they'd been coming back from over that road?" Jack said.

"We have no way of knowing. We can only hope he tells us when questioned." Amanda passed Jack a photograph of the belt buckle that had been taken earlier in the lab. "While I'm no forensic scientist," said Amanda, "looking at that belt buckle and the scratch we saw, I would say it's a strong possibility for a match. Even with the corner of the buckle gouging it, it could still have made a mark like what we saw. That scratch on his car wasn't from a bush or a shopping trolley or the usual suspects, and it certainly was not from a stone chip."

"Well, I vote we bring him in for formal questioning this afternoon and find out just where they were out for dinner on Friday night. And since it's only the two of them that live in that house, my suspicions are on Mrs Meady driving. Plus, we'll need to interview whoever else was at dinner and witnessed who got in the driver's seat."

"Any news on the mobile towers? Whose phone pinged, if any?"

"Let me check, hang on." Jack wheeled himself over to his desk to check the status.

Amanda could see the smile on his face as he rolled back to her.

"One Mrs Bethany Meady. Bingo," he said, shooting his hand in the air.

"Well, that puts at least Mrs Meady in the location at the right time. Add that to the car... I'll organise a couple of uniforms to pick them up, then I think I fancy another ride out there. Coming, partner?"

"May as well," said Jack, meeting her high-five slap. "I'll track down the collision specialist officer for when we get the vehicle, which we could do with getting hold of sooner than later, before that scratch disappears forever. He's likely still rubbing at it now."

"Well, the Meadys have got a bit of money and that means an expensive solicitor, which means this could be short and sweet. It's not a lot for the CPS. I'm relying on one of them slipping up somewhere really," Amanda said, concerned.

"We may have it if we act swiftly. That scratch is key to this."

"You know what gets me the most?" asked Amanda.

"What's that?"

"It's all after-the-fact evidence. They didn't stop, they threw away any chance of saving that girl's life, and we have no alcohol test, no drug test, nothing. It's a simple careless driving charge, death or not, and that means bugger all sentence for whoever was the culprit."

"I know. It stinks, doesn't it?"

"Maybe they know that, maybe that's why they fled?"

"Well, the law certainly encourages you to flee and not stop to hang around and call an ambulance, though you would hope people had scruples, some heart to do the decent thing if they'd hit another human being," Jack said, getting more worked up with each word. "Like the case of the old lady I keep talking about, there's some selfish individuals out there that have got nothing on their minds but themselves. I blame it on the narcissist social sites people put their lives on. Look at me doing this, look at me doing that." Jack added, animated for a moment, pulling faces and pointing to his own chest like a six-year-old. "I'm doing this and you're not, I'm better than you are," he finished. "It's pathetic."

Amanda raised her eyebrows at Jack – where was all this coming from? But maybe he was right. The world was turning into a self-centred mass, and she wasn't sure she liked it at all.

"Come on then, Jack," she said. "Let's get back to it. The sooner we start, the sooner we can finish."

"It's not turned out to be much of a day off has it?" he said.

"Nor was yesterday. We do it for the love of it, don't we, Jack?"

"Well, someone has to."

CHAPTER 55

Banker

Sunday afternoon

Eric sat back in his chair once more to mull things over. His friends had obviously been involved in the hit-and-run, that much was obvious, and the woman had been killed. This was serious. Even if he were a criminal solicitor, the code of conduct would prevent him from representing them anyway – his duty to act in the best interest of the client in relation to a matter conflicted with his own. Plus, Eric knew one of them was guilty. His friend Blake, on the other hand, could represent them at a push. The man didn't know the couple and had met them only briefly at dinner that night, so it was up to him whether he felt comfortable doing it.

"I think Blake is our best bet," he said finally.

"But now you know, Eric, obviously they're going to want to come and interview you. How will that sit? I mean, have you got to tell them seeing as you're not acting for us legally now?"

"No, I don't have to tell them unless they ask me directly. The problem is if I don't tell them the truth when asked, I could be arrested for assisting an offender under section 4 of the Criminal Law Act 1967, and I can't be getting involved in that. I've got my livelihood to think about, you understand. If I try to cover something up, it gets even worse, I'd be guilty of perverting the course of justice as well, and potentially other offences, so I need to keep way out of this. But no, to answer your question, I don't have to. I'm not obliged to tell the police unless asked. Let's hope they don't ask, eh?"

Bethany and Lee sat silent for a moment, pondering.

"What would you do then, Eric, if this was you, how would you sort it out?" asked Bethany.

"It is a tricky one, but I think I'd wait and see what evidence the police have got. They're obviously going to come back and likely arrest you if they think they've got enough. Perhaps they just need to finalise the last pieces. But they can't charge you unless the CPS thinks there is enough. So, while they're busy gathering evidence, we need to know exactly what that consists of." He fell silent again, thinking.

Lee and Bethany sat staring at the table in front of them as if it was going to give them the answer.

Eventually, Eric said, "When they call, as you think they will, go down to the station, but don't say anything until you've at least got the duty solicitor in with you – depends who it is, but they're usually pretty good. It sounds as though they've got evidence already, and depending on what that consists of, it could be hard to deny it. You did, in fact, hit the woman, Bethany. Blake may or may not advise you to plead guilty, depending on what you tell him, and that is something we should talk about now."

Bethany's head flipped up violently. "Guilty? Plead guilty?"

"Hear me out," he said, holding a hand up to stop her panic. "There are advantages to pleading guilty when they've got enough evidence. It saves the court a whole lot of time, and you get a third off your sentence. If the evidence is all circumstantial, they won't charge you, they need proper, hard evidence that you were at the scene of the crime and involved in the woman's death. If there's any doubt in what they have, then I would go with 'not guilty' and take the risk, because this is one of those cases that could go either to Crown court or stay in the magistrates'. They're called 'either way' offences. We don't need to get into all that now, a solicitor can't really advise you what to do, it has to be your own decision. But if a solicitor knows that you're guilty because you've admitted it to them, they then can't pervert the course of justice, he or she can't then represent you on a non-guilty plea."

"It's not as easy as buying a house is it?" Bethany said, maudlin.

"I'm afraid not, it's far more serious. Blake would be able to tell you an awful lot more, it's his area of expertise. So, when they come knocking to arrest you and take you in for further questioning, see what evidence they produce while you're in with the duty solicitor, he'll be with you during questioning, and I'll talk to Blake in the meantime. Nothing may happen for a day or two, or they could come back in an hour. We don't know."

"What will I be charged with?"

"It could be a couple of things, death by careless driving or death by reckless driving, perhaps. They might even add failure to stop and report an accident. But again, let's see what Blake comes up with. That's about all I can tell you for now," he said, closing his pad and putting his pen and paper away. "What I suggest you do now is just try and relax, and when the police come back make sure you've got legal representation with you at all times. Both of you. I'm guessing at this stage they don't know exactly who was driving, but that's only a guess. So Lee," he said, turning to him, "what will you say when they ask you?"

"I don't know," he said in all certainty, "but they know one of us was at the wheel, though I don't feel like I can throw Bethany under the bus." He winced at his words, words Bethany had used earlier. "But I also don't want to get in trouble myself. I've got my career to maintain and as the breadwinner..." His words trailed off as he realised how he must have sounded.

A solitary tear began to trickle down Bethany's cheek – realisation that her husband wasn't going to lay his coat over a puddle for her. What did she expect really? Could she ask her husband to do prison time on her behalf? That was some tall order. She doubted whether anyone would do it in reality. This was real life, not a movie. The very thought of being locked up was a frightening one, but it was all her mess, she had been the one at the wheel, nobody else was responsible, no matter whether she'd had a drink or had been coerced, she'd been driving, and there was no getting away from that. Whatever the pressure had been from Lee, she could have spoken up sooner and possibly saved the young woman's life. As a mature and sensible adult, the end result was hers alone.

Resignedly, Bethany raised her hands and let them drop dramatically on the table. "I'll just admit it, it was me at the wheel," she said matter-of-factly. "They're bound to find out sooner or later, and I can't have Lee being charged wrongly."

Eric raised his own hands in horror. "Now, don't go shouting 'I did it' just yet, let Blake see the evidence first. I'd strongly advise against ridding yourself of your own guilt at this stage, just stay quiet and hold yourself together."

She looked at Eric. "What would the sentence be?"

"I don't know, it's a question for Blake, but I would have to hazard a guess at anywhere between six months and five years. A guilty plea gets a third off whatever the sentence is, so it's definitely something to think about, but as I say, let's see first. Don't rush the process."

Bethany closed her eyes for a moment and held them tightly shut. Even doing half of the maximum would be two and a half years. It seemed like an eternity. Her career would be gone, she'd be a completely different woman when she came out.

Sooner than either she or Lee expected, the knock at the door started the ball rolling.

CHAPTER 56

Banker

Sunday evening

When Lee and Bethany Meady entered the police station for questioning, Darrel was on his way out. Not that either of them knew who the man was. He was just an individual they passed in a corridor who looked like he'd spent a good deal of time in a cell.

Uniformed officers had brought them in, and they each sat in separate interview rooms to be questioned individually. The duty solicitor, a man called Jerry Sage, had heard the latest and updated version of their story from Bethany, who'd managed to stay strong and hold back any emotion and guilt. Yes, they had travelled that road; yes, she'd been driving; and no, they hadn't seen anything. Blake Kipple was on his way, as per the plan that Eric had suggested they follow.

On the other side of Bethany's interview room wall, Lee worried about his wife. He knew she wasn't as strong mentally as him and had been fretting, quite understandably, since the accident had happened. While he was sitting alone, he pondered what would be happening to her and hoped she was sticking to their story. There would be awkward questions, they both knew, particularly when the police enquired about why they'd not come forward when they'd seen it on the news – they had travelled that route after all. Their answer was to be they hadn't seen anything to report – plenty of vehicles travel that road, and they simply weren't involved. Nobody in their right mind was ever going to admit to hitting another human in an accident after-the-fact, they'd simply hope it all went away and they'd never get caught. Nothing good could come of it, only bad. The police were never going to say 'well done for telling us you drove that route, and what a lovely car you have, go home and have a happy life,' it didn't work like that.

And that's exactly what Lee and Bethany did.

CHAPTER 57

The police station
Sunday evening

Blake Kipple walked into the station with a confident air about him. He was well known to the police as an extremely clever man, not only legally but generally – he had been a competent *Master-mind* contestant some years ago. He was tall with a full head of grey hair that he combed back from his forehead, so it rested on his ears but not on his collar. His dark eyebrows told the tale that at one time that same hair had been almost raven black, but it was the thick moustache stretched across his mouth that Jack always remembered him by. In his opinion, Blake's was probably an inch too wide for his face. The man was almost casually dressed, wearing a white shirt buttoned up to the neck, but his tie was distinctly absent. Jack had never seen him wear one, as was his easy style, and it seemed to put people at ease. Blake Kipple could be described as disarming, charming, and extremely likeable, and that's why he was notorious for doing well in court. To the detectives, he was a pain in the backside because he had the reputation of a smart man that usually got his way. If you were represented by Blake Kipple, you were one lucky person.

Amanda turned to Jack as they watched him arrive and said, "That's all we need, Mr Bloody Smarty-Pants. He reminds me of somebody off an old movie from the thirties, riding in on his white charger. Could you imagine him? All cape and dark hair flowing, rescuing the damsel in distress?" Amanda didn't try to hide her distaste.

Jack simply grunted. They were both standing, arms crossed, watching as he entered the corridor and was escorted down to an interview room.

"I guess he'll be taking over from Sage?" said Jack. "Amazing what money can buy."

"Well, if I ever needed a criminal solicitor, I'd call him too. You can't blame people, can you?"

"If you've got the money, yeah, fine. But I pity the guy who is in the middle, the one that hasn't got the money."

"What do you mean, in the middle?"

"I mean, like you've got the lowlife, and the poor that we deal with, those that haven't got two pennies to rub together, they get legal aid. And then you've got people like the Meadys in their big house. 'Big house and no knickers', my mother would have said."

"I think you mean 'big *hat* and no knickers'."

"Whatever," said Jack, shaking his head, irritated slightly, "you understand what I'm trying to say. The folks in the middle, they're the ones that will need to sell their house to raise funds for this guy to represent them," he said, flicking his head lightly over his shoulder in the direction Blake had just gone. "As the guy in the middle, the man trying to scratch a living together, he or she, they're the ones that miss out on legal aid and can't afford expensive lawyers. So, what are they supposed to do?" Jack wasn't about to wait for an answer. "I'll tell you what they do, they try and defend themselves. It's becoming all the more common now. Damn dangerous if you ask me."

"Where's all this coming from?" asked Amanda. "You've been

ever so maudlin these last few days and this again, it's more of the same."

"It's not maudlin, it's just downright not fair, but it's how the system works. It depresses me sometimes. Take me, for instance," he said. "If I was wrongly accused of something, how the hell could I defend myself, what money have I got tucked away in a bank to pay solicitors and barristers at however much per hour? I've no savings to speak of, and you can't just sell your house overnight. So, what am I to do?"

"I don't know, Jack. I hope neither of us ever gets in that situation."

"But it happens," said Jack persistently. "Look at your Ruth and the trouble she was in. People get accused of things all the time. We of all people should know that."

Amanda visibly smarted at hearing Ruth's name so casually added to the conversation. "I don't know," said Amanda, recovering herself and dismissing the discussion, "but I'd like to be a fly on the wall listening to what Sage and Kipple are talking about."

It was the perfect thing to say to get Jack off his high horse. He began to snigger.

"What's amusing you now?" she said as they started to walk back towards the squad room.

"Sage and Kipple. It sounds like breakfast cereal, doesn't it?" Amanda couldn't help but laugh. "Sage, Kipple, and Pop," said Jack, carrying on comically. Amanda dragged him back to the job at hand.

"Come on, are you ready for this, because in a moment we'll be called through."

"It'll be interesting to see what she says. My money's on her. Who's your money on?"

"I don't put money on suspects," said Amanda sternly.

"Well, I'm thinking she looks good for it because she seems far more nervous than he does. On a Friday night driving home, he's a big CEO and probably had too much to drink, and she gets behind the wheel because it's only around the corner, and they take the back road just in case. They wouldn't come across much other traffic."

Amanda gathered up the relevant files, and they proceeded back towards the interview rooms to wait until Blake Kipple was ready. They were almost there when the man himself came out and met them in the corridor.

"I just need some time with Mr Meady and then back with Mrs Meady."

"Are you representing them both?" asked Amanda.

"For the moment, yes. So, if you can direct me to Mr Meady, please, I'll have a quick word with him. In private."

"Follow me then," said Amanda, looking at Jack, thinking he'd probably win the bet. Amanda opened the door. Lee Meady was sitting with his head in his hands, but he lifted it up abruptly on hearing someone enter the room. He visibly relaxed when he saw Blake's face but noted Amanda. Blake entered the room and said, "I'll be a moment with my client," and shut the door behind him. Approaching the table, he shook Lee Meady's hand.

"Now, tell me what, if anything, went on on Friday evening."

CHAPTER 58

The police station
Sunday evening

Blake Kipple's conversation with Lee was over rather quickly, as was his conversation with Bethany. Both denied any involvement in the accident on Friday night but admitted to driving home that way – there was no law against that, was there? With Bethany Meady seemingly a good deal more nervous than her husband, Amanda had opted to question her first in the hope that she'd crumble and save them all a good deal of time. Sunday evening or not, Amanda was anxious to tie the whole thing up and move on.

But it hadn't gone as well as she'd hoped, and Blake Kipple had an argument for everything. After twenty minutes, Amanda had almost run out of steam, and the largely circumstantial evidence she had was not going to be enough. She should have waited, gathered more somehow, something stronger, before bringing either of them in for formal questioning. It was too late now; they'd shown their hand.

"Well, Detective Sergeant Lacey," Blake said, "if that's all you have and you're hoping to charge my client on that basis, I think we're done here," he said, collecting his pen and pad together. A victorious grin filled Blake's face, making his moustache seem even wider than before. The grey-haired man stood to leave and encouraged Bethany to stand as well. Amanda was almost helpless to stop them and stayed seated, feeling somewhat beaten. Jack opened his mouth to speak, but Amanda caught his eye and gently shook her head. The pair watched them Blake and Bethany leave the room.

When they were out of earshot: "Damn and blast!" Amanda seethed. "We need more, something definitive to tie their vehicle to the actual accident location and being involved in it. We need a hair trapped in a wiper blade or something, anything, but more than we have. He just made chutney out of us both." Amanda took a moment to catch her breath after blurting her dissatisfaction out in a rush. "Her phone in the vicinity around midnight is too loose since she's not disputing the fact that she drove them home and went that way around."

"It stinks, is what I say. Bloody toffee-nosed solicitor, I knew he'd pull something like this," said Jack, equally annoyed.

"It's our own fault," admitted Amanda. "We were too hasty, but really, with the scratch, her mobile in the location, and the two registration plate letters..."

"All simply explained, apparently. Those CCTV camera pictures are pretty unclear and, again, she's not disputing driving that way."

"There were only a handful of vehicles up that road that night."

"Precisely, and it could have been any one of them. The paint in the belt buckle could have come from another incident, unrelated. And her own uncle has a Firenze-red Range Rover, remember? And a Jag. Perhaps it came from there, totally unrelated, as Blake suggested. Melody had likely been in either of his vehicles before."

The room fell silent while they digested their disappointment. It tasted as bitter as their own bile. Amanda slammed her folder shut and stood.

"Come on, we'd best tell Buddy where we're at. No doubt he'll be chuffed... not," she said, laying on the sarcasm.

Jack rolled his eyes and stood alongside her. Telling the boss that you'd screwed a case up on lack of evidence never went down well. They could only hope he was full of Sunday roast, and he'd had a glass of wine or two to relax.

"Well, there's no hope charging Mr Meady either, not now," said Amanda. "Same evidence, and he wasn't the driver anyway. It's bullshit, is what it is."

"Let's get out of here. Fancy a drink?"

"No thanks, not for me," she said as they walked.

"Win some..."

"I know. But I look at it this way – it's not over yet. Every contact leaves a trace, remember?"

Jack nodded wearily. Locard's principle? He wasn't convinced. Not in this case. He dreaded telling Ron.

CHAPTER 59

Baker
Sunday evening

Considering the mess, Natalie was more supportive than Kit could ever have dreamed. He was extremely worried about what would happen next. His dealings back at the police station with the duty solicitor, Ned Pickle, hadn't filled him with any confidence. The tacky polyester suit and general sweaty demeanour of the man made him an unlikeable character, and his talent, if Kit could call it that from what he'd seen, was that of a bumbling idiot. Pickle had had trouble working his own Biro, not to mention getting the correct documents filled in, and everything else the man touched seemed to crumble like Cheshire cheese.

On Monday morning, Kit was to appear in front of the magistrates' court, and in the absence of decent legal representation, he was all on his own. He and Natalie had sat at the kitchen table thrashing scenarios out and learning what they could about the way the legal system worked from various websites. It was all totally confusing, and depending on what you read, or how you read it, one post appeared to contradict another you'd only just read somewhere else. By 6 pm, the plan was for Kit to plead not guilty, based on extenuating circumstances that he needed to explain. If he pled guilty, he could be imprisoned for up to six months, and he didn't want to do that. It did not sit right, and he did not want to go to prison. Pleading not guilty gave him time, then, for a real court case, not in front of a jury per se but in front of the magistrates at a later date, and he hoped by that stage he'd have something to offer them, and that he would have learned a great deal more about the legal system himself. How the hell he was going to take a crash course in such a short space of time he had no idea; it took many years to become a competent solicitor.

Tomorrow, he'd have no option but to take his chance and see what happened next. And pray. He hoped it wouldn't all crumble apart, and with that, Cheshire cheese came back to mind.

A little later, Natalie and Kit were in the lounge, mulling things over, sipping on leftover Christmas whiskey.

"At least it will be over tomorrow, not too long to worry over," said Natalie, trying to encourage her husband. The first appearance at the magistrates' court was only a brief one; it was only really to state his name and give his plea. If he pleaded guilty, he could be sentenced there and then, and that's what Kit was hoping to avoid. Natalie wasn't sure she agreed with his decision since he did take the car, and he could get a third of his sentence off straight away by not wasting the court's time. But it wasn't up to her. They'd been over it more times than he wanted to record.

"I know, and while I did it, I need the time to get things right. I'm not ready to plead guilty and get my sentence tomorrow. There's too much to sort out, too much to think about, and extenuating circumstances to explain. I need to get my head round this," he explained. "If I had a decent solicitor, perhaps I could plead guilty and get it over and done with, and they'd help me say the right things, but I haven't so it's got to be dragged out. It's the only way I can see."

"Doesn't it mean, though, if you plead not guilty, you'll get a harsher sentence if you are then found guilty?"

"From what I've learnt so far, yes. There is a gamble, and I did do it, all the evidence points to me as guilty, but I'm willing to take that risk. It buys us precious time, Natalie, in the hope I can avoid prison entirely."

"I don't want you to go to prison any more than you do," she said, "but it is *kind of* your first offence. It's not like you robbed a bank."

"First offence for theft, yes. Second offence in total. It depends what the magistrates think, it will be something as simple as that. Whether they like my suit, whether they like the look of me or not. My outcome is literally in the lap of the gods." Put like that, it didn't matter if Kit had a fancy solicitor or not, it wouldn't really do any good.

"I keep racking my brains to think of someone that we know, someone that can help us out, and I can't come up with anybody," Natalie said. "I bet one of your customers would be a solicitor, but I don't know which one."

"Me neither. We just don't have those people in our circle, and they wouldn't do it for free anyway. Plus, it's very different being a solicitor for selling a house, or for setting up a trust, than it is representing someone against car theft in magistrates' court. I'm guessing it's a criminal solicitor I need. And that shows how little we both know on the subject; we don't know what type of represen-tation to find, even if we could afford it."

Natalie tapped her fingertips against her glass gently – it helped her think.

"It's funny though, when these experiences materialise, you come to realise that you know nothing of the legal system and its implications and what can happen. We don't care until something arises to affect someone close enough to worry about."

"What do you mean?" she asked.

"I mean like this afternoon. We spent time googling the

possible length of prison sentence I could get for car theft, and it's six months."

"Look, Kit, it's your first theft offence, they're not likely to throw you in prison for it. It's there for those joyriding idiots that run cars round lamp posts every Friday night, not for the individual like you, the business owner, the family man."

"The sentence is the sentence though, there are guidelines to adhere to, and I don't want to be the one they feel the need to make an example of."

"Yes, and you also hear of people getting off from wicked crimes with home detention or a community order or whatever you call it, and they've killed someone. You hear of drunk driver or rapists that get six months or home detention. It's all twisted up and depends on so many factors that you have no control over. Stupid technicalities get cases thrown out because paperwork is either not there or incorrect. You've seen the headlines yourself."

"I know you're trying to cheer me up, Natalie, but I am worried, seriously worried, about what this could mean for us as a family and for the business." He took a deep, cleansing breath to release the tension he was feeling, and it was only the start of it, tomorrow would be ten times worse. He paused for a moment, then added, "I guess we'll know more tomorrow. It's only a short appearance anyway, then it's out of the way for a while, and we can figure out what goes on next." Kit looked across at Natalie with appreciation and, meeting her eyes, said, "I love you, Mrs Morris. I couldn't wish for more, and I thank you for your support. It means the world to me."

"That's what we do, Mr Morris," she said, smiling, and reached across to him for a hug.

CHAPTER 60

The police station
Sunday evening

Amanda and Jack watched as Lee and Bethany Meady left the building.

"Well, in my view, they're the scum of the earth," said Jack. "She was as nervous as a kitten. Definitely hiding the truth, and she knows it. She's lucky she can afford to pay someone like Blake. It stinks."

"The evidence we had was torn to shreds. We need more, Jack. In hindsight, I rushed things, eager to get them in before the scratch got dealt with permanently. I guess I'll bear the brunt of it, lesson learned," she said resignedly.

"Don't go blaming yourself. You know as well as I do that she's the one that killed young Melody, and we weren't able to have a good crack at her. That's all. You'd have brought a suspect in with that evidence in the past, and you'll likely do so again in the future. A damn good solicitor is what got in the way of justice being served on that one, not you, Amanda. Not you."

Amanda gave a low grunt. He meant well, but was Jack right?

Jack changed the subject. "Handy man to know though."

"Let's hope we never get to know him up close and personal then."

"I don't intend doing anything dodgy, but like I said earlier, sometimes the innocent get accused. Though I can't say that in this particular case. Guilty all the way."

"What was all that about earlier, do you need a holiday, Jack? Only, you seem down in the dumps at the moment, everything seems to be preying on you. I thought you were happy, at home and at work."

"Ay. Maybe I'm losing my tolerance of the human race. After all these years as a policeman, maybe it's finally catching up with me."

"You've got a good deal more in you yet, Jack," she said, slapping him on the shoulder. "You're one of the best detectives around, and there's no one else I'd rather work with. I hope you're not going to hang up your coat just yet, are you?"

"No, I don't think so," he said slowly. "I've still too much to do, though the time off would be nice."

"There's not many that care as much as you do, Jack," she said, "and that goes a long way." She thought for a moment then asked, "Why did you never want promotion?"

"Just wanted to be a good copper, didn't want the paperwork or the hassle, and the higher you climb, the less policing you actually do. Who wants to sit at a desk all day sorting numbers? Not me. Plus, my maths is pretty shite."

Amanda couldn't help grinning at that one.

"Got any plans this evening, what's left of it?" she enquired, grabbing her coat.

"My bed and a book, I think," he said, rubbing his lower back. "Maybe I need to get a new mattress."

"Well, you are supposed to replace your mattress every ten years. How old is the one you've got?"

"A hell of a lot older than ten. Maybe you're right. Maybe I do need one. Anyway," he said, yawning, "the more I think about it, the more I just want my bed, no book."

Jack pulled his phone out to look for messages. There were several missed calls, all from the same number again. Ron Butcher. He groaned.

"What's the matter?"

"Ron Butcher, looking for an update no doubt. Nothing I can't take care of, just more hassle."

Amanda frowned her disapproval at the man's involvement and Jack allowing himself to be pushed about, something else that was out of character. She grabbed the rest of her things, and they both headed out to their respective cars.

As always, Jack made sure she was safely in her car even though they were parked in the police car park. Nutters lurked in all sorts of corners.

As the two cars pulled out the car park and went their separate ways, Jack put his CD player on to wind down to one of his favourite tracks before he got home. Even though he'd been set up with Spotify and Bluetooth, he enjoyed the occasional motion of pushing a CD into the slot and wouldn't part with them for the world.

All the thoughts he'd had of recent, of Nelly Raven, an old lady dying alone, of Melody Holden, a young woman dying alone, had made him think about his Janine and, after all the years, how much he still missed her. While Vivian was indeed lovely to have around, and he was happy in her company, the two women were totally different, and no matter how things progressed with her in the future, he knew he'd never stop loving his Janine. Not ever.

ELO's 'Sweet Talkin' Woman' filled the car, and he sang along as he always did, blasting out every word. Whether he was feeling maudlin or happy, the song sent him to a place where he could remember her privately, the woman he'd spent so much of his life with. Cancer had eventually taken her, and not a day went by without him thinking of her at some point.

By the time he pulled up on to his driveway, the song had

changed to 'Wild West Hero'. Jack pulled the handbrake on and sat for a moment singing along to the words of the chorus, stringing out the last one, hhhheeeerrrro, before switching off the engine. Tomorrow morning, when he started the car up again, the song would carry on, and he'd likely sing it on his way into work as he often did. He never tired of the music.

He was so wrapped up in his little world of Janine and ELO that he didn't notice the car parked opposite. But then, why would he? There were cars parked all along the street. As he got out of his own vehicle, he heard the door of another slam nearby. His security light lit up at movement, and he stood for a moment, looking to see what was happening. It wasn't a neighbour. It was Ron Butcher, and he was walking towards him. Jack instantly felt unease. What was this man doing at his house? That was a breach and it riled him, but he'd see what the man wanted without causing concern, though he didn't like it. Ron Butcher was not a man anyone wanted to cross. Jack went with pleasant.

"Evening, Ron," he said. There was no point being defensive straight off.

"You don't answer your phone, Jack," said Ron. "I don't like being ignored."

"I've been interviewing. I just got out and saw somebody had called a few times, that was you, was it?"

"Like I said, I've been trying to call you, but you don't pick up your phone." It sounded almost threatening, and the man's tone took Jack back a little. "Can I come in for a minute?"

No way!

"That's not a good idea," said Jack. "But we can talk here for a moment. What's on your mind?"

"An update, Jack, just waiting for an update. Where are things? I hear somebody's been down the station being interviewed?"

"Well, if you already know that, you've obviously been in touch with whoever is on the inside for you, so you probably know as much as I do. Yes, someone's been interviewed and that's it. That's all I can tell you."

"Can't or won't?"

"There's nothing to report, and I can't report on an open case anyway, you know that. I did say, right at the beginning, I wouldn't be of much help to you."

Ron hung his head for a moment. When he raised it again, Jack was shocked to see tears in the hard man's eyes. He instantly felt bad. The man was obviously grieving. He'd lost his niece.

"Look," said Jack, "there really is nothing to report at the moment. Yes, someone's been interviewed, but I can't say any more than that."

"I miss her so much already, Jack," said Ron. "She was the little diamond in my life, and now she's gone. Everyone I've loved seems to be leaving me, and there's nothing I can do about it." He took a folded handkerchief from his pocket and dabbed at his eyes. Jack waited for the man to compose himself and carry on. "So, you'll understand that I'm anxious to find out who killed her, who took Melody's life, my sweet, sweet Melody. Another death in the family is just too hard to bear." Ron blew his nose, and Jack, being a compassionate man, knew how he felt. After all, he'd just been thinking about his own Janine. While time supposedly healed, you never forget the ones you love. Jack took a step forward and placed his hand on Ron's shoulder.

"I know, Ron," he said. "You're hurting now, but take it from someone that has experienced the death of a loved one, it does get easier eventually, the pain will ease."

"I'm not sure if that's helping, Jack."

"No, maybe not, not yet. But I can tell you that it does go away."

"All the way? Does it all go?"

Jack thought for a moment as Janine popped into his head in a cartoon speech bubble – she was wagging a finger at him.

"No, not quite."

"Then you'll know I need this to be closed quickly."

"I know that, Ron. As soon as I can tell you something, you know I will. Now, why don't you go home, grab yourself some of that single malt I'm sure you've got a bottle of, and have a toast to young Melody." Jack gave his arm an affectionate squeeze and pulled away. "Maybe we'll have some more news in the morning," Jack said as an afterthought, more to give the man something to cling to than the truth. "Now go home."

"That's probably what I'll do, Jack. Thanks. I appreciate your wisdom."

He stood watching as Ron turned back to his car and noticed the man's black Lexus looked almost red under the amber glow of a street lamp.

CHAPTER 61

Baker

Sunday night

Even though Kit was bone-tired, he knew he wouldn't be able to sleep. He had an important day tomorrow, and he needed to be prepared with as much information squashed into his head as possible. So, rather than struggle on trying to count sheep and watching shadows on this bedroom ceiling, he crept out of bed and went back downstairs to the laptop and fired it up. His precious family were sound asleep, and a large part of him wished he was right there with them. But his mind was doing somersaults, turning over various scenarios that could send his life spiralling in quite a different direction to the one he had planned.

He put a mug of milk in the microwave to heat up. His first Google search was to go through again what would happen in his first appearance. He'd been through the process several times with Natalie earlier on, but still, he felt the need to learn the process inside out. It had been some time since he'd been in front of the magistrates; he'd only been a young man back then and was only being charged with drunk and disorderly, a minor blot in his copy-book by comparison. Maybe it was because he was getting older, but he was worrying a great deal more this time around, and he might not get a slap on the wrist like he had back then. Tomorrow, he'd go up in front of the magistrates and plead not guilty.

The microwave pinged, and he added a couple of spoons of cocoa powder to the milk and stood at the sink sipping his hot drink. It was quiet all around him, the house still and not a sound out in the street. The town had droopy eyelids to match his own, though sleep escaped him. He took his drink back to his laptop and carried on researching how the system worked.

He never realised that the magistrates' court was run by what amounted to volunteers, supported by a legally trained adviser. They didn't necessarily possess formal legal qualifications and yet could sentence someone to prison for up to a year, although it was usually only six months. Still, to stand there in front of three peers who could be just like you, a bakery-shop owner, a car mechanic, and a doctor, and let them define his future didn't seem right. It was only a district magistrate that actually had to hold legal qualifica-tions, but who fancied putting their future in the hands of just one person? Thoughts of what that one man or woman had had for breakfast floated through his mind, and he wondered just how true the saying was. They'd see all sorts each and every day, the lowlife as well as the higher life, and he wondered what their mood was like at any given moment. Having a series of junkies, petty shoplifters, drunk and disorderly persons, et cetera paraded in front of you, day after day, must get wearing. And then there were those with their polished shoes and Armani suits zipping through a contraflow system at twice the speed they should have been in their high-end cars with their fancy solicitors dressed equally nice. They got a slap on the wrist and were told not to do it again. The homeless, the great unwashed, all mixed together with the highflyers and their fancy advice. Was there anybody in between? Were there people like him, Kit Morris, trying to do an honest day's work?

He'd been told to turn up at nine o'clock, no doubt with everybody else, and wait his turn. There was no appointment system, there was no 'it's 10.15 am and we'll see you straight away.' It didn't work like a doctor or a dentist or even a solicitor's office. It seemed it depended on how many people needed to be seen. There was every possibility his case might not even be heard tomorrow, if it got floated, but he didn't want to think about that. After the weekend, Monday was apparently a busy court day. He just hoped he could be back at work by lunchtime.

Finally feeling like he could sleep, he sipped down the last of his cocoa and wandered back upstairs to bed and the warmth of Natalie beside him. Everything he'd done, he'd done for his family, and he wasn't looking forward to the next few days. It was sleep he needed now; he had to be up again in a few hours to get the bakery ready as normal. After that, he'd leave for the magistrates' court and a decision that could change the rest of his life.

CHAPTER 62

Baker

Monday morning

By four o'clock on Monday morning, Kit Morris was back in his bakery, once again lost in his thoughts. His eyes stung from lack of sleep, and he knew he probably didn't look his best on the visual front. He had considered using some of Natalie's concealer to rub over his bags but decided against it, figuring the magistrates might take offence at him wearing make-up. It wasn't worth the risk of antagonising someone who could change the rest of his life.

At a little after five, the back door opened and Jakub and Elizabeth both entered and said their good mornings. Neither of them knew what lay ahead for Kit today; he'd decided not to tell them as there was little point in explaining and causing unnecessary worry on their parts. All they needed to know was he had to pop out for the morning.

By six o'clock the bakery was filled with the welcoming smell of freshly baked bread, and each person was busy with their own designated area, so Kit decided to take a moment and have a quiet cup of coffee on his own. He'd been rehearsing possible court scenarios all morning, and his nerves were already jangling like wind chimes in the breeze. The caffeine likely wouldn't help, but the taste and the break just might. He'd barely eaten any breakfast earlier and so took a warm crusty bread roll to have with his coffee and sat in the window, tearing bits off absentmindedly and nibbling with as much gusto as an ill child. Behind him, Elizabeth and Jakub exchanged glances. It was obvious something was wrong, but neither had asked, not wanting to pry. If Kit wanted them to know, he would have surely said.

The front door opened and distracted Kit from his thoughts as a wave of cool air filled the nearby area. It was Ron Butcher. He called his 'good morning' and went back to his bread roll and his thoughts, knowing that Ron would sit a couple of stools down from him in his usual space. Kit wasn't in the mood for conversation, but moving now would appear rude, so he stayed put. A moment later, the front door opened again, but this time he sensed somebody standing nearby before they spoke. He looked up and was somewhat surprised to see Natalie. She had a piece of paper in her hand.

"Morning," he said. "What are you doing here at this hour? And where are the children? Is everything okay?" he asked, panic adding to his frazzled state.

"Relax and just breathe for a moment," she said, smiling. "I wanted to give you this." She handed over the piece of paper. "I got up not long after you left to do my own bit of research. I know you're worried about this whole thing so just hear me out before you say anything, okay?"

Kit nodded. He knew better than to interrupt her when she had something on her mind.

"Like I said," she continued, "I did my own research this morning, and I know you're thinking of pleading not guilty, but there is another option to put this behind you fairly quickly. It's called a plea in mitigation."

Kit sensed her vigour, a renewed energy, and he tried to soak some of it from her for himself. It was clear she was excited by what she'd found. He let he carry on.

"You basically plead guilty, and then you are allowed to have a few words to tell, 'your plea in mitigation', the reasons why you did what you did. Your side of the story. And I think it's the best option."

Kit looked at Natalie and the warmth in her eyes. Could she be right? But the 'plead guilty' part had him worried. He took the piece of paper and read the notes she'd written out. The piece was split into four areas: an apology, some personal information, the circumstances of the offence, and a summary. He quickly scrolled through it all. She'd done a good job and made some excellent points, and reading it, if he were a magistrate, he'd let himself off. He raised a slight smile and then grinned back at Natalie.

"You have been busy. So, you think I should do this?"

"I think it's worth it. It will put it all behind you. You get to say your piece, but you don't have to wait for a court trial later on, and by pleading guilty, any sentence will be less than if you plead not guilty and are then found guilty. After all, you did do it."

"So, if I did this as you suggest, when do I do this part specifically, directly after I've pleaded guilty?"

"Pretty much. The court clerk will ask for your plea then the magistrates will ask if there's anything you want to say, and that's when you say you want to enter into a plea in mitigation. It gives everyone all the information from your side. But you get your say, Kit, that's the important part."

"I don't know, Natalie, it's a bit of a risk."

"It's a risk either way, Kit, but at least the sentence will be reduced and everything will go back to normal as soon as possible."

Kit folded the piece of A4 paper in two and put it in his apron pocket. It was certainly something to take into account and think about, and he was grateful that Natalie had spent the time doing more research, it was an option that he hadn't known about. Maybe he'd take her advice. He took her in his arms and held her close for a moment, drinking in her perfume and the feel of her body against his own. When he pulled back, he said, "I appreciate you doing that, Natalie, really I do. But let me think on it, eh?"

"You know I'll support you whichever way you choose, Kit Morris," she said, smiling. "Look, I'd better get back to the girls, they're in the car just outside, but I wanted to get this to you as soon as I could."

Kit put his arms around her shoulders again and pulled her in tight. "You're the best," he said. "I don't know what I'd do without you keeping me on the right course. I should have told you what I was thinking before I pulled off this stupid plan, you'd have known what to do."

"It's just what we do," she said, beaming up at him, not for the first time. "Now, let's not worry about it any more, there's plenty of time for talk later. Just make sure that you come home tonight because I love you, Kit Morris." She planted a firm kiss on his lips before turning so Kit couldn't see the tears welling as she left.

He watched her go then caught the eye of Ron Butcher, who was looking his way. The man got up off his stool and walked over.

"You and I should have a chat."

CHAPTER 63

Baker

Monday morning

Kit really didn't want to rehash the whole story again, particularly to Ron Butcher, a man he only vaguely knew. He was an acquaintance rather than a friend, but nonetheless, the man had overheard what Natalie had suggested. In fact, he'd overheard the whole conversation, and it was obvious he knew something serious was up. Maybe the man could help him? Though he didn't quite know how. But since Ron had been a loyal customer, he figured what the hell.

He moved his chair closer to Ron's, and they sat huddled together, looking almost conspiratorial. Kit told him the sorry tale about the business needing money, about the car, about his ex-business partner Darrel, the false documents, the cash, and all the shit that had happened since then. He wasn't proud of it as he recited it yet again, and it seemed pathetic and stupid to be telling the whole story out loud. On that, Natalie had been correct, it had been a poorly thought out plan; they could have found a better way to raise the cash.

"So, tell me about Darrel, then," Ron said as he bit into his second doughnut. Sugar settled on his upper lip, but the man did nothing to remove it.

"We were friends and then business partners, and everything was going just fine. And then we had a hell of a row one day, mainly over our expansion. He didn't want to do it, I did, and we just couldn't see eye to eye on it. If we were to grow a business for our families, something to hand down to the next generation perhaps, then we couldn't do it with just one big store. I want to open six or seven, go national if I can, but I'm hamstrung without finance." Kit took a breath and remembered Lee Meady. "Though I did meet a chap in here a couple of days ago actually. He's the CEO of a bank, reckons I've got a great product and said if I didn't get the funding I needed, I should give him a call. But I digress," he said, getting back to the story. "So, we had a stupid row. Then we had another and another and another until it got to the stage where we just hated the sight of each other, which didn't work for either of us being in the same place all day. The staff didn't like it, and our customers could sense the tension between us, so I scrabbled some money together and bought him out. Just before we went our separate ways, I sold my car to him. He made one payment, and I stupidly signed the documents over. He never paid me another penny."

"And that's why you decided to steal the car back," Ron finished the sentence for him, "because you figured it was still yours. I get that, I would probably have done the same. But it didn't go according to plan, then?"

"No, it didn't," said Kit. "Hence why I'm up in front of the magistrates this morning."

"So, did you do it all on your own?"

"No, I had help, but I'm not going to admit that to anybody else, there's little point. It won't reduce my sentence, and it is all my doing."

Ron nodded his approval. Kit was loyal.

"But somehow this Darrel man figured what was going on, that it was you?"

"He saw me move the car apparently. What he didn't know was that I'd already seen what he'd got hidden in the boot."

Ron tilted his head enquiringly, "And what was that?" he asked.

"Not sure if I should say really. No offence."

"None taken. I'm just being nosy really and trying to help you out at the same time. Sometimes it's good to talk, and it's an intriguing story," he said, smiling. It was one of the few smiles Kit had ever seen Ron offer.

"Oh, what the hell," said Kit, "it doesn't matter now anyway. He'd got forged documents and a wad of cash in the boot – the documents had his photo but a different name. I guess he was planning to run off someplace, I don't know, I haven't asked him."

"Or maybe he's just planning to use them to buy something, a property maybe. What's his surname?" Ron asked almost nonchalantly.

"Poynter, Darrel Poynter. Why do you ask? Do you know him?" Did Kit detect a little recognition of some sort?

"I'm just thinking," Ron said, finishing the last of his doughnuts and licking his lips. He wiped his fingers on a serviette before carrying on. "I once knew a man that dealt with false documents. I wondered if this Darrel had perhaps got them from him, being local."

Kit shrugged, he'd no idea. "So, that's really where we're up to, and I'm in court later. Maybe I'll see him there; he got arrested over the weekend too. I'm sure they'll have charged him with something."

"Well, if they have the documents in his boot, he will at least have been charged with 'possession with intent to use' or something like that. Or even 'using a false instrument', I think they call it. I guess it depends if they can prove he's used them or was planning to. Not that you don't use false documents you lashed out hard-earned cash for. As for the cash, did the police think it was yours?"

"I told them it wasn't mine. They'll not find my prints or DNA on it, and I wouldn't be stupid enough to drop myself in it by mentioning what was under the tyre unnecessarily, now, would I? They believed me, it fitted with Darrel's problems rather than mine. He'd likely say he was saving for a holiday and can keep his cash wherever he wanted to, no harm in that. Unless it's traced to a crime say, through serial numbers or whatnot, what can they do about it?"

Ron grunted his understanding as he listened.

"You seem to know a lot about forgeries, though, Ron."

"I know a lot about a lot of things. It's my business to know." Ron smiled for the second time. As he stood to leave, Kit once again marvelled at how such a slim man could eat two doughnuts for breakfast, day in, day out.

"I don't want to keep you any more, Kit, and I've got things to do, people to see, as they say. So, good luck later. I'll be thinking of you."

"Thanks, Ron, I appreciate it. When this is all over, can I buy you a pint sometime?"

Ron nodded his approval then headed out to his own car parked out front.

Once in his Lexus, Ron wasted no time in dialling Felix.

"We might have some trouble," he said when his son answered.

"What?"

"Did you supply some docs to Darrel Poynter by chance?"

"Name doesn't ring a bell. What name was he using on the docs, any idea?"

"No, I don't. Do you think your mate Barry could have done them?"

"First off, Dad, that weirdo's not my mate, he's a dirty paedo. And I guess it could have been. Why?"

"Can you find out for sure?"

"If you really want me to. Why the interest?"

"Just trying to do a favour for somebody, trying to do the right thing."

"You gone soft in your old age?" asked Felix.

"Don't get cocky. I'm always your father. Remember that."

Felix chuckled and said, "I'll see what I can do."

CHAPTER 64

Banker

Monday morning

Bethany felt as if she hadn't slept in days, which was because, in reality, she hadn't. It was beginning to take its toll on her, but there was little she could do. At least she was back at home now and not sat in a cell, which is where she would have been if she'd admitted the offence to the detectives. Blake had worked his magic, and both Lee and Bethany had been able to sleep in their own bed. A little after 7 am, she was making coffee in the kitchen when Lee came down the stairs. She'd decided not to go into work though wouldn't tell her boss the real reason why. How could she say she'd been answering questions at the police station in relation to killing a woman? Keeping her job was the least of her worries right now.

She poured a mug of coffee, took it to the window seat, and watched the light coming up from behind houses and trees in the distance. At least it wasn't raining, but it wasn't set to be a nice day either. She felt Lee's hand on her shoulder and ignored it, waiting for him to remove it. Finally, he moved away from her without saying a word. They'd rowed and then rehashed the whole thing over and over again until the wee small hours when there was nothing left to say. They were barely speaking to one another. Behind her, she could hear him making himself something to eat.

"Would you like a slice of toast?"

A peace offering, perhaps?

She doubted she could get it down into her empty stomach that was churning like the ocean in a storm, but she knew she needed to at least try and so accepted. "Have we got any marmalade?" she asked. The bitterness of the rind might be less queasy on her stomach than sugary jam.

"I'll check," he said. "The sugar will help, good idea."

That hadn't been what she'd been thinking, but it didn't matter; she went back to her coffee.

She'd stopped googling careless and reckless driving offences sometime ago, not able to bear the stories she'd discovered, the number of drivers that had been sent down for long sentences, hardly any of them had got off scot-free. It made depressing reading, but had the boot been on the other foot, had someone hurt or killed one of her loved ones through their careless actions, she too would have wanted the full weight of the law to fall down on them.

Lee handed her a piece of toast, and she bit into it, forcing it down to soak up the acidic coffee that lay there. Her stomach hurt from being continually clenched with stress, and the amount of coffee and alcohol she'd drunk since her arrival back home last night hadn't helped. Lee sat down beside her and sipped his own drink in silence. She knew he was probably wondering if it all did come out, how it would affect his life, his work even, as well as what it would be like living on his own for a period of time while she was in prison. How would he cope with his high-pressure job as well as the house? Perhaps he'd move into town? Would he bother?

They might have both been released last night, but would the police find more evidence of their involvement and come knocking again? There were so many unanswered questions floating around, bashing and colliding inside her skull, each one demanding an answer that she couldn't give it. She felt like ripping the top of her head off and throwing it against the side of the wall to keep the thoughts at bay. But that was only something that happened in stupid cartoons. Hopefully her day in court would never come.

Lee reached across and took her hand as they sat together watching the morning light rise. The slight contact made her shiver inside, and she fought to overcome the sensation without outwardly showing any signs of her discomfort.

Lee had put her in this upsetting and stressful position, and she was starting to feel a bitterness developing deep inside. Some days he was the kindest man, attentive, loving, and giving, and yet other days he was the polar opposite, particularly if he'd had a drink or two.

Like Friday night...

Perhaps she needed to go away for a while, take a break, but would that draw attention from the police? It was okay for Lee, he had his own ways of coping and relieving his stress. He thought she was oblivious to his extramarital relationships, but on that he was wrong. After finding a condom in his jacket pocket one day, she'd installed a tracking app on his phone. The same hotel location had shown on several occasions and confirmed her suspicions. Just before she'd removed the app, she'd visited the hotel and waited outside in the car park. On that particular evening, there had only been couples and single men leaving around the same time as Lee had. It explained a lot. What was strange, as she sat there thinking about it now, was that she didn't feel unsettled by it any longer. Had she those few weeks ago though?

She was conscious of his voice dragging her back to the moment.

"I'll see you later," Lee called, all business, briefcase in hand.

"Bye," she said without turning. And he was gone.

It was going to be another grey day. Heavy slate-coloured clouds hung in the distance and looked almost as heavy as her heart. She hoped neither would burst any time soon.

CHAPTER 65

The police station
Monday morning

There hadn't been much of a lie-in for Amanda or Jack. They were both in at the usual hour, sipping their drinks from the coffee cupboard. The air was filled with disappointment, and even though Amanda had tossed and turned thinking for much of the night, neither she nor Jack had come up with any other further ideas to investigate. The foul weather had washed away any trace evidence there may have been, and Lee Meady had cleaned his vehicle. They had nothing but a mobile phone pinged on a road the Meadys had admitted travelling along anyway. They had nothing.

"I'm going to have a chat with Felix Butcher," said Amanda. "Just to ask the question, for my own sanity."

"I doubt it will help your sanity when he tells you Melody hadn't scratched his car."

"No, but if she had..."

"It would make you think the Meadys weren't involved? Were perhaps innocent? Unlikely."

"Something like that. Hey, maybe they are innocent. Like you said on Sunday, while we watched Blake Kipple arrive, people get accused all the time."

Jack nodded, but he wasn't convinced. The door opened to the tiny room, and Raj popped his head around it. "Room for a small one?" His customary pale blue shirt dazzled against his dark skin as he slipped inside, not waiting for permission to join in. "What's happening? It looks like a funeral in here."

"Drowning our sorrows in coffee," said Amanda sullenly.

"The hit-and-run driver, I'm guessing?"

"The same."

"It's the tough part of the job, I agree. But, on the flip side, there's the huge amount of other cases we solve every year. I know your victim wouldn't say the same, nor her family, but sometimes we just can't get to the bottom of it, no matter how much we want to or how hard we try."

Amanda stared at the floor as Raj's words sunk in. She knew he was right, but Melody Holden hadn't been a simple burglary or a broken wing mirror. She'd been a young woman who'd been killed.

"Well, I'll not let it rest," said Jack. "We might not get the driver responsible today, but there's always another time."

Amanda and Raj both looked at Jack, their eyes catching his in turn, and they knew he meant it.

Amanda threw back the last of her coffee and said, "Come on, there's plenty of other cases we can be working on. I'll go and see Felix anyhow, just to be sure. Then we move on, agreed?"

"Yes, boss," said Jack. They had no choice but to.

Amanda had never actually met Felix Butcher in person but had seen him from a distance. While he didn't scare her, she wasn't particularly looking forward to asking him about a scratch on his vehicle. She'd phoned first and arranged to meet him at home, the house he shared with his dad, Ron. Having parked on the drive, she'd approached the front entrance then stopped a moment to admire the huge fountain where water tinkled down the stone layers. The sound was almost therapeutic, and she was tempted to dip her fingers in and swish them around, as if to test the temperature. The front door opened, and Ron Butcher stood watching her. Ignoring him, she carried on in her own world until he was standing beside her.

"I love the sound of it," he said. "I'd like to be laid to rest by a fountain when I go, so I can listen to the bubbling permanently."

There was something in the way the man spoke that made Amanda think his wish might be imminent.

"You've come to see Felix, I believe. Come on in, he's out the back."

Amanda followed Ron right through the house towards the far end that Felix officially called his home. Opening a door off the kitchen, Amanda found herself in another, much smaller kitchen that was decorated quite differently to the older man's. Felix looked up from reading the newspaper and, without standing, simply said, "Hello." Amanda introduced herself. Ron stayed put in the doorway. It didn't really matter whether he heard the conversation or not, and at this stage, the reply didn't much matter to the closed investigation either.

"What do you need?" he asked rudely. "I thought you lot had given up on the case?"

How the hell did he know that so early on? They'd only let the Meadys go last night.

"Only through lack of evidence, not because we want to."

Ron scoffed behind her, and she felt him leave, though the door remained open.

"One last question to tidy away though," she said. "Do you ever recall Melody scratching your Range Rover at all, or maybe the Jag? Maybe with her bag or belt or some such?"

Felix rose from his chair with a face like thunder. Amanda guessed what he was thinking.

"Relax, Mr Butcher, no one is accusing you of having anything to do with the accident," she said hurriedly, her palms and splayed fingers out front in defence. Felix backed down, and Amanda breathed a sigh of relief. "If you could just answer the question though. Like I say, it's needs to be tidied away."

Felix sat down but stayed quiet for a long moment, and Amanda wondered what was going on in the younger man's head. Surely he hadn't had anything to do with it?

"She did cause a small scratch, but it's all fixed up now," he said finally, meeting her eyes. "I was livid at the time since I'd not long bought the damn thing, but it was repaired quickly enough." Amanda wasn't sure whether to be happy or sad about the news.

"Do you know how she did it?"

"Fooling around with that boyfriend of hers, she said. I suspect it was more than fooling around, if you understand my meaning."

"Where was the scratch?"

"On the back door of the Range Rover. If her belt buckle did catch it, she'd have to have been facing it, boyfriend behind her."

Amanda tried not to envisage the scene too clearly. If Melody had been wearing the same belt, it was another explanation though.

Damn it!

"And you say it's all repaired now? Do you have the invoice for the repair?"

"All sorted. And yes. Do you want to see it?"

"Please."

Felix left the room without a sound and was gone for a couple of minutes. When he returned, he slipped Amanda the receipt. There, in blue and white, was the repair for one scratched boot door. It was dated some weeks back. What were the chances? Had they got the Meadys wrong after all? Had they been telling the truth?

"Does that answer your question?"

"It does, thanks," Amanda said, handing the receipt back.

"So, they drive a Firenze-red vehicle of some sort, do they?"

Amanda tried not to show her surprise. The man was quick to figure things out.

"I'll be going. Thanks for clearing that up," she said and moved to leave.

Standing quickly, Felix shouted, "We'll not let this go, even if you lot do," as Amanda headed towards the door.

There was nothing she could do except say, "Thanks for your time," and hope Ron wasn't going to berate her too as she walked through. Thankfully, he was sitting with his vape pen looking peaceful. "I'll show myself out."

"You do that."

CHAPTER 66

Amanda
Monday morning

It was almost 8.00 am, and Amanda needed some air after her brief meeting with Felix so she drove into the town centre rather than back to the station. The man could be an intimidating character, as could his father, Ron, but she'd kept her cool as well as the upper hand. Felix had been quick to put two and two together with the car colour they'd been searching for. Now though, with another reasonable explanation of where the paint on Melody's buckle had come from, there was doubt as to whether the Meadys had been involved at all.

Perhaps Amanda had been too hasty in bringing them both in for questioning with so little to work with, but that was often the case with hit-and-runs. She'd hoped one of them, probably Mrs Meady, would have cracked and told the story of events that had happened that night, but it hadn't been the case, the woman had stayed strong and admitted nothing. Their smart lawyer had then pulled on the dangling threads of what little evidence they'd obtained until it unravelled like a ball of string. She would not make that amateur mistake again.

Amanda opened the door to the bakery and stepped inside. Warm bread mixed with the aroma of coffee, two of her most favourite aromas in the world, and she approached the counter. A red-haired man with a friendly face stood there, and for a moment, Amanda was mesmerised by the man's freckles, he had hundreds.

"What can I get you today?" he asked.

Amanda paused for a moment to browse the cabinet. It all looked so good. As if reading her mind, he said, "People say our jam doughnuts are the best, if you're unsure what to have?" His eyes twinkled as he spoke; Amanda didn't doubt his word.

"In that case, I'll have one to eat here, and can you do a box to go, maybe a dozen?"

"Coming right up," he said and turned to put one on a small plate for her. "I'll pack a box up for you. Are you having coffee, perhaps?"

"Why not. Cappuccino, please."

"I'll bring it over, take a seat."

Amanda turned to do as he suggested and headed over to a vacant stool by the window. Like many, she found people-watching therapeutic and sometimes enlightening. No sooner had she sat down than a voice she recognised greeted her from behind. Turning, she came face to face with Blake Kipple, his moustache the size and shape of a small banana as he smiled.

"I thought it was you, detective. Taking a break from fighting crimes on the streets of Croydon and beyond, are we?" A small section of his expertly styled grey hair had come adrift and was dangling unattended to, off to one side. She was tempted to reach out and put it straight, tuck it back behind his ear. His suit, as always, fitted him perfectly, but then made-to-measure was meant to. His shoes shone as brightly as her own Docs did.

"Taking some doughnuts for the team actually, the team that worked so hard on a recent case." She couldn't help the sarcasm that dripped from her words, she meant them all. At that moment, a tray of cakes to take away and her own refreshments were placed by her side. Kit left quickly, no doubt sensing a little hostility between the two. Blake eyed the box suspiciously but nodded his approval.

"The best in town."

"So I believe." After a long moment, Blake still hadn't moved on and she asked, "Is there something I can do for you, Mr Kipple?"

"Me? No. Simply being pleasant, that's all. There's no point in being rude when you're on opposite sides, now, is there? And we are often on opposite sides, you detectives and myself." He leaned in almost conspiratorially and added, "We both want justice, but we have to make sure there isn't an *in*justice during the process. Wouldn't you agree, detective sergeant?" he said, smiling, before delivering a two-fingered salute like he was a cub scout. Amanda wanted to roll her eyes but refrained. Jack's words about never knowing when you might need someone like Blake Kipple entered her head, and she smiled in acknowledgement instead.

"Indeed. Now have a nice day," she said, dismissing him.

He took the hint, returned another beaming smile, and headed for the door, leaving Amanda shaking her head. She turned back to her coffee and doughnut and watched him walk off, no doubt towards his car parked nearby. "Fighting crimes on the streets of Croydon," she mimicked, then smiled again. It was the sort of thing Jack would have done. Blake Kipple likely knew either one of the Meadys had been guilty of driving and hitting Melody Holden that night, and just like Jack, Amanda had suspected it had been Bethany. Since her chat with Felix, she was no longer so sure. It was finished now though, there was nothing else to be done but focus on something else she could still put right. Ten minutes later, she'd finished her doughnut and the last of her coffee, then headed back to the counter to pay.

"You know him, do you?" Kit asked. "Only he comes in here regularly, though we've never really spoken."

"You could say that, though I hope I never *need* him," she said, "Blake Kipple is a criminal solicitor," she added with a grimace.

Leaving Kit open-mouthed, she gathered the box of doughnuts and headed for the door herself.

He wondered if he might meet the man again later. In court.

CHAPTER 67

Baker

Monday morning

At 8.55 am, Kit Morris made his way up the front steps of the magistrates' court with bats beating a hole inside his stomach. He needed the toilet again, not that he'd much left in his system, and he felt nauseous and dehydrated all at the same time. The inside of his mouth felt like the bottom of a birdcage. He paused at the smeared glass front doors. They needed washing. It amazed him that even at a time such as this, he was criticising the ugly building's cleaning standards. He pulled a door open and went inside. It was time.

Far from what he'd seen on TV shows, there was no grandeur in this town courthouse. Instead, the halls looked more like Saturday night in a busy A & E department without the blood and bandages. Individuals from all walks of life were hanging around, some seated, many simply wandering almost vacantly as they either killed time or checked in with a court usher upon arrival. Kit stood for a moment to take the scene in. Monday was the busiest day after a weekend's brawling and petty crime, and that didn't include those, still banged up in police cells, who were deemed a tad more dangerous to have out on bail than a drunk. Homeless people gathered in a corner, in no rush to go anywhere and finding warmth for the day. Nobody was bothered, nobody moved them on.

As Kit moved further along, a different breed of human being was evident. Men and women smartly dressed in designer labels, with privately funded solicitors in tow, gathered outside a particular courtroom: traffic court. No doubt they'd quickly pay their fines and scurry off back to their day jobs, moaning at the inconvenience of it all. Hadn't the courts got better things to do, like sentence murderers and rapists? It was a travesty of the current government and a waste of public money, they'd say.

And then there was Kit and a handful just like him.

The whole place was stuffy, overcrowded, and claustrophobic.

Kit found his voice and asked a nearby usher which court he should go to. He gave her his name.

"Court ten. Wait to be called."

"Any idea when that might be?"

"None. Just wait to be called." And then she was gone. Staring after her as she hurriedly walked, files and documents balanced within her thin frame and arms, he ambled towards his designated courtroom and took a seat to wait. It was 9 am. Proceedings would start soon enough. He hoped the magistrates had a short list to get through but, more importantly, that they were well fed and in decent moods.

From his seat, Kit dared not move and used his phone to entertain himself while the clock ticked on. Others joined him nearby, everyone in the same holding bay and no doubt hoping it would be a quick visit. A tannoy directed someone to the cells, and Kit wondered how many people were down their waiting their turn in the queue, them likely to be first on the magistrates' list, way in front of him. If you ever found yourself detained from Friday lunchtime, you'd be in that pokey cell until round about now. Monday was the first opportunity for those refused police bail, the really rough lot, and those who had been rounded up and held after they'd failed to attend their court appearance. A woman's voice broke into his thoughts as he scrolled aimlessly.

"What ya here for?" He looked up into a face of spots, topped off with a head of greasy hair. Her breath smelled of cigarettes and mints all mixed up, the mint not up to the job of totally disguising her habit. She sat next to him and tried the question again. "Well?"

"I'd rather not say if you don't mind." He went back to his phone in an attempt to dismiss the woman, but like a leech, she clung on to him.

"I'm here for being drunk, again," she giggled. "I'm making a habit of it."

"Right," Kit said, not sure what else to add. Then he thought about what she'd just said – she was a regular. "What's the process then? How long do we all wait?"

"Relax, it'll be ages yet. Gotta get them from the cells done first. Depends, like, but a good couple of hours yet. Or, might not even get to us. Had that before."

"Pardon?"

"If they run out of time, like. Might have to come back again. Happened to me last time."

It wasn't the news Kit wanted to hear. After psyching himself up and researching until the wee small hours, and with Natalie's extra effort, he wanted to get it over and done with, preferably today. "I hope not."

"Where's your solicitor? I ain't got one. Well, I have, the court one. He's a bit shit though."

That was precisely why Kit was taking his chances on his own. His only experience with the duty solicitor had not been a great one, and the court one would likely be about the same. They were barely paid for their time, he knew that from experience. Who in their right mind would want to do the job when the more lucrative private practice called? You got what you paid for.

"I'm representing myself," he said and left it at that. The court door opened, and a female usher called a name. A youth walked towards her, his trousers hanging off his skinny hips, threatening to fall to his ankles. He yanked them up with both hands. Kit could see ink on the lad's knuckles as he passed, DIY tattoos. He disappeared into the courtroom, and Kit and his friendly cling-on stared after him.

"That's a good sign," she said. "They've started. Fancy a coffee?" Kit assumed from her general shabby appearance that she was asking him for one rather than offering to pay herself. "There's a café. Coffee's okay. Not like I'm a connoisseur," she said, laughing. Not wanting to lose his place if he was called, he stood to retrieve his wallet and took out a note. Unsure as to whether he'd see the coffee or the change, he handed it over.

"Get us both one. With sugar for me."

He watched the note disappear into her palm and returned to scrolling through his phone as she strolled towards the little café. He breathed in clearer air and resumed his wait.

CHAPTER 68

Baker

Monday morning

He never saw the young woman again nor his £10 note. He'd been had. Even while he'd been sitting in the court waiting room he'd been scammed. He guessed people like her preyed on people like him, those with more important things on their minds. With little knowledge of the system, he was literally a sitting target, and she'd known what to do. He hadn't wanted to lose his place and risk not appearing in court and have that count against him. From the young woman's perspective, it had all worked perfectly.

Natalie had sent several texts asking for an update, but he'd no news to give her in reply. Part of him wished she was sitting beside him and another part, a larger part, was glad she wasn't. He didn't want her to see him so nervous and in what he hoped would be the worst situation they'd ever have to cope with. He still had his health, that was the main thing. Plus, he still wasn't entirely sure which way to plead yet.

The only time Kit moved was when the courts adjourned for

lunch at around one o'clock. He went straight to the gents before heading to the small café in the building to get something to eat. The curry smelled good so he bought himself a portion, and his stomach seemed to appreciate the gesture of proper food. By 1.30 pm he was back in his spot, refuelled and ready to wait. He just hoped it wouldn't be several more hours. He'd read and re-read the work that Natalie had put together for a mitigating plea so many times he could almost recite it rote fashion, but he took the page from his pocket once more and studied it again. Finally, with nothing else to do, he'd looked up the courthouse website and read some of the comments of people who had 'checked in' and been waiting on other days. The average waiting time at Croydon magistrates' court was between two and four and a half hours; he'd been there that already, it couldn't be much longer now.

There were only a few people left hanging around the waiting area. Every time the courtroom door opened, each lifted their head as the usher called a name. The woman in the doorway checked her clipboard. It was Kit's turn.

"Kit Morris," she shouted. "Kit Morris," she shouted again. This was it, his moment of glory. He stood and gave a polite nod as he headed her way, so she didn't have to yell his name down the corridor for a third time. The two went inside.

It was a nondescript room that contained a bench at the front, a few empty chairs, and a handful of other people hanging around that could have been solicitors or the general public, he wouldn't know. He didn't much care either. As per Natalie's instructions, he knew to introduce himself to the prosecution when he arrived so he asked the usher who he should aim for, and she pointed in a gentleman's direction. Kit headed over.

"Good afternoon," Kit said, holding out his hand to a man dressed in a sharp navy suit. He looked all of thirty years old. "I'm Kit Morris, I'm representing myself today."

The man shook his hand and introduced himself as the Crown prosecution solicitor. "Trevor Kipple," he said, "pleased to meet you."

Kit was grateful for his friendly comments, the man seemed polite enough. He wanted and needed to be on good terms with him because he had yet to demonstrate his sincerity.

"I know Blake Kipple, any relation?"

"That's my father, though we play for different sides. Makes for exciting dinner conversations," he said, smiling once again. Changing the subject to the business at hand, he asked, "Are you ready?"

"As ready as I'll ever be, I guess," Kit said, trying to smile a little.

"Good luck then," Trevor said and carried on to his seat.

Kit was pleased to see the faces of the magistrates that would decide his future from here on in. He scanned them quickly, giving a brief smile and a nod, hoping his politeness and sincerity would work. He got nothing back from either of the three. It seemed the one in the middle would be in charge, a woman. She looked to be around fifty-five, Kit surmised, with pale blonde hair cut in a short style that suited her serious face. He didn't doubt she saw some riff-raff to fill her hours; it must be a dour job at times.

All too soon, the proceedings were under way and the charge read out. The court clerk asked him how he wanted to plead. But Kit was still unsure and stood speechless in the dock for a moment. Even though he'd gone through this very scenario so many times in his mind, he really wasn't sure what to say now he was living it. To plead not guilty would not be telling the truth and would only delay things. And even though he didn't feel that he *was* guilty, he *had* taken the car that wasn't rightfully his. Not on the legal documents anyway. He thought about what Natalie had done, how much work she'd put together only this morning, and why she thought he should plead guilty. The clerk nudged him and asked him again for his plea. He was running out of time. He had to decide – and fast.

Finally, remembering what was written on the piece of paper tucked in his breast pocket, Kit found his voice.

"Guilty," he almost shouted. As the word left his lips, there was no turning back, and at that moment, something clicked inside of him and he knew he'd done the right thing. The magistrate looked directly at him and asked, "Is there anything you'd like to add?"

"A plea in mitigation, please, madam," he said clearly, though careful not to appear cocky.

Raising an eyebrow, she said, "Go ahead," and Kit tried to remember everything that was written down in his pocket, all the things he wanted to say, and in what order. It seemed the bench wanted to hear about certain things – without any waffle. He ran down the piece of A4 paper burned into his mind and started with his apology.

"I'm embarrassed to be here, and I really want to say sorry and do the right thing," he started. "My name is Kit Morris, I'm thirty-five years old, a self-employed baker and owner of a local store. I've got two young daughters and a rather lovely wife. My business is currently struggling financially, and it's as I fight to keep a roof over our heads that I find myself in the circumstances I am in today. My financial worries are not your concern, but they most definitely are mine. I sold the vehicle in question to my now ex-business partner sometime ago, and he paid just one instalment out of the three owed to me. I stupidly signed across the ownership documents and never saw any further money. I merely thought I could retrieve the vehicle and sell it on, then give him his first payment back and everything would be okay. I needed the money for my business expansion so that I can build a better life for my family, and I've pleaded guilty as I know I've done wrong. I have cooperated throughout and told the truth, and I'm extremely sorry for my actions. If I get convicted, I will likely lose my business, and that means my family will suffer even more. I'd just like to say again how extremely sorry I am that my own actions have led me here today."

When he'd finished, Kit hoped he'd said enough, covered the points he needed to without rambling or sounding insincere.

It felt almost cleansing to apologise and explain himself in front of the three blank faces in front of him, and Kit looked for a sign on each that he'd struck a nerve. They were likely poker players. Kit waited for what seemed like an eternity for a direction of what might happen next. One of the magistrates looked across at the prosecution and asked if they had anything to add.

"No, madam," was all Trevor Kipple said. He was happy that Kit had pleaded guilty and had told the story straight, as he himself had understood it. For Kit, there was nothing to add, nothing to subtract, nothing else for him to do but wait for his sentence to be handed down to him. It would take another hour for the magistrates to come to their decision.

CHAPTER 69

Baker

Monday afternoon

Kit was almost out of the court building when he heard someone yell his name from behind. From the tone, it didn't sound at all pleasant, and when he registered who it was something dropped to the bottom of his stomach with a thump. It was Darrel and he didn't sound too happy. Kit glanced to his side at a security guard that had obviously heard a name being called and had himself not liked the manner in which it was said. Kit wondered whether to turn around or carry on walking, and he glanced again at the guard before making his decision. He stopped and coolly turned.

"Hello Darrel."

"I thought I might see you here," he said. "You're a bloody joke!"

"Why don't you calm down and stop making a fool of yourself or even risk getting yourself in more trouble. If you hadn't been at my house swinging the punches, neither of us would be here today."

"If you hadn't stolen my car, neither of us would be here today. Get it right," he said vehemently.

Kit could see out the corner of his eye that the security guard was watching the altercation, hoping it didn't get any more heated in case he had to intervene. The older guy didn't look like he could achieve much on the intervention front.

"Anyway, I'm tired so I'm going to say goodbye now, Darrel. Let's leave it there, eh? Be sensible, go home."

"Like hell we'll leave it there. I could go to prison for this."

"That's not my concern, Darrel, you got those documents and cash for a reason. Nothing to do with me."

Kit had turned to walk away when he felt the first punch land on the back of his head. He went down instantly as the security guard made his way over to intervene and other members of the public stood well back. Darrel, it seemed, was intent on being a complete nuisance. Kit lay on the floor on his stomach for a moment, wondering what to do. He knew deep down that the best thing would be to get up and walk away, but now Darrel had assaulted him in a public place and there were witnesses. It was one time he was glad of CCTV camera footage being available should he have to defend himself. Again. He'd only just left one courtroom, and he certainly didn't relish the prospect of finding himself in another one, particularly after what the magistrates had just told him. He could be in a messy situation extremely easily. Behind him, he could hear grunts and voices as another security guard had come to the older guy's aid. The two men were escorting Darrel away, no doubt to a room somewhere to cool down or maybe even a cell downstairs. He didn't know, and he didn't care. He got to his hands and knees and rubbed the back of his head where he'd been punched. It was throbbing already. Eyes were suddenly averted and those that had just witnessed the scene made for the exit.

Thanks for your concern everyone.

A thin man standing by the far wall had seen the altercation. Darrel was obviously one angry man, aggrieved at being found out, his plans now scuppered, and a hefty charge to face. He was lucky to still be walking around and not be sitting in a remand centre. While it would have been nice to have a quick chat with Kit, Darrel was the one Ron Butcher was looking for. Kit had told him about the forged documents, and that meant Darrel's sentence could be up to ten years' imprisonment, the guy was looking at a long stretch. With that knowledge, maybe the man was looking to bargain too. He tipped a nod to the security guard, and two minutes later, Darrel was once again in the building foyer.

Ron followed him for a few steps before calling his name. Darrel turned, and recognising Ron's thin face, didn't say a word. Ron held out a Post-it note.

"Give this man Felix a ring. There may be something in it for you to reduce your upcoming sentence if you calm down and stop being such a prat."

"What's it to you?" Darrel stuttered, showing his nerves but trying to be the harder man.

"Calm your arse, and remember who you're speaking to." There was no mistaking the chill on Ron's words, and Darrel dropped his attitude in a flash. He took the piece of paper. It was just a mobile number. Nothing else.

"Felix is your son, right?"

"Like I said, call him, get it sorted."

Darrel scoffed slightly but started walking. Ron was tempted to follow him and give the man a slap for his attitude, but he had business in the opposite direction.

Even though home was a fair walk from the courthouse, Kit wanted the fresh air, having stagnated all day in a claustrophobic room that needed urgent refurbishment. That and the added stress of defending himself, and all that had gone on over recent days. He was completely drained. He needed a long drink and not more coffee. Walking away from the court building, he wondered where the nearest pub was and remembered the Slug and Lettuce not too far behind him on Park Lane. It wouldn't be too much of a detour from there to home afterwards. Natalie would be worried right now, he knew, but he just needed five minutes alone time and a long glass of something cool that would take the edge off both his thirst and his anxiety before calling her.

Entering the pub, he sniffed in the familiar odour of beer and wood polish and approached the bar. While he waited for his pint, he slipped his phone out. There was a message from the bakery and a couple more texts from Natalie. He listened to his voicemail; it was Elizabeth wanting to know if he'd be back that afternoon because there was an order that needed doing for supplies. She didn't want to do it on her own and get it wrong. Kit smiled at the mundane question; it was just what he needed. His pint arrived and he drained the first half in one long pull before licking the foam that stuck to his upper lip and wiping his mouth on the back of his hand. He caught the eye of the barman who raised his brows questioningly and smiled – he'd likely seen the look of relief and satisfaction many times before.

Kit called Natalie to tell her the news.

CHAPTER 70

Banker
Monday afternoon

Lee couldn't concentrate at work. Even though he'd arrived a little later than usual, after the stresses of being questioned by detectives the previous night, his blood pressure felt like it was simmering somewhere just above the top of his skull. He threw his pen down, exasperated, and watched it roll off the edge of his desk. Coffee wasn't going to fix his wound-up state, but he knew one thing that would. He'd find an excuse to leave the office.

He sent a brief text and waited for a reply.

In the daytime, so unlike you! Love to, same place as usual?

He tapped back.

Yes. How about 1pm? I'll arrange it.

Perfect. See you then.

Lee sat back and smiled to himself. He'd feel much calmer later on he knew, his liaisons did that to him, and if anybody needed calming down today it was him. He thought back to Bethany and how she'd been at breakfast, distant somehow, in a world of her own even, but that was understandable under the circumstances. The questioning had been a stressful and upsetting experience for them both, and she'd likely find her own way to deal with it.

He made the hotel booking and checked his watch. He'd arrive with plenty of time to spare. Perhaps a soak in the bath would be a soothing appetiser. It had been a while since he'd last indulged himself.

After an afternoon with his lover in a hotel room, Lee made his way across the car park feeling much more relaxed, a smile on his face. Dressed in a sharp navy suit, he could have been any one of the number of businessmen that regularly met clients at the venue, although Lee's meeting had absolutely nothing to do with any business dealings. He clicked the key fob to his red Jaguar and slid inside. A moment later and Lee Meady pulled leisurely out of the hotel car park, heading home. Bethany would be thrilled to see him back so early.

Watching him go from the window, it struck Felix that the man he'd been seeing of recent drove the exact same car as him, and it was the same colour too. How he'd never noticed before, he couldn't think, but the realisation now was a jolt to his system. Since DS Lacey's visit earlier on in the day, he knew they'd been investigating the colour aspect, why else had she been so interested in the scratch on the Range Rover? Could it be a coincidence? Something told him it wasn't. He needed to find out more – and quickly.

It was two long hours before Felix finally had the answer and disappointment rippled through his veins. There was no mistaking it, only yesterday Lee and Bethany Meady had been questioned in relation to Melody Holden's death.

He needed to talk to Ron.

CHAPTER 71

Baker

Monday afternoon

Natalie, understandably, was ecstatic, and with a six-month suspended sentence and a hefty fine, Kit was happy enough too. It could have been a hell of a lot worse. Now he needed to make sure he kept out of trouble, and Darrel smacking him one on the way out was not a good start. All he had to do now was pay his fine and meet up with his probation officer when he was supposed to.

It did, however, look like his expansion plans were not going to materialise any time soon, but at least he still had an income, a business, and a family that was standing by him. He rested the remains of his pint back on the bar and stared into it as if the answers would somehow rise from the remainder of the amber nectar liquid. The barman kept his distance, he'd obviously seen people deep in thought or worried and knew to leave them be. Being a pub near the magistrates' court, he likely saw a lot of people drowning their sorrows or celebrating with relief. Kit felt the front door open and the breeze wash in. Instinctively, he turned to see who else was joining him late in the afternoon. Instantly, he recognised the vanilla vape trail of Ron Butcher.

"Hello Ron," said Kit. "What brings you over here at this hour?"

"I thought I'd see how you got on. I figured you'd be in here; most people are after a day in court, it can be a pretty stressful event." He leant his elbows on the bar and nodded to the barman who poured him a pint.

"Stressful isn't a word I'd use, it's downright nerve-racking and gut-wrenching."

"Yes, but you did okay on your own though, didn't you?"

"I did as it happens, but how do you know I was on my own?"

Ron tapped the side of his nose like he knew everything, and Kit didn't bother asking any further, knowing full well that the tentacles of such a man probably reached tight corners. A dark brown pint was set down in front of Ron, and it was a moment or two before he took his first mouthful. He drank it like a bird sipping from a bird bath, which seemed out of kilter with what the man emanated. In fact, the more Kit thought about it, Ron wasn't really a beer drinker at all but likely a spirits man. It was all immaterial anyway.

"So, what did you get then?" asked Ron, taking another sip.

"Six-month suspended and a thousand-pound fine. Not quite sure where I'm going to raise a grand from, but I'm not complaining. I'll find it somehow."

"Let me know if you struggle," said Ron.

"Thanks, Ron, but I can't afford your rates," he said, chuckling.

"We'll sort something out, got to keep the doughnuts rolling, and if you've got no money, I won't get my breakfast."

Both men grinned at that. It was a stupid business proposition, but it made some sense. "I'll let you know then."

"Whatever suits you," he said. "I'm just glad to help. I'd hoped to be in court myself this week."

"Hoped? Why, what's happened?"

"Disappointingly, I believe the driver that killed my Melody was released without charge from the police station last night. I thought they had their man. Or woman."

"Oh, Ron, I'm sorry to hear that."

"I wanted to see them in court, to look them in the eye. I wanted to cause them grief, grief like they've never experienced before." The words leaving his mouth were heavy with threat, and they chilled Kit to the centre of his body. "They took my diamond away, and I want to make sure they pay for it."

Kit knew Ron had a reputation, and he wouldn't want to be someone who'd let the man down. Whoever had killed someone close to him would be in danger.

"Melody was the young lady that died last week, I'm guessing." It was beginning to register with Kit, the penny dropping. "I'm so sorry Ron, I didn't know anything about it. I've been so busy with my own worries I haven't thought about anything else going on in the world. I wish there was something I could do."

"Thanks, Kit," he said. "But yes, that was my Melody, left on the roadside to die." Silence took over for a moment or two while each digested the sadness of it all. Then Ron picked up his drink and took a last sip. The atmosphere between the two men changed in an instant, back to normal as Ron said, "I just wanted to check in with you, so I'll be off." His phone was ringing.

Kit thanked him for his concern. Watching Ron slowly walk from the building, he wondered how he'd known he was in the pub. Had he been waiting? Following? And why did he offer him money? Just being friendly? Ron also knew what was going on with his niece's case, things Kit felt only the police might know. Had Ron somehow been behind his own case too? He thought back to seeing the man at breakfast.

"Whatever," Kit said resignedly and turned back to finish off the last of his drink before heading home.

Ron knew that Felix hadn't been telling the truth about whether he'd supplied the documents. Call it father's intuition, he knew the

lad well enough to know when he was fibbing. Even though Felix
hadn't been stood in front of him, his voice, his tone gave it away.
How many times he'd had to tell him he'd no idea, but it seemed
the message hadn't quite got into his skull. He wasn't a young lad
any longer but a grown man, he should know better.

He spoke to Felix as he walked. "Expect a call from Darrel
Poynter. You know what to do. Move the heat away from us, plant
it somewhere else, preferably somebody that should be locked up
anyway. Anyone that fiddles with kiddies is more than deserving in
my book. I don't tolerate that sort of behaviour, call it karma. But
get the job done, and make sure Darrel takes the initiative. I'll
manage things at this end, you just sort the message out."

There was a long pause before Felix finally spoke. "How did you
guess it was us?"

"Felix, I've been in this business long enough to know when
someone is not telling the truth. I'm just disappointed you didn't
tell me yourself."

"Sorry, Dad," he said, sounding six years old all over again.

"I don't know when you'll learn though Felix, that's my problem.
It's a worry. I'm not going to be here forever; life can be short, like
young Melody would testify to if she could, hers over already. She
hadn't the chance to even get hers going, so just be honest next
time when I ask a simple question."

There was no malice in Ron's voice, only sadness, and Felix
picked up on it. While he wasn't an old man, Ron felt much older
than his years and it was beginning to show. His bones creaked, his
muscles hurt, and often he was just bone-tired. But Ron kept going,
there was too much to do.

Now he had to make sure that Darrel Poynter's sentence was
reduced for giving up a counterfeiting paedophile. It wouldn't be
that hard.

*And it'd deflect the heat from his own involvement with dodgy
documents.*

Ten years in prison for counterfeiting wasn't much different to
what Darrel would expect to get for using the forged documents.

But once the police found the child porn that was no doubt on Barry's computer, as well as all the document-making gear itself, it would be an easy one, a gift from God they might say. If Darrel was stupid and didn't reach out to Felix? Well, then Ron would have to pay him a visit too. It wouldn't be hard to find out where the guy lived, and Ron could still be persuasive, he hadn't lost the knack.

He thought of his new friend Kit and the mess he'd got himself in. He liked the man —a good business head, a family man, a decent sort that didn't bullshit. In whatever line of work you were in, those traits were important. Ron would keep a special eye out for him.

"I'll leave it with you then," said Ron. "Don't disappoint me."

"Before you go, I've got some other news," Felix said, and he proceeded to fill his dad in with the details of a local man that drove a Firenze-red Jaguar.

"Good work. Leave it with me."

CHAPTER 72

Baker

Monday evening

By the time Kit had reached home he felt a lot better. The walk and pint had done him good, getting rid of the day's cobwebs that had clung to him from earlier. Natalie and his girls were waiting for him excitedly, and he paused for a moment in the hallway as everyone clamoured for a hug and a squeeze, and he enjoyed the moment. Damn, they all three felt great, and his heart swelled in his chest at what he had waiting for him. He'd go to the ends of the earth for any one of them – and then some.

"Dinner is nearly ready," said Natalie. "I thought you'd probably be hungry. I figured you may have missed lunch, so we'll eat early if that's okay?"

"I'm ravenous actually," he said. "I managed some quite nice curry at the little courthouse café, but because my stomach was in knots, I couldn't eat it all." He sighed with pleasure and relief at being home. "I'm absolutely knackered."

"Well, you will be, but it's all over now," she said, placing her hand in his and leading him down to the kitchen, the two girls back to their own play, whatever they'd been doing before he arrived home. With short memories and no idea what was going on in their father's life, everything was normal to them, and Kit was grateful for that. He flopped down on a kitchen chair.

"So, now I've just got to find £1,000 from somewhere, though I've no idea where."

"I can help with that," said Natalie, beaming.

"How?" Kit asked, surprised. "I know you're super amazing at times, but where are you going to get a spare thousand pounds from?"

"It's our holiday fund actually," she said. "I've been trying to put some away so that, when the holidays do come, we've got something to play with." Her face lit up with mischief.

"Natalie Morris, I've said before, and I'll say it again, you're the best. How much have you got squirrelled away?"

"About £1,500, so there's more than enough, still leaving a bit for later."

"Hell's bells!"

"I'll get it now," she said and busied herself in a cupboard before resurfacing with the cash.

"I'll take it tomorrow, pay the bill, and get it over with. Then it's finished, and I'm completely out of it."

She handed him the various notes, all stacked neatly.

"Thanks, I'll put it in an envelope in a moment," he said, laying the money on the table in front of him. Changing the subject, he asked, "What's been happening in your world? Tell me something that is nothing to do with my trials and tribulations. Literally."

And so she filled him in on the mundane things that had happened through her own work day, what the children had been up to at school, and their plans for the week ahead. Kit sat smiling like a cat with fresh fish for dinner and enjoyed the moment. Had it all gone quite differently, he could well have been waiting for a trial date and a stiffer sentence. He was glad he'd taken Natalie's advice with the mitigation plea.

After an early meal and having put the girls to bed, Kit announced he needed to pop back to the bakery and double-check everything was okay ready for the morning.

Jakub and Elizabeth no doubt would have done a good job, but still he had to be sure.

"I'll feel better if I just go and double-check everything, with so much going on my mind has been elsewhere. Do you mind?"

"Of course I don't mind, but don't be long, have an early night, eh?"

"Just a quick check and then I'll be straight back." Kit grabbed his jacket from the hall cupboard and pulled the collar up around his neck. The October evenings were getting chillier and chillier, but at least it wasn't raining as he ventured out to his car out front. He wondered what would happen with the Audi now – nobody had said anything. He'd likely never see it again, and maybe that was for the best.

A few minutes later, he pulled up outside the bakery, which was all in darkness, everything looking as it should do. He drove around to the small rear car park and sat for a moment thinking back to his meeting with Jakub only a couple of nights ago and what they'd been planning to do with the car. It seemed like a lifetime ago. The bright outside security light lit up the space as he let himself in and closed the latch behind him. He flicked the light switch on and headed to the storeroom-cum-office and made sure that the safe was locked properly. Glancing around the inside of the bakery, everything was as he knew it would be, all cleaned down ready for the morning. The coffee machine stood silent, the rest of the shop neat and tidy. He had a great team, and he enjoyed working with them. Kit pulled out a stool and sat in the window, in Ron's spot, for a moment, looking out into the shadowy street, street lamps giving an eerie glow as they always did. There wasn't much call for people up and down the street at night, but in the day it was a different story, and he couldn't wait to be back in amongst it first thing in the morning. No doubt Ron would be in for his breakfast as usual and maybe they'd have a chat again. He seemed like a decent bloke from the dealings he'd had with him so far, perhaps others had the man all wrong.

A homeless person shuffled by, unaware Kit was watching. All his belongings stuffed in an old shopping trolley, he'd be looking for somewhere to sleep tonight. Life on the streets would be lonely, monotonous, and downright cold at times, he figured. He wondered whether the man would spend the night in a doorway further along, or maybe double back and sleep in Kit's own doorway. Kit made a mental note to take him a coffee and something to eat if he was nearby tomorrow. And then he was gone, dragging Kit back to the present and his relief the case was over as long as he stayed out of trouble. Maybe he had Ron to thank for that.

Kit finally climbed into bed feeling a good deal better than he had the previous night. Natalie snuggled up to him and flung her arm protectively over his chest, and he felt good, secure, and more than that he felt loved. She was always there for him, always with the right answers when he needed them most. He hoped in the future he could confide in her more, but he didn't want to give her the worry, she had enough on her own plate with her job and looking after the family. She took on so much with his early starts, and he rarely saw the children in the morning, but their lives were richer for the parts they each played in creating a stable environment for one another. He silently thanked God as he stared up at the ceiling, then listened a while to Natalie's breathing. Tomorrow, he'd go back to the court and pay his fine.

While his court case was over and done with, there was still the small matter of finding funds for his expansion plans. Or maybe there weren't going to be any. Maybe that was just it, maybe there was someone or something telling him he should pull out while he still could, revisit the idea again in another year or so, when he was financially better off. Perhaps when interest rates changed, or when the economy picked up, or whatever the excuse would be at that time. Nothing was ever set in stone, but right now, it was time to forget it.

But as he finally drifted off to sleep, Kit was just glad to be at home in his own bed with Natalie lying next to him. He could have easily been spending his first night in a prison cell somewhere.

CHAPTER 73

Jack's place
Tuesday morning

Jack was just leaving home when his phone buzzed. It was Amanda.

"Hello boss," he said casually. "What's up?"

"I've just heard the strangest thing," she said. "We've had a tip-off. Well, the fraud squad have. They contacted me to see if I knew much about the man."

"Oh?"

"Apparently, we've got a counterfeiter in town, one making the illegal documents that were involved in a case with a man and a car theft over the weekend. One of Raj's cases apparently. The guy we had in here has been charged with various offences but wasn't giving up the name of his supplier, and then this happens. Not that I'm complaining. So anyway, long story short, the boys in blue have been round there, and guess what they found?"

"Let me guess," said Jack sarcastically. "They found counterfeit-document-making equipment."

"Go to the top of the class, but guess what else they found?"

Jack thought for a minute, wondering what she was prodding at, raking through what else could be in the man's home, a man that was into illegal documents.

A computer. What might be on that computer?

"Don't tell me he's got indecent photographs on his computer?"

"Hundreds, if not thousands, of them," said Amanda excitedly, "and by all accounts underage girls. And get this, Barry Cribbins isn't his real name."

"Barry Cribbins? I've never heard of him."

"No, you haven't, it was a false ID of his own making, but I know you've heard of Bernard Evans."

"Bernard Evans," Jack rolled the name over his tongue and through his head. "Where've I heard that name before?"

"Funny you should ask," she said teasingly. "Cast your mind back, a long way back, to the turn of the century, in fact."

"I wasn't alive at the turn of the century."

"Not the nineteenth century, the twentieth century," said Amanda, slightly exasperated. "Do your sums."

"I told you I'm crap at sums, but anyway, how do I know his name for goodness sake, or have I got to carry on guessing?" He could hear Amanda chuckling at the other end of the line. She was enjoying this.

"Remember when several girls went missing back in 1999, at Christmas time? Does Leanne Meadows ring a bell? Chloe was her sister. Dave Meadows went to prison? That Meadows?"

"Holy shit," said Jack. "That is a blast from the past. Bernard Evans ran off to Europe somewhere, and we never found him. No wonder if he changed his name. God only knows what he's been up to for the last however many years. And he's been in Croydon, here, making fake documents? Under our noses?"

"Yep, and he's anxious to cut a deal."

"They're all anxious to cut a deal, they all watch too much TV. I daresay he's shit-scared of going to prison, is he? Being a paedophile and all?"

"Well, he's looking at ten years plus for counterfeiting on its own, never mind the paedophile angle and whatever else might be on this computer. He'll likely stay there for the rest of his life."

"It's funny you should mention that case, though, because I was only thinking about Mary a couple of days ago. She was part of that screwed up mess, poor kid."

"Well, he's here at the station so I just thought I'd let you know, though he won't be going anywhere for a while yet. When they're finished with him, he'll be going straight to a remand centre. Good news though."

"Don't tell me he's got Kipple representing him?"

"I don't know, though I'd doubt it. Not many would want to represent a man with his background, it turns my stomach," she said, "I think it turns most people's stomachs actually." Changing the subject, she asked, "So anyway, that's my news, what are you doing now?"

"Well, I was going to run a quick errand, but I'm tempted to come back now and meet the scumbag that caused so much distress that Christmas. I wonder if he knows where his accomplices are? We only got one of them, and he resembled a burnt sausage."

"Now, you know you can't just rock up here and have a chat with him, serious crimes are dealing with it."

"No harm in watching though, eh?"

"I guess not. Well, whoever grassed him up did the right thing. At least he's off the streets now, so that's the best news this week."

Jack knew what Amanda was alluding to. He also wondered about the timing of the tip-off, particularly after all these years. He smelled a rat. Could Ron have had a part in it perhaps? Though what did he stand to gain if it had been him? Ron certainly wouldn't get involved if there wasn't something in it for himself.

Jack scratched his head, but only a speck or two of dandruff came to the surface.

CHAPTER 74

Baker

Tuesday lunchtime

Just after the lunchtime rush finished, Kit took the money and made his way across to the court to pay his fine. The sun had started to peek out from behind the thick dark clouds and provided a much-needed blanket of mild warmth. In another couple of hours, the temperature would plummet again for the night. The autumn days seemed to get colder and shorter as the years went on, and Kit wished it was spring that was coming and not winter.

He walked up the same steps he'd climbed nervously the day before and headed inside. He nodded to the security guard, the same one that helped rescue him from the grip of Darrel only the previous day. Searching around, it soon became apparent he'd no clue where he should head, and with no signs to direct him, he fell back to the security guard to ask.

"The machines have all gone, sorry. You have to do it online now."

"I thought there'd be a cashier or something," Kit said.

"A few years back, yes, there would have been. Then the machines came, and now there's neither. Progress, they call it," he offered, rolling his eyes to the top of his head and back, "though not having them makes my job easier."

"Eh?"

"Vandals."

"Right, of course," Kit said, nodding. "I guess I'll have to sort it online then."

"Sorry. Anyway, how's your head today?"

"Sore, but thanks for asking."

"Enjoy your day," the guard said, and Kit turned to leave. It was then he spotted Ron Butcher standing over by the wall, looking in the opposite direction. He checked his watch even though he already knew roughly what time it was – he hadn't been gone long and could spare a few more minutes. He wandered over and Ron turned towards him, no doubt sensing his arrival before hearing him.

"Hello Ron, what are you doing here?"

"Daydreaming at the moment, if I'm honest," he said, raising a tight smile.

Kit looked confused and cocked his head at his friend.

"Wishing the scum that took my Melody away was appearing today," he said with sudden venom.

Kit remembered Ron had said the same thing yesterday, in the pub.

Noticing Kit's confused look, Ron mellowed instantly and added, "No such luck. A spot of business actually, that's all. A client needed my help."

Kit noticed the man seemed twitchy, not quite himself, and not really in the mood to chat.

"What are you doing back in this hole?" Ron asked.

"Thought I'd pay my fine, but apparently you can't pay it here any longer," Kit said with a shrug.

"Progress, eh?"

"Something like that."

Kit couldn't help but notice Ron's demeanour and wondered what was going on in that head of his. Sensing Ron wasn't up for any more conversation, he made to go.

"See you in the morning then. I'll leave you to it," he said and reached out to give the man's arm a quick pat.

It felt like pure bone under his jacket sleeve.

CHAPTER 75

Baker

Tuesday evening

Kit felt like celebrating. Recent events could have been a lot worse and made him realise just how close he'd come to losing his business and his freedom. He needed to keep out of trouble for the rest of his life, not just for the next six months; prison was not a place he ever wanted to end up in. He turned to Natalie over dinner and said, excitedly, "Let's go out."

She scoffed light-heartedly and said, "Just like that? What about our two children?"

"We'll drop them at your mum's. They always want them anyway."

"But it's a school night."

"A missed day won't hurt them. Come on, let's do something spontaneous, let's go out for a couple of hours have a few drinks, get a taxi home. I just need to do something. *We* need to do something," he urged.

Natalie looked at him wide-eyed and open-mouthed, and he took the chance to encourage her.

"Go on, get yourself ready, I'll ring your mum," he said, and she didn't need asking twice. Giggling like a teenager, she ran up the stairs. It had been a while since the two of them had been out on their own. He turned to his two children, who were smiling excitedly, and said, "Hurry up and finish your dinner then we'll pack a little bag for you each and you can stay over at gran's. What do you say?"

"Yeah!" they chorused loudly. There was no disputing their enthusiasm.

Forty-five minutes later, everybody was in the car, backpacks packed. When they'd dropped the two off at their gran's for the second time in recent days, Kit turned to Natalie and asked, "Where do you fancy going first? The town is your oyster."

"A wine bar. Do we even still have wine bars?" she said. "It feels so long since we've been out."

"Then we'll find a wine bar, or whatever they're called now."

"But not a sports bar, not with a game on. Let's have a couple of nice drinks then find somewhere and have dessert."

She looked the happiest he'd seen her in weeks.

"Natalie Morris, you know how to push the boat out," he said teasingly, wrapping his arm around her shoulders as they laughed. It felt good.

One drink turned into another and then another, and it was almost eleven when they finally staggered out of the last pub, all thoughts of dessert long gone. Having had quite enough to drink and thoroughly enjoyed their impulsive time together, they walked in search of a taxi rank to get a lift back home. No doubt they'd have sore heads in the morning. Sometimes, though, you just had to let your hair down and enjoy yourself.

It was while they were walking that Kit thought he saw Lee Meady looking rather worse for wear. As they got closer, Kit could see it was definitely him in the shadows, the amber street lamps lighting up his face. Kit wondered whether he should approach him, check if he was all right. Would the man even remember him though? Still, something pulled at Kit and told him he should make sure Lee got home safely. He was about to call out when he noticed a young woman approach the man. A short conversation ensued, and something changed hands.

"That's the bank guy I was telling you about," he said. "For the loan."

"Well, he's been out having a good time looking at the state of him," Natalie said, laughing. They carried on a few more steps though Kit kept watching.

"What's going on over there?" he said, pointing. "He just gave her some money."

"Maybe she's a hooker?" asked Natalie.

"She's a rough-looking hooker. Anyway, you can't call them hookers any more. Not PC. It's sex worker now."

"Righto, I'll remember that for next time," she said, teasing.

As they got closer, Kit realised he recognised the woman. It was the same one that had fleeced him of the £10 note at the magistrates' court on Monday.

"Bugger," he said.

Natalie looked up at him enquiringly.

"She owes me ten quid."

"She owes you ten quid, for what? She doesn't look your type," she said, laughing.

"She scammed me that the magistrates', went to get us both the coffee and never came back with my money." As an afterthought, he added, "Though it does look like she could use it more than us."

"Looks to me like she just got paid anyway," Natalie said. "Whatever they're up to, don't get involved, just leave it alone. You don't know either of them." Natalie, the voice of reason. "Stay clear, eh?"

Taking her advice, they carried on past, got into a waiting taxi, and headed for home.

CHAPTER 76

Banker

Tuesday evening

Lee Meady had spent the evening drowning his sorrows. After arriving back from the office, he'd called Bethany to say he was meeting a colleague for a few drinks in Croydon, and he'd get something to eat with him. Bethany of course wondered just who 'he' was but had found herself really not caring. She'd enjoy her own quiet night in without him yammering on, it would soothe her still jangling nerves.

As it turned out, Lee was in fact all alone, there was no work colleague or anyone else for that matter. Being dumped by text was a coward's way to end a relationship, but that's exactly what Felix had done, and he wasn't returning Lee's frantic calls.

At around 11 pm, Lee staggered alone along the pavement, barely able to support himself, headed for the taxi rank. It was time to go home.

"Need a pick-me-up, mister?"

Lee struggle to focus on the thin face in front of him. Or were there two faces, both the same? He couldn't tell and blinked away the double image that eventually settled into one. She was spotty and not particularly attractive, not that he was looking for company or would even be capable in his state.

She spoke again. "A pill will see you right. Here," she said, holding out a small package that was mainly plastic film. "Only cost you a tenner. You'll be flying in a few minutes, not staggering," she said, smiling. "Take it." She pushed the tiny package towards Lee who was staring at it knowingly. He'd experimented a little in the past with Felix, though that was all over now.

He felt himself swallow the drool that was gathering in the corner of his mouth. His breathing was heavy.

The woman urged him to take the packet again. Her instructions were to make sure he took it, even if he didn't pay.

He'd certainly pay for it later.

"Here, I'll even unwrap it for you," she said, fumbling with it. The naked pill lay in the palm of her hand, and she again offered it.

With glazed eyes, Lee picked it up and slipped it in his mouth as the young woman vanished into the shadows.

Lee stood for a moment or two, waiting for the effects of it to take over. When they came, they were far stronger than anything he'd experienced in the past. His heart began to race rapidly as sweat beaded on his forehead, the rest of his body turning wet and clammy. He tried to steady himself, his breathing, to bring himself under control, but his heart rate spiked dangerously, bringing on a severe headache. A migraine? He grabbed his head in an effort to remove the pain. It was unlike anything he'd experienced before. He glanced around him, but his vision was distorted, sending a kaleidoscope of patterns to his brain, and he struggled once again to stay balanced, to stay upright. He failed and tumbled to the ground. Vomit rose from his stomach violently and flew out on to the pavement in front of him, and he shielded his eyes from the bright lights of the dim amber street lamps. He lay down on the cold pavement, unable to control what was happening to him.

Vomit met his sweaty hair while he lay there, closing his eyes tightly to chase the pain away, and the left side of his body turned numb.

To a passer-by, he looked like any other drunk sleeping it off in his own mess, though one in an expensive suit. No one touched him until the following morning, when a council worker tried to rouse him, and he was eventually taken away in an ambulance. Lee Meady had had a near-fatal stroke. Had he been able to think, he'd have wished himself dead, particularly with what was still to come for him. Left in a permanently semi-paralysed state, with double incontinence, unable to talk, feed himself, or even swallow food, he'd need continuous nursing care until he ultimately choked on his own secretions.

He would never be in control of anything ever again.

CHAPTER 77

Butcher

Wednesday morning

Ron needed to get back on an even keel. There'd been too much going on for his liking, and none of it much good. With Melody's death, he'd wanted his revenge, but discovering Felix already knew the owner of the car that killed her had been almost as hard for Ron to bear. Finding Lee and Bethany Meady hadn't been that difficult, though he would never know who had actually been at the wheel that night. Nor had it been difficult to come up with a suitable way to hurt them. The Meadys would experience quite how deep pain could be felt. Or Bethany would; Lee would lack any further experiences, his life almost over.

Ron parked up just outside Kit's bakery, and even though it was slightly earlier than normal, he entered the warm shop. The smell of baked goods and hot coffee fuelled him; he'd barely slept a wink for thinking about his niece and the injustice of it all. That a person could take someone so precious so easily and without penalty wasn't right. No one knew for sure what had happened in the car that night, whether the Meadys were drunk, whether they were over the limit with drugs, distracted arguing, or speeding. With none of those hard facts and the weather playing its part in destroying any DNA evidence, the case had been dropped. It was a travesty, for sure. He'd intervened though, and he felt better for it.

He nodded to the young, pale lad behind the counter.

Kit, who had seen his friend enter the shop, said, "Morning, Ron. Your usual?"

"Yes, please. Would you bring it over for me?"

"Of course I will. Take a seat."

Curiously, the man had never asked Kit to be a servant before, and he wondered what was different this morning. He watched as Ron made his way over to his usual spot in the window and thought about how much he seemed to have aged in the last twenty-four hours. He busied himself making coffee, pouring one for himself in case Ron felt like a friendly ear, and placed doughnuts on a plate ready to go. Balancing the two mugs and Ron's breakfast, he made his way over.

"Do you want some company?" Kit asked. "Because I can easily take my break somewhere else. I thought I could perhaps lend a friendly ear if you wanted to chat, you look like you need it. Up to you."

"I'm not sure I'll be good company, but it's your shop so sit wherever you like."

Not quite sure what to do, Kit went with his original plan and pulled up a chair next to Ron. "Are you feeling any better?"

"I feel like shit actually," he said resignedly. "But wheels are in motion and nothing keeps me down forever, so I daresay by the end of the day I'll be back to my old self. Then I have a funeral to attend later on this afternoon."

"I'm sorry to hear that, Ron. Events in life seem to come in threes, don't they? Whether they're big or small, whether you stub your toe and your teabag bursts or something major happens, the boiler bursting, a funeral to go to, it always happens in threes."

"That's not going to cheer me up," said Ron, glancing over and catching Kit's eye. He smiled despite himself.

"I'm obviously failing. Perhaps I should leave you to your breakfast," said Kit, getting up to leave.

Surprisingly, Ron took his arm gently and said, "No, please take your seat. I've got something to chat to you about anyway."

"Oh?"

"Have you had any luck finding the cash you need for your development?"

"No, I haven't. The omens are telling me to leave it be for now."

Ron nodded knowingly. "I've got a proposition for you."

With Ron Butcher and the word 'proposition', Kit wasn't sure where this was about to go. He raised both hands, palms facing Ron, and said, "I'm not being funny, Ron, but I can't afford one of your loans."

"I'm not offering to give you a loan, so you can put your hands down."

"What are you thinking then?"

"I've been coming in here most mornings since you opened. Whether you've noticed or not, I don't know. But what I've noticed is this place is always busy. You have great trade and another location would no doubt serve you well as long as you can get the funds. So, while I was lying there last night tossing and turning, I thought you might appreciate a silent business partner, one that would invest money only."

That certainly wasn't what Kit was expecting to hear, and it took him back for a moment.

"That's very generous of you, Ron. I must say, though, you've surprised me a little, and I wouldn't have thought silent partner was your style."

Ron managed another smile; he was getting used to them. He liked Kit because the man wasn't afraid of him. He talked to him like a bloke with no ulterior motive, no plan of his own, unlike some he dealt with. He trusted Kit, who reminded him of his own younger self.

"Admittedly," he said, "silent partner would be a new step for me. But, you know, I'm not getting any younger and aggro can be hard work sometimes. Felix has taken over much of the business, so I can pull back a little bit but keep an eye on things. Plus, I see an excellent future here for you, and sometimes it feels good to do good, if you understand my meaning." Ron thought back to a comment his Felix had said and smiled. "Maybe I am getting soft in my old age."

Ron gazed out of the window, the world coming alive around him, though for him, there wouldn't be much more life left. He hadn't told a soul, and never would, that it wouldn't be much longer for him.

"Give it some thought. I'm not suggesting half partners. But it would be an end to your problems, and I'd get a free breakfast every day."

Kit couldn't help but smile. "Give me twenty-four hours to think and talk to Natalie. I do appreciate your offer, don't get me wrong, it's just my last business partner and I... Well, as you know, it didn't end well."

"What's happening with him and the car?"

"He'll wait for his day in court, I expect, I really don't care about him now. Or the car for that matter." Kit allowed himself to drift away for a moment. It could have all been different for so many reasons.

Ron picked up on the change. "Well, you think about it, and let me know when you're good and ready. Now, if you don't mind, I'm going to finish my doughnuts and coffee off in peace."

Kit realised he was dismissed, though the man wasn't being rude. Ron wanted his breakfast time alone, and Kit would give it to him.

CHAPTER 78

The police station
Wednesday lunchtime

Amanda and Jack were in the squad room working on the copious amounts of paperwork that came with each case when the news came in. Lee Meady had been found lying unconscious in the street in his own vomit and had been taken to hospital. With a suspected massive stroke, it wasn't looking good for him. Jack wondered again at the timing of events. Amanda was quick to disregard his initial thoughts.

"If he had high blood pressure, he'd have been at risk of a stroke," said Amanda simply. "Add to that recent stressors... I doubt there's anything sinister in it, just bad luck and maybe even life choices."

Jack couldn't help but think about Ron once again. It all made perfect sense. Could he have dealt his own justice somehow?

"Sad for him, though, and her," he said. "Having to look after your spouse in that condition. If he ever gets home again that is. He might not. In which case, it's a nursing home until he dies."

They both fell silent for a moment thinking about what-ifs, though Amanda didn't share the same reasoning as her colleague. Anxious to lighten the mood, Jack changed the tempo and announced it was time for lunch.

"I'll grab some fresh air with you," said Amanda. "In fact, I'm sick of sandwiches, let's go and find a café somewhere."

"Whatever works for you," said Jack. "I'll be right behind you." They were heading for the door as he asked, "What d'you fancy, greasy spoon or something a little more upmarket?"

"Not greasy spoon," Amanda admonished almost sternly, "and neither do you." She nodded to his shirt that was pulled tight over his belly. "Your fitness test must be looming soon, and I suspect Mrs Stewart's already cooked your bacon this morning or was it Vivian?" she said with a wink.

"Sod that for a game of smarties, I'm too old for running shuttle tests, and it was Mrs Stewart actually, no Vivian this morning." But he couldn't help the grin on his own face. "Plus, I know just the place."

"You know just the place, do you?" she said, acting surprised as they walked towards the back door. "Vivian must be having a positive influence on you if you're inhabiting healthy-food-producing premises."

"She is, yes, so there's no need to take the mickey. A man can't live by lettuce alone, and the occasional bacon sandwich shouldn't be considered a crime either."

"No, but your bacon sandwich is punishing you by dropping fat deposits around your arteries," she said.

"Well, look at you. Gone all healthy yourself, have we?"

"Doesn't hurt to get a bit more in shape, particularly as I get older," she said. "And before you ask, I'm just being a bit more careful in what I consume, though I am taking an evening fitness class. For strength mainly." There, she'd told him. She awaited the ridicule.

Jack glanced across as they walked and nodded. "Good on you, Lacey," he said. "Fill some time too, eh?"

Amanda rolled her eyes. That wasn't why she was doing it. Her own work fitness test was looming, and she wasn't going to fail it. As they reached the car park, Amanda had her keys ready so Jack figured he would be getting in with her and not the other way around.

He made his way to the passenger side. "I'll direct."

Ten minutes later, the two pulled into a side street and parked a few places down the road.

"Where is it?" Amanda asked, scanning the area.

"Back around the corner," he said, leading the way back up to the main drag.

They stopped outside a small vegetarian place, and Amanda looked at him with eyebrows raised in wonder.

"No need to look like that," he said.

"But there's no meat in here. Plenty of lettuce leaves though," she said, pointing it out as if Jack didn't know what vegetarian actually meant.

He opened the door for her. "There are other tasty options actually. I've been in here a couple of times and they do a nice home-made baked beans with poached eggs."

Amanda's eyebrows seemed to stay at the top of her forehead as they entered, and she had to admit the inside did have a nice feel about it. For lunchtime mid-week it was particularly busy. She glanced around at the diners. There was no one wearing tie-dyed clothing or looking like an earth mother. Men in business suits, women in smart dresses, and children were all enjoying food without meat. Picking up a menu from the counter, Jack announced he'd stick to beans and eggs.

A pretty young waitress wandered over and took their drink order. She was dressed in earthy colours and wore an apron that looked like it had been made out of old sacks, though somewhat softer material than that. Jack couldn't help but notice the stud in her nose and wondered if it hurt to put it in. Did she take it out when she had a cold?

"Beans and poached eggs for me, please," said Jack and waited a moment for Amanda to peel her eyes away from the menu.

"I can't decide between the beetroot and pomegranate salad or..." She lingered on the 'or', stretching it out while she picked a second option to choose from. "I'll have the same as Jack, since he recommended it," she announced, satisfied with her choice. The waitress left to process their order, and Jack watched her go, long hair tied in a ponytail almost down to her waist. For a moment he thought about Melody, it would be her funeral soon enough. The young waitress was about the same age, though an earthy girl Melody Holden certainly hadn't been. Amanda called him back to the present. Knowing Jack as she did, she knew he wasn't being inappropriate in any way.

"Jack?" she questioned.

"Sorry, I was miles away."

"I know, I just wondered what you were thinking, watching her go."

"I was thinking about young Melody actually, and the fact it'll be her funeral soon. Maybe I'll go."

"Talking of funerals, did you ever get in touch with the next of kin of the old lady?"

"No, unfortunately it always rings out. But I spoke to the young PC that notified Nelly's family. She thought she might go to the funeral herself, with Nelly being her first dead body. You never forget your first, do you." It wasn't a question but a statement.

"When is it?"

"Later on today. I thought I'd slip out if it didn't get too busy. It's only local, but I don't suppose there'll be many in attendance. We'll make up the numbers a bit."

"You go and pay your respects if that's what you want to do. Goodness knows you're owed some time. When is Melody's funeral exactly?"

"I don't know, I'll have to ask Ron."

"Have you still got his number?" asked Amanda.

"I've got his current number, it's just whether it's still

connected. He switches numbers like I switch underpants. But he won't be hard to track down."

"She was a very popular girl by all accounts. I had a quick look through her Instagram account. She was pretty enough," said Amanda. "I haven't got time to spend on social media with this job. Perhaps I should try and make some..."

Jack knew exactly what she was thinking: somewhere to meet someone new, perhaps.

Amanda caught on quickly. "I know exactly what you're thinking, Jack Rutherford, but I know Instagram and Facebook are not dating sites."

It was his turn to raise an eyebrow.

Amanda carried on: "And I'm not going to be putting a profile on Tinder any time soon either."

"Never said a word," he said, teasing, before they paused the conversation for food to be placed in front of them. Jack tucked in straight away; he was famished. Amanda followed suit and took a mouthful, and Jack watched her reaction as she chewed and savoured the food. He noticed the slight wrinkle in her eyebrows again. She had such an expressive face and obviously approved of his choice of lunch venue. He smiled inwardly to himself but didn't say anything. Vivian had introduced him to the place a couple of weeks back, and they'd been in several times since, enjoying the variation from what he normally ate. She was having a positive influence on him, his mind and his body, and he found himself thinking about her for a moment and about how well they were getting on together.

A speech bubble appeared suddenly in his head with Janine in it, and he wondered what she would say if she could see him eating in a vegetarian restaurant and dating an ex-sex worker. In the bubble, Janine threw her head back and laughed heartily, blew him a kiss, and was gone.

CHAPTER 79

The police station
Wednesday afternoon

At nearly three, Jack picked up his jacket and, on passing her desk, told Amanda he was off and doubted he'd be back for the rest of the afternoon, unless something urgent came up.

"No problem. Enjoy yourself," she said absentmindedly, head down, fingers tapping away at her keyboard. Jack paused for a moment and wondered if she'd any idea what she'd just said. He was, after all, going to a funeral.

The drive to Mitcham Road Cemetery didn't take long, and he found a spot to park easily. He wasn't expecting many people to be at Nelly Raven's funeral service, and he was right. Only a couple of cars were in the car park so there was plenty of space for anybody that felt like they'd attend out of morbid curiosity, nothing better to do. Getting out of his car, he stopped to take in the weak sun. The afternoon was clear for a change, and it was one of the warmer days they'd had recently. He was in two minds about whether to take his jacket off or leave it on and opted for on. It could be cold in the chapel. Slowly, he made his way to the funeral of a woman he'd never known but nonetheless wanted to pay his respects to. Up ahead, he could see a uniformed officer and, as he got closer, realised he didn't recognise her. She must be relatively new around the station and likely the one he'd spoken to earlier – her first dead body.

He ambled up to her and made his introduction. "I'm DC Jack Rutherford."

"Hello, I'm PC Paula Gill," she said, showing perfect teeth that were even and brilliant white.

"Gill," Jack said rolling another name around his head. "I used to know a lady called Gill."

"Really?"

Jack pondered a moment longer. "That's it!" he almost shouted as though it was a eureka moment. "She used to work in the office, Maureen Gill, we called her Mo. Sometime ago mind."

"That's my mum," she said proudly. "She's one of the reasons I became a police officer." The young PC's face glowed at her mother's name.

"Really, how is she?"

"She's good," said Paula.

"Say hello to her for me, would you? I was very fond of Mo. She helped me on a case many years ago, at Christmas. We didn't catch all the culprits but we got three young girls home safely. It was a horrible time," said Jack, thinking back to the winter of 1999. "In fact, I might have a bit of an update on that one. We got one of the missing men in custody only yesterday as it happens. Perhaps you can tell her."

"I will, yes."

Jack began to grin. "You know, the one thing I remember about your mum is she always had a digestive biscuit on the go," Jack said, smiling at the memory of Mo Gill's ample cleavage, crumbs and all.

"She still does," said Paula and they shared a giggle between them.

"So, I'm guessing you're the PC I spoke to about funeral details. Your first body?" asked Jack.

"Yes, that's right, and since she was all alone, I figured she shouldn't have an empty chapel when she gets sent off."

"You were at the scene?"

"I was, yes, briefly, and I notified next of kin as well, although it wasn't actually me. I'm not long out of training as you've probably gathered, so I accompanied another officer."

"And who is the next of kin? Only, I've been trying to get hold of him, but he never picks his phone up."

"Quite a gruff chap," she said. "Although perhaps I shouldn't say that. But he didn't seem to be too bothered. A Derek Williams. I wonder if he'll show up today? He's cutting it a bit fine if he's coming." she said, checking her watch.

"Derek Williams. It doesn't ring any bells."

The young officer shrugged.

"We'd better go inside, it'll be starting soon," she said.

The two made their way into the small chapel, organ music playing gently in the background, though there was no sign of an actual organ. In the centre was a simple coffin that contained Nelly Raven's frail old body. Paula and Jack sat together in a pew three rows back. With so few in the room, it seemed pointless sitting right at the rear. A moment or two later the piped music stopped, and the minister made his way to the centre of the room. Jack could tell that he wasn't surprised by how few were in the congregation. He'd obviously popped his head out earlier, and with nobody there in attendance, would have already surmised the woman was either not liked or died without any family. It seemed almost a waste of his time to say anything at all. Margaret, Nelly's neighbour, turned from her spot and gave Jack a polite small wave, and he returned the gesture. The only other person, a man, faced the front. All Jack could see was the back of a greying head. But Nelly deserved to have a send-off whether there was anyone there or not, the council likely footing the bill. The minister proceeded through his delivery, but he had little to go on. How could he talk about a woman he'd never known when there was no family willing to tell him about her? He simply couldn't.

The whole sorry event only took about twenty minutes. The singing from four people, plus the minister himself, was pitiful, but they did their best, and Jack hoped that Nelly appreciated both his and Paula's attendance. As Nelly's casket moved through the curtains, it was all over, and they made their way slowly back out into the weak sunshine.

Paula spoke first and said, "Thanks for coming. I think she would have appreciated it."

"Good on you for having the heart and taking the time to come. You'll go a long way as a police officer if you think along those lines," he said, smiling. "From experience, you'll remember Nelly for the rest of your life. We all remember our first."

"Thanks, and nice to meet you. I'll tell Mum you said hello," she said with a bright smile. Adding a light wave, Paula headed back to her vehicle. Jack watched her go before the hairs on the back of his neck rose. A familiar vanilla fragrance filled his nostrils. As he turned, he came face to face with the owner of the grey hair that been sitting in the front pew.

"Derek Williams," he said, the penny finally dropping.

"And that's why you're a detective, Jack."

"Why the change?"

"I didn't want a connection to be made. Shall we take a walk?" he said.

"If you have time, yes," said Jack, "because I'd love to know the story, particularly why a man as wealthy as you allowed your mother to die so cold and alone." He was finding it hard to be civil under the circumstances, given how they'd found Nelly Raven, what condition she had been in, with a son, daughter, and nephew all nearby and more than able to help out. "Why don't you tell me what went on."

CHAPTER 80

The crematorium
Wednesday afternoon

As always, it was peaceful at the crematorium. As they walked through the gardens at a leisurely place, enjoying the last of the afternoon sunshine, Jack waited for Ron to open his heart and tell him the full story of just who Nelly Raven was. There were two or three minutes of silence before Ron spoke, and the first words out of his mouth surprised Jack.

"She was a selfish, mean bully and made our childhoods a living hell."

Jack let the silence carry on, not wanting to tread on Ron's thoughts as he processed them and told him about his boyhood.

"She'd always been a bully for as long back as I can remember. And Dad never intervened. I think he was too scared to, she was a lot tougher than most woman back then, physically and mentally. For punishment, she used to lock Teresa and me in the cellar. It was bitterly cold down there, and I remember sitting for hours and hours on end, trying my hardest not to cry, but when you're only five or six, that's really tough. And Teresa got just the same treatment as I did. For the slightest thing, Mum would fly into a rage, and we'd find ourselves in punishment. She was horrendous. I don't think I have any fond memories of her and certainly don't remember doing anything nice together like all the other kids did. It's no wonder I had to start looking out for myself and looking after Teresa right from an early age. When Dad passed on, he was lucky to be out of it. At one stage though, he thought he was rid of her. We'd have been about ten or twelve when Teresa and I got home from school one day to find her gone. Dad came home later. Apparently she'd left a note saying that she had run off and wasn't coming back, and secretly Teresa and I were chuffed. We were really glad. We hated the woman with a passion, and I don't think Dad liked her much either." Ron paused for a long moment before pressing on, the words obviously hard to confide. "Everything was calm for a maybe two years, and then, wherever she'd gone, she must have got bored or short of money because she came back and all hell settled in again, like she'd never left in the first place. I felt sorry for Dad having to put up with her coming back too, particularly after having a couple years of peace and quiet and some sort of normality and proper food. I don't remember Mother ever cooking a decent meal in all that time. Dad did his best when he got home from work. So, when Teresa and I got to do home economics at school, we did our bit to put food on the table. Thank God for school dinners, that's all I can say. Otherwise we'd have starved." Ron grinned, and Jack noted the boyish smile he remembered from their youth. There weren't many kids that appreciated school dinners.

"So, what happened next?" asked Jack. "When she came back."

"We had about six months of her nastiness again, her bullying and her cruelty. And then I lashed out one day since I was getting bigger, and she fell and hurt her head on the side of the fireplace in the lounge. We'd had an almighty row and I'd told her that we didn't want her in the house, and she tried to fight back, but she slipped. Knocked herself out, totally unconscious, and I remember looking down and thinking, 'Good riddance. I hope you're dead.' But she wasn't unfortunately. It was probably twenty minutes before she woke up, and boy, did I know about it when she'd regained her strength and balance. I've still got the scars from where the buckle end of the belt gouged my backside. I thrashed like a madman lying on that bed on my belly. She'd tied my legs to the bedposts so I couldn't escape." Ron's voice caught, and he stopped while he gathered himself to carry on. Jack wondered if he'd ever spoken of his ordeal to anyone before.

"Teresa and I tried running away, but we couldn't stay away for long. We had no means, no money, nowhere to go. Then, when I was about sixteen, I met up with Chesney McAlister. Remember him, Jack?"

"Chesney," Jack said. "Now there is a blast from the past. I can see where you get some of your ideas from now," Jack said, smiling slightly. "He's dead now of course."

"He didn't last very long, no. He couldn't keep out of trouble; the police were always up in his business dealings. Then he got involved with trying to turn a bank over," he said with almost a laugh.

"You're a bit cleverer, aren't you," said Jack, eyeing him knowingly, "which is why you're still walking around the crematorium and not in prison."

"Ah, he was good for me at the time in my life when I needed someone, someone to play father figure, because Dad was a bit of a wet weekend and couldn't stand up to Mother. It's amazing Teresa and I have turned out in one piece. As we have."

"So, you just kept away, I'm guessing. No need to go back and visit your old mum?"

"It would have been hypocritical, and well, why would I have wanted to? When we walked out of the door for the last time, we swore would never go back and we didn't. Not ever."

"How long have you been estranged?"

Ron thought for a moment and said, "A little over forty years, but I knew she was in town, though I never bumped into her once. She moved away for a while when Dad died then came back again, but I'd still got no reason to keep in touch with her, nor desire. I'm not sure why I'm here now. Maybe making sure she goes up the chimney."

Ron stopped walking and turned to Jack. "Why are you here, Jack? Did you know her?"

"I didn't know her at all. No, I just thought that somebody should be at the poor woman's funeral because of the state we found her in at her home."

Ron dipped his head. "We used to know what cold was like locked in that cellar. Damn, it was bitter in winter particularly. It's ironic, don't you think? Teresa and I could have both died of hypothermia during those winters. I have no sympathy. There's nothing you can say to make me want to change my mind. I'm glad she died of neglect because we almost did."

It sounded harsh to Jack's ears, but he could understand why Ron felt justified. What went on in other people's families would never cease to surprise him. He was just glad that, even though he'd never had children himself, what precious family he did have were on speaking terms. He thought about Mary again, and he wondered what she was doing and what she'd turned out like.

Ron met Jack's eyes full force and said, "Family cruelty is something I can't abide. Have your enemies out on the street if you must. Hell, I've got a few of my own, but those that are meant to care and look out for you and love you should do so, so that love can be returned. It's a two-way process, and Mother couldn't make us love her because she never loved us in the first place."

Jack was startled to see tears forming in Ron's eyes once again. Things weren't always what they seemed. Ron looked gaunt, malnourished almost. Was that the added stress from recent events?

"Now, I must go, Jack. I've got another funeral to attend for someone that I actually cared a hell of a lot about," he said and pulled away. Whether he was in a hurry or didn't want Jack to see his tears, Jack would never know.

Jack stayed where he was thinking about all he'd just been told. Knowing the full story from Ron, he couldn't help feeling the man's sadness too.

Everybody hurts, sometimes.

CHAPTER 81

Jack
Wednesday afternoon

He thought of old Nelly Raven, and young Melody, and Ron off to his second funeral of the day, one that would be a good deal different to the one he'd just attended. Watching the man walk away, Jack reflected back on the lack of his own immediate family. Janine and he had never had children, though young Mary had come into their lives very briefly. It had been tempting for Janine and himself to adopt the little foundling, but they'd decided it best not to get involved in her life. All he could do was keep an eye out for her from a distance, her natural family found. Maybe it was time to say hello again. The last time he saw her she would have been six or seven, a pretty little thing living with her mum in the rather strange set up that was the girl's own family. He wondered if they still lived in town, whether Mary herself had gone off to university perhaps, what her life was like now. He felt glad she'd graced his life, if only briefly.

The closest he had to a daughter now was Amanda, and she was his boss. No matter what their actual relationship was, he'd always look out for her and that's why it saddened him that she was going through so much pain herself after the split of her marriage.

It can take a hell of a long time to find love, and once found, it should never be wasted or messed with.

He slipped his phone out of his pocket, looked up Ruth's number, and stared at it. Should he call? Should he interfere? He knew Amanda would be seething mad if this didn't work out.

"Sod it," he said and pressed call. A moment later Ruth's voice filled his eardrums. She sounded happy to hear from him.

"Hello, my favourite male detective," she said teasingly. "How the devil are you?"

"I'm not bad actually, Ruth," he said, "not bad at all. I thought I'd give you a call since it's been a little while. I thought you might like Chinese takeaway at my place, from Wong's, your favourite."

"You know me, Jack, I never say no to Wong's. When are you thinking?"

"How about tonight, are you free later?"

"I certainly am. How about seven?"

"Perfect. Jump in a taxi, we'll be drinking," he said. "See you later."

He hung up, found the next number and stared at it. If this went pear-shaped, he could lose two friends. He hit Amanda's number.

"What is it, Jack?" she said.

"I thought you might like to come around for dinner tonight, get a takeaway from Wong's, sweet-and-sour. Can you make it?"

"Well, seeing as my social calendar is fairly empty, I guess I can," she said. "What's the occasion?"

"Let's just call it family. See you at seven. Oh, and catch a taxi, you'll be drinking," he said, then hung up before she asked any more questions.

He had one more call to make and found Vivian's number. There was no hesitation when he dialled this one.

"Hello gorgeous," he said, smiling as he did so.

"Hello yourself. What are you doing?"

"I'm realigning the planets, and I need some help from your good self. Are you up for the challenge?"

"Sounds ominous. What do I need to do?"

"You need to be at my house tonight at 6.45. Bring a bottle of wine."

"What are we up to?" she asked.

"Like I said, realigning the planets, I'll explain more when I see you."

"It's a date. See you later." And she was gone.

Jack strode back to his car with a smug grin on his face, hoping like hell that his plan would work. It had been a couple of months since Amanda and Ruth had been in the same room together, and it was high time they sorted their differences out and made up. He knew they loved each other, and time was a great healer. After recent events, he knew more than ever that life itself was too short to be apart from the one you loved.

Janine popped into the speech bubble in his head and nodded her approval before slowly disappearing again. How he missed her, but at least he knew he was doing the right thing.

His plan would work.

ACKNOWLEDGMENTS

This book is most definitely a work of fiction, though some of the physical places featured are indeed real. If those places are not portrayed entirely accurately, that's my doing to make it fit the story, it is a work of fiction after all. The characters, however, are all figments of my imagination, though I'd love to meet Jack, Amanda, and the rest of the cast in person someday. Are you reading this, Netflix?

I'd like to thank Sarah Waters, a barrister who shared with me the correct process when it came to the technical court stuff. That said, any variation from actual legal procedure is for my creative purposes, because in reality some parts of the process are far too boring to write about. I'd also like to thank Rod Hayler, solicitor at Old Bailey Solicitors, for his valuable input on many points, it's much appreciated.

Having a stroke would be a truly terrible thing, particularly an almost fatal one like Lee Meady experienced, and I thank Dr Ben Swift for enlightening me on the devastating process a body goes through at such a time. Not forgetting my editors, Jenny and Jon, whom I thank for their sterling advice and accuracy. It's a pleasure to work with you both as usual. Jack would say you two sound like a breakfast cereal, as he did of Sage and Kipple, or perhaps even a cartoon duo.

To Angus McLean, for the police stuff, a mighty thanks as always.

Finally, thanks to you, the reader, because if you didn't buy my books, there would be little point in me writing any more.

And double-finally, thanks to Monkey the cat, who listened to this story read out loud so many times while she pretended to be asleep in my office. RIP Monkey.

ALSO BY LINDA COLES

Jack Rutherford and Amanda Lacey Series:

The Controller

Hot to Kill

The Hunted

Dark Service

One Last Hit

Hey You, Pretty Face

Scream Blue Murder

Butcher Baker Banker

The Chrissy Livingstone Series:

Tin Men

Walk Like You

ALSO BY LINDA COLES

If you enjoyed reading one of my stories, here are the others:

The DC Jack Rutherford and DS Amanda Lacey Series:

The Controller

It takes courage to change sides.

They're making big money. When a group kidnapping dogs for ransom hits South London, local detective Amanda Lacey investigates after an acquaintance alerts her she isn't the only victim of the upsetting crime.

But what starts out as a way to make quick money for the gang, quickly turns sinister when a local hard-man gets involved. And Pete didn't sign up for what happens next. With a past record, can he put his personal fears aside and involve the police before it's too late?

Hot to Kill

Just how many deadly pranks can one woman get away with?

Approaching 50, Madeline Simpson is totally hacked off and the English summer heatwave isn't helping with her hot flushes. While it was never her intention to kill, the body count increases as she doles out retribution to those that rub her up the wrong way.

Alerted by similarities in local deaths, someone close to home is hot on her tail to put an end to the carnage.

Often humorous and regularly deadly, read ***Hot to Kill*** to find out how one woman discovers the identity of a local sex offender while wreaking havoc on a carefully crafted mission.

A quirky and humourous story of life, revenge, dead bodies and a good few bottles of Bombay Sapphire Gin.

The Hunted

The hunt is on...

They kill wild animals for sport. She's about to return the favour. A spate of distressing big-game hunter posts are clogging up her newsfeed. As hunters brag about the exotic animals they've murdered and the followers they've gained along the way, a passionate veterinarian can no longer sit back and do nothing. To stop the killings, she creates her own endangered list of hunters. By stalking their online profiles and infiltrating their inner circles, she vows to take them out one-by-one. How far will she go to add the guilty to her own trophy collection?

Dark Service

The dark web can satisfy any perversion, but two detectives might just pull the plug...

Taylor never felt the blade pressed to her scalp. She wakes frightened and alone in an unfamiliar hotel room with a near shaved head and a warning... tell no one.

As detectives Amanda Lacey and Jack Rutherford investigate, they venture deep into the fetish-fueled underbelly of the dark web. The traumatized woman is only the latest victim in a decade-long string of disturbing—and intensely personal—thefts.

To take down a perverted black market, they'll go undercover. But just when justice seems within reach, an unexpected event sends their sting operation spiraling out of control. Their only chance at catching the culprits lies with a local reporter... and a sex scandal that could ruin them all.

One Last Hit

The greatest danger may come from inside his own home.

Detective Duncan Riley has always worked hard to maintain order on the streets of Manchester. But when a series of incidents at home cause him to worry about his wife's behaviour, he finds himself pulled in too many directions at once.

After a colleague Amanda Lacey asks for his help with a local drug epidemic, he never expected the case would infiltrate his own family...And a situation that spirals out of control...

Hey You, Pretty Face

An abandoned infant. Three girls stolen in the night. Can one overworked detective find the connection to save them all?

London, 1999. Short-staffed during a holiday week, Detective Jack Rutherford can't afford to spend time on the couch with his beloved wife. With a skeleton staff, he's forced to handle a deserted infant and a trio of missing girls almost single-handedly. Despite the overload, Jack has a sneaking suspicion that the baby and the abductions are somehow connected...

As he fights to reunite the girls with their families, the clues point to a dark secret that sends chills down his spine. With evidence revealing a detestable crime ring, can Jack catch the criminals before the girls go missing forever?

Scream Blue Murder

Two cold cases are about to turn red hot...

Detective Jack Rutherford's instincts have only sharpened with age. So when a violent road fatality reminds him of a near-identical crime from 15 years earlier, he digs up the past to investigate both. But with one case already closed, he fears the wrong man still festers behind bars while the real killer roams free...

For Detective Amanda Lacey, family always comes first. But when she unearths a skeleton in her father-in-law's garden, she has to balance her heart with her desire for justice. And with darkness lurking just beneath the surface, DS Lacey must push her feelings to one side to discover the chilling truth.

As the sins of the past haunt both detectives, will solving the crimes have consequences that echo for the rest of their lives?

Butcher Baker Banker

Two deaths. Three extraordinary problems. Questionable ways

to fix them.

A trio of individuals weave in and out of each other's lives without realising they have a connection. But they do.

Baker Kit Morris will do anything to keep his family business alive. Desperate for cash, he hatches a risky plan that lands him in trouble. As he struggles to stay out of prison, Kit forges an unlikely friendship with a tough man.

Local thug Ron Butcher rose to the top of London's gangland by "fixing things". But even his extensive crooked connections are useless when death knocks at his own family's door.

And where does the CEO of a high-street bank fit into all of this?

As DS Amanda Lacey and DC Jack Rutherford investigate recent deaths, Jack receives a last-minute history lesson and is left wondering where it all went wrong.

The Chrissy Livingstone series:

Tin Men

She thought she knew her father. But what she doesn't know could fill a mortuary...

Ex-MI5 agent Chrissy Livingstone grieves over her dad's sudden death. While she cleans out his old things, she discovers something she can't explain: seven photos of schoolboys with the year 1987 stamped on the back. Unable to turn off her desire for the truth, she hunts down the boys in the photos only to find out that three of the seven have committed suicide...

Tracing the clues from Surrey to Santa Monica, Chrissy unearths disturbing ties between her father's work as a financier and the victims. As each new connection raises more sinister questions about her family, she fears she should've left the secrets buried with the dead.

Will Chrissy put the past to rest, or will the sins of the father destroy her?

Walk Like You

When a major railway accident turns into a bizarre case of a

missing body, will this PI's hunt for the truth take her way off track?

London. Private investigator Chrissy Livingstone's dirty work has taken her down a different path to her family. But when her upper-class sister begs her to locate a friend missing after a horrific train crash, she feels duty-bound to assist. Though when the two dig deeper, all the evidence seems to lead to one mysterious conclusion: the woman doesn't want to be found.

Still with no idea why the woman was on the train, and an unidentified body uncannily resembling the missing person lying unclaimed in the mortuary, the sisters follow a trail of cryptic clues through France. The mystery deepens when they learn someone else is searching, and their motive could be murder...

Can Chrissy find the woman before she meets a terrible fate?

ABOUT THE AUTHOR

Hi, I'm Linda Coles. Thanks for choosing this book, I really hope you enjoyed it and collect the following ones in the series. Great characters make a great read and I hope I've managed to create that for you.

Originally from the UK, I now live and work in beautiful New Zealand along with my hubby, 2 cats and 6 goats. My office sits by the edge of my vegetable garden, and apart from reading and writing, I get to run by the beach for pleasure.

If you find a moment, please do write an honest online review of my work, they really do make such a difference to those choosing what book to buy next.

If you'd like to keep in touch via my newsletter, use this link to leave your details:

http://eepurl.com/gwfVqL

Enjoy! And tell your friends.

Thanks, Linda

Keep in touch:

www.lindacoles.com

linda@lindacoles.com

Follow me on BookBub

Made in United States
Orlando, FL
03 December 2021

10926186R00219